Praise for Anita Shreve's
The Weight of Water

"Mesmerizing . . . quietly spellbinding. . . . A kind of mystery forged of romance and danger. . . . Part of the book's power is of the conventional whodunit variety. . . . Equally strong is Shreve's evocative prose style. . . . *The Weight of Water* is well-crafted entertainment that also plumbs the depths."
—Dan Cryer, *Newsday*

"Spellbinding. . . . Shreve's triumph here is in creating a pace that brilliantly mimics the frenzy of one who acts in a moment of searing passion."
—Leah Odze Epstein, *Nashville Bookpage*

"It's impossible not to keep turning the pages, as Shreve, with somber voice, leads us on."
—Susan Dooley, *Washington Post Book World*

"Spare, tightly plotted, and compactly written . . . a novel powerfully driven by plot and language. . . . Shreve displays an intriguing range of style and tone. It is as if an Ibsen drama had eruped in an Ann Beattie novel."
—Maureen McLane, *Chicago Tribune*

"Riveting . . . haunting. . . . Shreve is equally adroit at spinning a yarn and etching fine prose."
—Kate Callen, *San Diego Union Tribune*

Also by Anita Shreve

THE WEIGHT OF WATER

ANITA SHREVE

Little, Brown and Company
BOSTON | NEW YORK | LONDON

This novel is a work of fiction. Names, characters, places, and incidents are either the product of the author's imagination or, if real, are used fictitiously.

Originally published in hardcover by Little, Brown and Company, 1997
First Back Bay paperback edition, 1998
First Little, Brown mass market edition: March 2001

Library of Congress Cataloging-in-Publication Data

Shreve, Anita.
    The weight of water / Anita Shreve. — 1st ed.
      p.   cm.
    ISBN 0-316-78997-6 (hc)   0-316-78037-5 (pb)
    I. Title
PS3569.H7385W43   1997
813'.54—dc20   96-21326

10 9 8 7 6 5 4 3 2 1

Printed in the United States of America

For my mother and my daughter

Author's Note

DURING THE NIGHT of March 5, 1873, two women, Norwegian immigrants, were murdered on the Isles of Shoals, a group of islands ten miles off the New Hampshire coast. A third woman survived, hiding in a sea cave until dawn.

The passages of court testimony included in this book are taken verbatim from the transcript of *The State of Maine* v. *Louis H.F. Wagner*.

Apart from recorded historical fact, the names, characters, places, and incidents portrayed in this work are either the products of the author's imagination or, if real are used fictitiously.

The matter of who killed Anethe and Karen Christensen was settled in a court of law, but has continued to be debated for more than a century.

THE WEIGHT
OF WATER

I HAVE TO LET this story go. It is with me all the time now, a terrible weight.

I sit in the harbor and look across to Smuttynose. A pink light, a stain, makes its way across the island. I cut the engine of the small boat I have rented and put my fingers into the water, letting the shock of the cold swallow my hand. I move my hand through the seawater, and think how the ocean, this harbor, is a repository of secrets, its own elegy.

I was here before. A year ago. I took photographs of the island, of vegetation that had dug in against the weather: black sedge and bayberry and sheep sorrel and sea blite. The island is not barren, but it is sere and bleak. It is granite, and everywhere there are ragged reefs that cut. To have lived on Smuttynose would have required a particular tenacity, and I imagine the people then as dug in against the elements, their roots set into the cracks of the rocks like the plants that still survive.

The house in which the two women were murdered burned in 1885, but when I was here a year ago, I photographed the footprint of the house, the marked perime-

ter. I got into a boat and took pictures of the whitened
ledges of Smuttynose and the black-backed gulls that
swept and rose above the island in search of fish only they
could see. When I was here before, there were yellow
roses and blackberries.

When I was here before, something awful was being
assembled, but I didn't know it then.

I take my hand from the water and let the drops fall
upon the papers in the carton, dampened already at the
edges from the slosh. The pink light turns to violet.

Sometimes I think that if it were possible to tell a story
often enough to make the hurt ease up, to make the words
slide down my arms and away from me like water, I
would tell that story a thousand times.

I T IS MY JOB to call out if I see a shape, a rocky ledge, an island. I stand at the bow and stare into the fog. Peering intently, I begin to see things that aren't really there. First tiny moving lights, then minutely subtle gradations of gray. Was that a shadow? Was that a shape? And then, so shockingly that for a few important seconds I cannot even speak, it is all there: Appledore and Londoners and Star and Smuttynose — rocks emerging from the mist. Smuttynose, all of a piece, flat with bleached ledges, forbidding, silent.

I call out. *Land,* I guess I say.

Sometimes, on the boat, I have a sense of claustrophobia, even when alone on the bowsprit. I have not anticipated this. We are four adults and one child forced to live agreeably together in a space no bigger than a small bedroom, and that space almost always damp. The sheets are damp, my underwear is damp. Rich, who has had the boat for years, says this is always true of sailing. He gives me the impression that accepting the dampness, even taking a certain pleasure in it, is an indication of character.

Rich has brought a new woman with him whose name is Adaline.

Rich gives instructions. The sailboat is old, a Morgan 41, but well-tended, the teak newly varnished. Rich calls for the boat hook, shouts to Thomas to snag the buoy. Rich slows the engine, reverses it, guns it slightly, maneuvers the long, slim boat — this space that moves through water — alongside the mooring. Thomas leans over, catches the buoy. Adaline looks up from her book. It is our third day aboard the sloop: Hull, Marblehead, Annisquam, now the Isles of Shoals.

The Isles of Shoals, an archipelago, lie in the Atlantic, ten miles southeast off the New Hampshire coast at Portsmouth. The islands measure three and a half miles north and south by one and a half miles east and west. There are nine islands at high tide, eight at low; White and Seavey are connected. The largest island looked to its first residents like a fat pig wallowing in the sea, and hence the name of Hog. Smuttynose, our destination, derived its name from a clump of seaweed on the nose of a rock extending into the ocean. It has always been an off-putting name, though the others read like poetry from a ship's log: "We passed today the islands of Star and Malaga and Seavey and Londoners; and navigated to our success the treacherous rock of Shag and Eastern and Babb's and Mingo."

In 1635, the Isles of Shoals were formally divided between the Massachusetts Bay Colony, which included Maine, and the territory subsequently to be known as New Hampshire. Duck, Hog, Malaga, Smuttynose, and Cedar went to Maine. Star, Londoners, White, and Seavey went to New Hampshire. The division has always held. In

1635, when the ordinance was first declared, nearly all of the residents of Star fled to Smuttynose, because it was still legal to drink in Maine.

From the guidebooks, I read startling facts: On the island of Star, in 1724, a woman named Betty Moody hid herself and her three children from Indians in a cavern. She crouched near to the ground and held one of the children, an infant girl, tightly to her breast. Mrs. Moody meant to silence her baby to keep the child from giving away their location, but when the Indians had gone, she discovered that she had smothered the girl.

Rich looks like a wrestler: He is neatly muscled and compact. His head is shaved, and he has perfect teeth. I do not think he resembles Thomas at all — an odd, genetic quirk; there are ten years between them. Rich tickles Billie unmercifully, even on the Zodiac. She squeals as if she were being tortured, and then complains when he stops. Rich walks about the Morgan with athletic grace, and he gives the impression of a man for whom nothing has ever been complicated.

We have come only from Annisquam and arrive in the early morning. I watch Thomas bend over the stern to snag the mooring. His legs are pale with whorls of brown hair above the backs of his knees. Over his bathing suit, he has on a pink dress shirt, the cuffs rolled to the elbows. It is odd to see Thomas, my husband of fifteen years, engaged in chores upon this boat, a second mate to his younger brother. Without his pen or his books, Thomas seems disarmed, disoriented by manual labor. As I watch him, I think, as I so often do, that my husband looks too tall for his surroundings. He seems to have to stoop, even while seated. His hair, cut longish, now nearly colorless, falls forward onto his forehead, and he pushes it away with a gesture I am fond of and have seen a thousand times. Despite his seniority, or perhaps because of it, I sometimes see that Thomas is unsettled by the presence of Rich and Adaline, as a father might be in the company of a grown son and a woman.

What does Adaline think when she observes Thomas? My husband is a poet of the first tier, already a kind of emeritus at the university, even though he is only forty-seven. Adaline is not a poet, but seems to have great admiration for Thomas's work. I wonder if she knew Thomas's verse before, or if she has learned it for the trip.

When there is time, I read about the islands. I carry pounds of paper in my camera bag — guidebooks, accounts of the murders, a trial transcript — materials from Research, who seem to think that I am writing the piece. When the murders occurred, in 1873, the newspapers wrote of the crime, and later it was called in these same papers "the trial of the century." This is a familiar turn of phrase this summer as we witness a courtroom spectacle that has all but benumbed even the most avid observers. My editor thinks there is a link between the two events: a double murder with a blade, a famous trial, circumstantial evidence that hinges on tiny factual details. As for me, I think the similarities few, but a magazine will make of something what it can. I am paid to take the pictures.

My expense account is lavish, but Rich, who publishes technical journals, will not hear of money. I am glad that Thomas has thought of his younger brother and his boat: I would not like to be in such close quarters with a strange captain or a crew.

How long, I wonder, has Rich been seeing Adaline?

I read many accounts of the murders. I am struck most by the relativity of facts.

When I think about the murders, I try to picture what might have happened that night. I imagine there would have been a gale, and that the wind from the water would have battered against the glass. Sometimes, I can hear that wind and can see the wooden house under the high cirrus of a full moon. Maren and Anethe would have lain on their backs on either side of the double bed — or could it have been that they were touching? — and in the next room, Karen would have called out suddenly with fright.

Or was it that the dog barked first?

Sometimes I imagine the murders to have been a thing of subtle grace and beauty, with slim arms raised in white nightgowns against the fright, white nightgowns against the snow, the rocks sharp and the gale billowing the thin linen like sheets on a line. I see an arm raised along a window, the moon etching smudges on the panes, and a woman calling to another and another, while below them, at the waterline, the waves slap fast and hard against the dory.

I love to watch my daughter move about the boat in her bathing suit, the fabric stretched and limp, riding high over her butt, her body plump and delicious, often salty if I lick her arm. At five, Billie is entranced by the sloop, a space with lots of cubbyholes and clever places to store the few toys she has been allowed to bring along. She sleeps in the quarter berth beside the companionway. Adaline and Rich are in the forward cabin, the owner's prerogative. Thomas and I have less privacy, stowed amidships as we are, in the open, on a bed that is put away each morning to become a breakfast table.

Occasionally I find Billie's sandy footprints down below. Sand in the fridge. Does Rich mind? I think not. Billie's hair has lightened in the sun and curls continuously from the damp. More and more, I notice her enlarged pupils and the way they cause her eyes to appear nearly black. She has extravagantly long lashes that exaggerate every blink. The loss of her two top front teeth has widened her grin and produces a delicate lisp.

In the mornings, I can hear Adaline and Rich in the forward cabin: a rustle of cloth, a murmur, rhythmic movements. The sounds from Adaline are surprising — guttural and sometimes frantic. I begin to anticipate the sounds and to move away from them. I go above to the cockpit in my robe. I wonder if Billie would be afraid if she awoke — afraid that Adaline were being hurt.

I think that Evan, who was Anethe's husband, would have moved urgently toward the door on the morning after the murders, reports of the unthinkable pushing him forward in a kind of frenzy. The high cirrus would have blown out by then, and the sun would have been on the rocks, beginning to melt the snow. Evan would have been the first man inside the door. He would have insisted.

In 1852, Nancy Underhill, a schoolteacher, was sitting on a ledge at Star when a wave washed her into the sea. Her body was found, a week later, at Cape Neddick, in Maine.

This morning, after we have tied up, Adaline stands in the cockpit, her hands at her waist, her eyes searching the shoreline of Smuttynose, as if something profound might reveal itself to her. When she speaks, she has a residue of an Irish accent, and her voice lends her an aura of authority I do not necessarily feel in myself. Her words rise and fall and dip some more, and then come back to where you can hear them — like soft church music, I often think, or like the melodious beat of water on the hull.

Adaline moves like a dancer, swaying for balance. In the mornings, when she comes up the ladder and emerges from the companionway, she seems to glide into the cockpit. She wears long skirts in thin cottons, with blouses that fall loosely around her hips. She wears a gold cross at her throat, jewelry that is somewhat startling in a woman of her age and stature. The cross draws the eye to the hollow above her clavicle, a hollow that is smooth and tanned. It is as though she once wore the cross as a girl and simply forgot to take it off.

Adaline, Rich tells me, works for Bank of Boston, in an international division. She never talks about her job. I imagine her in suits, standing at gates in airports. She has scars on her wrists, slightly crooked vertical threads in smooth flesh, as though she once tried to trace her veins with a razor or a knife. She has an arresting mouth, with full curved lips of even dimensions, and barely any bow at all.

Sometimes I imagine I can see Maren Hontvedt at the end of her life. In the room in which she is sitting, the wallpaper is discolored but intact. She wears an eyelet cap to cover her hair. I note the languid drape of the shawl folding into her lap, the quiescent posture of her body. The floor is bare, wooden, and on the dresser is a basin of water. The light from the window falls upon her face and eyes. They are gray eyes, not yet faded, and they retain an expression that others who knew her might recognize.

I think that she is dying and will be gone soon. There are thoughts and memories that she hoards and savors, holding them as one might a yellowed photograph of a child. The skin hangs from her face in folds, her skin a crushed velvet the color of dried hydrangeas. She was not beautiful as a young woman, but her face was handsome, and she was strong. The structure of her face is still as it was, and one can see the bones as one might be able to discern the outline of a chair covered by a loose cloth.

I wonder this: If you take a woman and push her to the edge, how will she behave?

After we moor the boat, Rich offers to take me over to Smuttynose in the Zodiac. Billie begs to go along. I shoot from the dinghy in a crouch, leaning against the side of the boat for balance. I use the Hasselblad and a telephoto with a polarizing lens. From time to time, I shout to Rich to cut the engine so that the vibrations will be lessened, or I gesture with my hand in such a way that he knows to push the throttle forward.

There are two houses on the island. One is a small, wooden-frame house called the Haley house. It is not habitable, but is of historic note and has a great aesthetic purity. The other is a shack with rudimentary supplies for shipwrecked sailors.

Rich beaches the Zodiac expertly inside the crumbled breakwater of Smuttynose. The beach is tiny, narrow, blackened by dark stones and charred bits of wood. The air is sharp, and I understand why years ago sea air was prescribed as a tonic for the body. Billie removes her life jacket and sits cross-legged on the sand in a lavender T-shirt that doesn't quite cover her belly. Rich is tanned already, an even red-gold on his legs and arms and face.

There is a line at his throat. We have left Thomas and Adaline on the Morgan.

In the winter months on the Isles of Shoals, the windows were never opened, nor were the children ever let outside, so that by March the air inside the houses was stale and putrid and old with smoke, and the children could hardly breathe.

Rich takes Billie by the hand and guides her past the breakwater so that he can help her search for mussels among the rocks and put them in her pail. I heft my camera bag onto my shoulder and head out toward the end of Smuttynose. My plan is to turn around and frame a shot of the entire island. At my destination, the easternmost tip of the island, there is a rock shaped like a horse's fetlock. Inside the square-cut boulders is a sheltered space, a sea cave, that sloshes with water when the tide is high. It is slippery on the rocks, but after I have left my camera bag on a dry ledge and anchored it in a crevice so that the wind will not blow it away, I crawl like a crab to the sea cave and squat inside. On three sides of me are the shoals and roiling water, and straight out to the east nothing but Atlantic Ocean. Unlike the harbor and the place where we have landed, this side of the island is unprotected. There is lichen on the rock, and small flies lift in a frenzy whenever a wave crashes and sprays.

At the rock, which is known as Maren's Rock, I shut my eyes and try to imagine what it would be like to huddle in that cave all night in winter, in the dark, in the snow and freezing temperatures, with only my nightgown and a small black dog for warmth.

I crawl from the rock, scraping my shin in the process.

I collect my camera bag, which has not moved from its notch. I take a roll of color slide film, thirty-six shots of Maren's rock. I walk the length of the island, the going slow in the thick, scratchy brush.

On January 14, 1813, fourteen shipwrecked Spanish sailors, driven to Smuttynose by a winter gale, tried to reach the light from a candle in an upstairs window of Captain Haley's cottage. They died in a blizzard not forty feet from their destination and are buried under boulders on the island. One man made it to the stone wall, but could go no further. Captain Haley discovered him the following morning. Six more bodies were found on January 17, five more on the twenty-first, and the final body was discovered "grappled up on Hog Island passage" on the twenty-seventh. According to the *Boston Gazette* on January 18, the vessel, named *Conception,* weighed between three and four hundred tons and was laden with salt. No one in America ever knew the dead sailors' names.

When I find Rich and Billie, they are sitting on the beach, their toes dug into the sand. I sit beside them, my knees raised, my arms folded around my legs. Billie gets up and stares into her pail and begins to leap in stiff-legged jetés all around us.

"My fingers are *bleeding*," she announces proudly. "We pulled off a million of them. At least a million. Didn't we, Uncle Rich?"

"Absolutely. At least a million."

"When we get back to the boat, we're going to cook them up for supper." She bends over her pail again and studies it solemnly. Then she begins to drag the pail down to the water's edge.

"What is she doing?" Rich asks.

"I think she's giving the mussels something to drink."

He smiles. "I once read an account of a pilot who said the most beautiful sight he'd ever seen from the air was the Isles of Shoals." He runs his hand over his shaved head. His skull is perfectly shaped, without bumps or dents. I wonder if he worries about sunburn.

"Adaline seems very nice," I say.

"Yes, she is."

"She admires Thomas's work."

Rich looks away and tosses a pebble. His face is not delicate, in the way that Thomas's is. Rich has dark, thick eyebrows that nearly meet in the center. Sometimes I think that he has Thomas's mouth, but he doesn't. Rich's is firmer, more pronounced in profile. "Childe Hassam painted here," he says. "Did you know that?"

"I wouldn't have thought that someone who worked for Citibank would know so much about poetry," I say.

"Actually, it's Bank of Boston." He tilts his head and looks at me. "I think poetry is something that's fairly universal, don't you? Enjoying it, I mean."

"I suppose."

"How is Thomas?"

"I don't know. I think he's convinced himself that each poet is given a finite number of words and that he's used up his allotment."

"I notice that he's drinking more," Rich says. Rich's legs are brown and covered with dark hair. Looking at his legs, I contemplate the trick of nature that has caused Thomas and Rich to receive what appear to be entirely separate sets of genes. I glance out toward the sloop, which floats four hundred feet from us in the harbor. The mast teeters in the chop.

"Adaline was married once," Rich says. "To a doctor. They had a child."

I turn to him. He must see surprise on my face.

"I think the girl must be three or four now. The father has her. They live in California."

"I didn't know."

"Adaline doesn't see the girl. She's chosen not to."

I am silent. I try to absorb this information, to put it together with the gold cross and the lilting voice.

"Adaline came over from Ireland for him," he says. "For the doctor."

He leans over and brushes a dried smear of muck from my calf. He smooths my leg with his fingertips. I am thinking that the calf is not a place that anyone touches much. I wonder if he shaves his head every day. What the top of his head would feel like.

"She's kind of detached," he says, withdrawing his fingers. "She doesn't stay with people long."

"How long have you two been together?"

"About five months. Actually, I think my tenure is almost up."

I think of saying to him that to judge by the sounds emanating from the forward cabin, I cannot agree.

In front of us, Billie lies down at the waterline. Mostly, I think, to get sand in her hair. I tense and begin to rise. Rich puts a restraining hand on my wrist.

"She's OK. I've got my eye on her."

I relax a bit and sit back down.

"Did you want something more?" I ask. "From Adaline, I mean."

He shrugs.

"She's very beautiful," I say.

Rich nods. "I've always envied you," he says. "You and Thomas."

He puts his hand to his face to shade his eyes, and he squints in the direction of the boat.

"I don't see anyone in the cockpit," I say.

A few minutes later, I take a photograph of Rich and Billie and her pail of mussels. Rich is lying on the small piece of rough beach, his knees raised, dark circles inside the wide openings of his khaki shorts. The eye is drawn to those dark circles. His arms are spread at his sides in a posture of submission. His head has fallen into a depression in the sand, so that his body seems to end at his neck. Billie is standing over him, perfectly bent at the waist, her arms stretched out behind her for balance, like two tiny wings. She is talking to Rich or asking him a question. Rich seems vulnerable under her scrutiny. Beside Billie is her green plastic pail of mussels, perhaps enough to make an appetizer for two. Up behind them both is the Haley house, small and old, the trim neatly painted in a dull brick red.

When I look at the photographs, it is hard not to think: We had seventeen hours then, or twelve, or three.

Immediately after the photograph is taken, Rich sits up. He remembers, he tells Billie, that a pirate named Blackbeard once buried his treasure on the island. He gets up and searches through the scrub, examining this branch and that, until he has made two forked sticks. He sets off with Billie while I wait on the beach. After a time — fifteen minutes, twenty? — I hear a cry from Billie. She is calling to me. I get up to look and then walk over to where she and Rich are standing together, about two hundred feet from the beach. Billie and Rich are bent over a hole they have dug in the sand. In the hole is a treasure: five quarters, two dollar bills, a gold-colored toothpick, a chain with a single key attached, a bracelet made of copper wire, and a silver-colored ring. Rich pretends to read the inscription under the band of the ring. "To E from E with undying love."

"What's 'E to E' mean?" Billie asks.

"Blackbeard's real name was Edward, which begins with *E*. And his wife's name was Esmerelda, which also begins with *E*."

Billie ponders this. Rich tells her that the silver ring belonged to Blackbeard's fifteenth wife, whom Blackbeard himself murdered. Billie is nearly levitating with excitement and fright.

The boundaries of the Hontvedt house — also known, before the murders, as simply "the red house" — have been marked with stakes. The boundaries delineate an area approximately twenty feet by thirty-six feet. In this small space were two apartments, separated by a doorless wall. The northwest side of the house had two front doors.

After the brief ride back, I step up onto the Morgan from the Zodiac, Rich catching my hand. Thomas and Adaline are sitting opposite one another, on canvas cushions in the cockpit, seawater dripping from their bodies and making puddles on the floor. They have been swimming, Adaline says, and Thomas seems mildly out of breath.

Adaline has her hands up behind her head, wringing out her hair. Her bathing suit is red, two vibrant wisps of fire-engine red on glistening skin. Her stomach, a lovely, flat surface the color of toast, seems that of a young girl.

Her thighs are long and wet and have drops of seawater among the light brown hairs.

She twists her hair and smiles at me. Her face is guileless when she smiles. I am trying to reconcile the image of her smile with the frantic, guttural sounds that emanate in the morning from the forward cabin.

I remember these moments not solely for themselves, but for the knowledge that beyond these memories lies an instant in time that cannot be erased. Each image a stepping stone taken in innocence or, if not in innocence, then in a kind of thoughtless oblivion.

Rich goes immediately to Adaline and puts a proprietary hand on the flat of her belly. He kisses her on the cheek. Billie, too, takes a step forward, drawn to beauty as any of us are. I see that Billie will find a reason to drape herself across those long legs. With effort, Thomas keeps his eyes on me and asks about our small trip. I am embarrassed for Thomas, for the extraordinary whiteness of his skin, for his chest, which seems soft. I want to cover him with his blue shirt, which is lying in a puddle.

On March 5, 1873, approximately sixty people lived on all the islands composing the Shoals: the lighthouse keeper's family on White; workmen building a hotel on Star; two families — the Laightons and the Ingerbretsons — on Appledore (formerly known as Hog); and one family, the Hontvedts, on Smuttynose.

We run the Zodiac into Portsmouth. We are hungry and want lunch, and we don't have much in the way of provisions. We sit in a restaurant that has a porch and an awning. It seems as close to the water as one can get in Portsmouth, though I think there is not much to look at beyond the tugs and the fishing boats. A sharp gust of wind catches the awning and lifts it for a second so that the poles that anchor it come off the ground as well. The awning tears loose at one corner and spills its wind. The canvas flaps in the breeze.

"*The heavens rent themselves,*" Thomas says.

Adaline looks up at him and smiles. "*Uncovered orbs and souls.*"

Thomas seems surprised. "*Mullioned waters,*" he says.

"*Beveled whispers.*"

"*Shuttered grace.*"

"*Shackled sunlight.*"

I think of Ping-Pong balls hit hard across a table.

Adaline pauses. "*Up-rushed sea,*" she says.

"Yes," Thomas answers quietly.

At the restaurant, Billie eats a grilled cheese sandwich, as she almost always does. She is hard to contain in a restaurant, an effervescence that wants to bubble up and pop out of the top of the bottle. I drink a beer called Smuttynose, which seems to be a brand that capitalizes upon the murders. After all, why not name a beer Appledore or Londoner's? The drink is oak colored and heavier than I am used to, and I think I become slightly drunk. I am not sure about this. The boat itself produces a kind of inebriation that stays with you for hours. Even when you step foot on land, you are still swaying, still feeling the thump of water against the hull.

I read in the guidebooks that America was discovered at the Isles of Shoals, on Smuttynose, by vikings.

On Star Island, there is a cemetery known as Beebe. In it are buried the three small daughters of George Beebe who died separately and within a few days of each other in 1863 of diphtheria.

At the restaurant I have a lobster roll. Thomas has fried clams. There is a lull in the conversation, as though the strain of the trip into the harbor in the Zodiac has drained everyone of words. Adaline eats a salad and drinks a glass of water. I notice that her back is straight while she eats. Rich, by contrast, is easily slouched, his legs stretched in front of him. He pushes his chair slightly closer to Adaline's and begins idly to stroke her arm.

Captain Samuel Haley settled on Smuttynose several years before the American Revolution. While he was building a seawall to connect Malaga and Smuttynose, he turned over a rock and discovered four bars of silver. With this money, he completed the breakwater and built the pier. The breakwater was destroyed in February 1978.

Edward Teach, also known as the pirate Blackbeard, spent his honeymoon with his fifteenth and last wife on the Isles of Shoals in 1720. He is said to have buried his treasure on Smuttynose.

"Don't tear your napkin."

Thomas's voice is ragged, like the bits of paper on the table.

Adaline gently removes the wad from Billie's fist and picks up the debris around her plate.

"How did you get a name like Billie?" she asks.

"It's Willemina," Billie answers, the name spooling off her lips in a pleased and practiced way.

"I named her for my mother," I say, glancing at Thomas. He drains his wineglass and puts it on the table.

"My mom calls me Billie because Willemina is too old," she adds.

"Fashioned," I say.

"I think Willemina is a pretty name," Adaline says. Her

hair is rolled at the sides and caught at the back with a clip. Billie stands on her chair and tilts her head to examine the rolls and the way they seamlessly fold into the nape of Adaline's neck.

Smuttynose is twenty-eight hundred feet east and west, and a thousand feet north and south. It consists of 27.1 acres, almost all of which is rock. The elevation of the island is thirty feet.

Thomas is thin and stretched, and seems, physically, not to have enough leverage in life. I think that Thomas will probably be thin until he dies, stooped perhaps in the way some tall men become as they age. I know that it will be an elegant stoop. I am sure of that.

I wonder if Thomas is as sad as I am when he awakens in the mornings and hears Adaline and Rich in the forward cabin.

We are waiting for the check to come. Billie is standing next to me, coloring on a place mat. "Were you born in Ireland?" I ask Adaline.

"In the south of Ireland."

The waitress brings the check. Thomas and Rich reach for it, but Thomas, distractedly, lets Rich have it.

"This assignment you're on must be gruesome for you," says Adaline. She begins to massage the back of Billie's neck.

"I don't know," I say. "It seems so long ago. Actually, I wish I could get my hands on some old photographs."

"You seem to have a lot of material," Thomas says.

"It was foisted upon me," I say, wondering why my voice contains a defensive note. "Though I must confess I find the accounts of the murders intriguing."

Adaline reaches up and removes a gold hair clip from

the back of her head. Her hair is multihued, a wood grain that curls slightly in the humidity, as does Billie's. On the boat, Adaline most often wears her hair rolled at the back of her head or at the nape of her neck in intricate knots and coils that can be loosened with a single pin. Today, when she removes the clip, her hair falls the length of her back, swaying with the fall. The settling of all that hair, the surprising abundance of hair springing from a knot no bigger than a peach, seems, at the time, like a trick, a sleight of hand, for our benefit.

I look over at Thomas. He is breathing slowly. His face, which normally has high color, has gone pale. He seems stunned by the simple fall of hair from a knot — as though the image itself, or the memories it evokes, were unwanted news.

I do not have many personal photographs of Thomas. There are dozens of other pictures of him, photos of a public nature: book-jacket portraits, for example, and formal snapshots in magazines and newspapers. But in my own collection, Thomas has almost always managed to avert his eyes or to turn his head altogether, as if he did not want to be captured on any day at any place in time. I have, for instance, a picture of Thomas at a party at our apartment after Billie was born: Thomas is stooped slightly, speaking with a woman, another poet, who is also a friend. He has seen me coming with the camera, has dipped his head and has brought a glass up to his cheek, almost entirely obscuring his profile. In another photograph, Thomas is holding Billie on a bench in a park. Billie, perched on Thomas's knee, seems already aware of the camera and is smiling broadly and clasping her tiny fists together with delight at this new activity, at this strange face that her mother has put on — one with a moving and briefly flickering eye. Thomas, however, has bent his head into Billie's neck. Only his posture tells the viewer he is the father of the child.

For years I thought that Thomas avoided the camera because he has a scar that runs from the corner of his left eye to his chin — the result of a car accident when he was seventeen. It is not disfiguring, in the way some scars can be, ruining a face so that you no longer want to look at it; instead, Thomas's scar seems to follow the planes of his face — as though a brush had made a quick stroke, a perfect curve. It is almost impossible not to want to touch that scar, to run a fingertip along its bumpy ridge. But it is not the scar that makes Thomas turn his face away from the camera; it is, I think, that he cannot bear to be examined too closely by a lens. Just as he is not able to meet his eyes for any length of time in a mirror.

I have one photograph of Thomas in which he is not turned away. I took it on the morning after we met. He is standing in front of his apartment building in Cambridge, and he has his hands in the pockets of his trousers. He has on a wrinkled white shirt with a button-down collar. Even in this picture, the viewer can see that Thomas wants to pull away, and that it is with the greatest of effort that he has kept his eyes focused on the camera. He looks ageless in the photograph, and it is only because I happen to know that he is thirty-two that I would not think he was forty-seven or twenty-five. In the picture, one can see that Thomas's hair, which is naturally thin and of no distinct color, has recently been cut short. I took the picture about nine o'clock in the morning. He looks that morning like someone I have known a long time — possibly since childhood.

We met for the first time, appropriately, in a bar in Cambridge. I was twenty-four, and worked for a Boston paper, assigned recently to Local Sports. I was on my way home from a shoot in Somerville of a high school girls' basketball team, but I needed a bathroom and a pay phone.

I heard his voice before I saw his face. It was low and measured, authoritative and without noticeable accent.

When he finished the reading, he turned slightly to acknowledge a nod, and I could see Thomas's face then in the light. I was struck by his mouth — he had a loose and generous mouth, the only extravagance in a spare face. Later, when I was sitting with him, I saw that his eyes were set closely together, so that I did not think he was classically handsome. His irises, however, were navy and flecked with gold, and he had large pupils, dark circles that seemed to have no protection.

I went to the bar and ordered a Rolling Rock. I was lightheaded and hollow-stomached from not having eaten anything. It seemed that every time I had thought of eating that day, I had been called to yet another assignment. I leaned against the bar and studied the menu. I was aware that Thomas was standing next to me.

"I liked your reading," I said.

He glanced briefly at me. "Thank you," he said quickly, in the way of a man who has no skill with compliments.

"The poem you read. It was very strong."

His eyes flickered over my face. "It's old work," he said.

The barman brought my Rolling Rock, and I paid for the beer. Thomas picked up his glass, leaving a wet circle on the highly varnished surface of the bar. He took a long swallow and set the glass back down.

"This is a reading?" I asked.

"Tuesday night. Poet's night."

"I didn't know."

"You're not alone."

I tried to signal to the barman, so that I could order a snack.

"Thomas Janes," he said, holding out his hand. I noticed the fingers, long and strong and pale.

He must have seen the confusion on my face.

He smiled. "No, you've never heard of me," he said.

"I don't know poetry very well," I said lamely.

"No apologies."

He had on a white shirt and a complicated cable-knit sweater. Dress slacks. Gray. A pair of boots. I told him my name and that I was a photographer for the *Globe*.

"How did you become a photographer?"

"I saw a show of AP photos once. I left the show and went out and bought a camera."

"The baby falling from the third-story window."

"Something like that."

"And you've been taking pictures ever since."

"It helped to put me through school."

"You've seen a lot of terrible things."

"Some. But I've seen wonderful things, too. I once caught the moment that a father lay down on the ice and pulled his son from a fish hole. You can see the clasped arms of the boy and the man, and the two faces with their eyes locked."

"Where was this?"

"In Woburn."

"It sounds familiar. Could I have seen it?"

"Possibly. The *Globe* bought it."

He nodded slowly and took a long swallow of his drink. "Actually, it's much the same, what you and I are doing," he said.

"And what would that be?"

"Trying to stop time."

The barman beckoned to Thomas, and he walked to a small platform at one end of the room. He leaned on a podium. The audience, to my surprise, grew quiet. There was not even the chink of glasses. Thomas pulled a piece of paper from the pocket of his trousers and said he wanted to read something he had written just that day. There were words that stayed with me: *Wainscot* and *redolent* and *core-stung*.

Later there were a great many glasses on the table, mugs of cut glass that refracted the dregs. There seemed to be endless circles of liquid oak. I thought that nearly half the people in the bar had come to the table to buy Thomas a drink. Thomas drank too much. I could see that even then. He stood and swayed a bit and held the table. I touched him on the elbow. He had no shame in his drunkenness. He asked me if I would help him get to his car. Already I knew that I would have to drive him home.

A sink with a rusty stain leaned along one wall. A small bed that sagged and was covered with a beige blanket stood in the center. Thomas lay on his back on the bed, which was too short for him. I removed his boots and sat on a chair by the desk. Thomas's feet were white and smooth. His stomach was concave and made a slight hollow under his belt. One of the legs of his trousers had ridden up to expose an inch of skin above his sock. I thought he was the most beautiful man I had ever seen.

When I knew that he was asleep, I slipped a hand into his trouser pocket and removed the folded piece of paper. I took it to the window, where there was a slit in the curtain. I read the poem in the street light.

After a time, I put a finger to the skin at his shin. I traced the scar on his face, and he twitched in his sleep. I put my palm on the place where his belly dipped. The heat of his skin through his shirt surprised me, as though he were running a temperature, as though the inner mechanisms of his body burned inefficiently.

I slipped into the bed and lay beside him. He turned onto his side, facing me. It was dark in the room, but I could see his face. I could feel his breath on my skin.

"You brought me home," he said.

"Yes."

"I don't remember."

"No, I know you don't."

"I drink too much."

"I know." I brought my hand up, as though I might touch him, but I didn't. I laid my hand between our faces.

"Where are you from?" he asked me.

"Indiana."

"A farm girl."

"Yes."

"Seriously?"

"I've been in Boston since I was seventeen."

"School."

"And after."

"The after sounds interesting."

"Not very."

"You don't miss Indiana?"

"Some. My parents are dead. I miss them more."

"How did they die?"

"Cancer. They were older. My mother was forty-eight when I was born. Why are you asking me these questions?"

"You're a woman in my bed. You're an attractive woman in my bed. Why did you stay here tonight?"

"I was worried about you," I said. "What about your parents?"

"They live in Hull. I grew up in Hull. I have a brother."

"How did you get this?" I reached up and touched the scar on his face.

He flinched, and he turned onto his back, away from me.

"I'm sorry," I said.

"No, it's all right. It's just . . ."

"You don't have to tell me. It's none of my business."

"No." He brought an arm up and covered his eyes. He was so still for so long that I thought he had fallen asleep.

I shifted slightly in the bed with the intention of getting up and leaving. Thomas, feeling the shift, quickly lifted his arm from his eyes and looked at me. He grabbed my arm. "Don't go," he said.

When he rolled toward me, he unfastened one button of my shirt, as though by that gesture he would prevent me from leaving. He kissed the bare space he had made. "Are you with anyone?"

"No," I said. I put my fingers on his face, but I was careful not to touch the scar.

He unfastened all the buttons. He opened my shirt and

laid the white cloth against my arms. He kissed me from my neck to my stomach. Dry lips. Light kisses. He rolled me away from him, pulling my shirt down below my shoulders. He lay behind me, encircling me, pressing his palms into my stomach. My arms were pinned beneath his, and I felt his breath on the nape of my neck. He pushed himself hard against my thigh. I bent my head slightly forward, letting go, letting this happen to me, to us, and I felt his body stretch with mine. I felt his tongue at the top of my spine.

Sometime later that night, I was awakened by a ragged moan. Thomas, naked, was sitting at the edge of the bed, the heels of his hands digging angrily into his eye sockets. I tried to pull his hands away before he injured himself. He fell back onto the bed. I turned on a light.

"What is it?" I asked. "What's wrong?"

"It's nothing," he whispered. "It'll pass."

His jaw was clenched, and his face had gone a sickly white. It couldn't simply be a hangover, I thought. He must be ill.

He raised his head off the pillow and looked at me. He seemed not to be able to see me. There was something wrong with his right eye. "This will pass," he said. "It's just a headache."

"What can I do for you?" I asked.

"Don't go," he whispered. "Promise me you won't go." He reached for my hand, catching my wrist. He gripped me so tightly, he raised welts on my skin.

I prepared him an ice pack in the tiny kitchen of his apartment and lay down next to him. I, too, was naked. It's possible I slept while he waited out the pain. Some hours later, he rolled over, facing me, and took my hand.

He placed my fingers on the scar. His color had returned, and I could see that the headache was gone. I traced the long bumpy curve on his face, as I was meant to do.

"There's something I want to tell you," he said.

In the morning, after our long night together, after the migraine, the first of dozens I would eventually witness, I persuaded him to get up and take me out to breakfast. I made him pose for a photograph at the front door of the apartment house. At the diner, he told me more about the scar, but the language, I could hear, had already changed, the telling of it was different. I could see that he was composing images, searching for words. I left him with a promise to return in the late afternoon. When I came back, Thomas had still not showered or changed his clothes, and there was an unmistakable exhilaration about him, a flush on his face.

"I love you," he said, getting up from the desk.

"You couldn't possibly," I said, alarmed. I looked over to the desk. I saw white-lined papers covered with black ink. Thomas's fingers were stained, and there was ink on his shirt.

"Oh but I do," he said.

"You've been working," I said, going to him. He embraced me, and I inhaled in his shirt what had become, in twenty-four hours, a familiar scent.

"It's the beginning of something," he said into my hair.

In the restaurant in Portsmouth, Thomas turns slightly and sees that I am watching him.

He reaches across the table. "Jean, do you want a walk?" he asks. "We'll go up to the bookstore. Maybe we'll find some old photographs of Smuttynose."

"Yes, that's right," says Adaline. "You and Thomas go off for a bit on your own. Rich and I will take care of Billie."

Rich stands. My daughter's face is serious, as if she were trying to look older than she is — perhaps eight or nine. I watch her smooth her T-shirt over her shorts.

"Fat repose," Thomas says. He speaks distinctly, but there is, in his voice, which is somewhat louder than it was, the barest suggestion of excitement.

At the next table, a couple turns to look at us.

Adaline reaches around for a sweater she has left on the back of the chair. *"Spaded breasts,"* she says.

She stands up, but Thomas cannot leave it there.

"Twice-bloated oaths on lovers' breath."

Adaline looks at Thomas, then at me. *"The hour confesses,"* she says quietly. *"And leaves him spinning."*

Thomas and I walk up Ceres Street to the center of the town. Thomas seems anxious and distracted. We pass boutiques, a microbrewery, a home-furnishings store. In a storefront window, I see my reflection, and it occurs to me there are no mirrors on the boat. I am surprised to see a woman who looks older than I think she ought to. Her mouth is pressed into a narrow line, as if she were trying to remember something important. Her shoulders are hunched, or perhaps that is simply the way she is standing, with her hands in the pockets of her jeans. She has on a faded navy sweatshirt, and she has a camera bag on her arm. She might be a tourist. She wears her hair short, hastily pushed back behind her ears. On the top of her hair, which is an indeterminate and faded chestnut, there is a thin weave of dew. She wears dark glasses, and I cannot see her eyes.

I am not, on the afternoon we walk up Ceres Street, or even on the evening I first meet Thomas, a beautiful woman. I was never a pretty girl. As my mother once said, in a moment of honesty that I used to resent but now appreciate, my individual features were each lovely or passable in themselves, but somehow the parts had never formed an absolutely coherent whole. There is something mildly disturbing, I know, in the length of my face, the width of my brow. It is not an unpleasant face, but it is not a face that strangers turn to, have to see. As Thomas's is, for instance. Or Adaline's.

Thomas and I do not touch as we walk up Ceres Street. "She seems a pleasant person," I say.

"Yes, she does."

"Billie likes her."

"And Rich."

"He's good with kids."

"Excellent."

"She has a beautiful voice. It's interesting that she wears a cross."

"Her daughter gave it to her."

At the top of the street, Thomas pauses for a moment and says, "We could go back." I misunderstand him and say, looking at my watch, "We've only been gone ten minutes."

But he means, *We could go home.*

There are tourists on the street, people peering into shop windows. We reach the center of town, the market square, a church, a tiny mall with benches. We round the corner and come upon the facade of a tall, brick building. The windows are long and arched, multipaned. There is a discreet card in the window.

"That was an interesting game you were playing with Adaline," I say, studying the card for a moment.

"Not really," says Thomas. He leans in toward the window and squints at the sign.

"THE PORTSMOUTH ATHENAEUM," he reads. "READING ROOM OPEN TO THE PUBLIC." He examines the hours listed. He seems to study the card a long time, as though he were having trouble understanding it.

"Who was the poet?" I ask.

"Fallon Pearse."

I look down at my sandals, which are spotted with drops of oil from cooking in the kitchen at home. My jeans have stretched and wrinkled at the tops of my thighs.

"If any place would have archival photographs, this would be it," he says.

"What about Billie?" I ask. We both know, as Rich and Adaline do not, that even a half hour with Billie can be exhausting. All those questions, all that curiosity.

Thomas stands back and scans the building's height. "I'll go back and find Adaline," he says. "I'll give her a hand with Billie. You see if they've got what you need, and we'll meet back here in, say, an hour?"

Underneath my feet, the ground seems to roll slowly up and away as it sometimes does in children's cartoons.

"Whatever you think," I say.

Thomas peers into the front window as if he might recognize something beyond the drapes. With a casualness and tenderness I suddenly mistrust, he bends and kisses me on the cheek.

Some weeks after Thomas and I met each other in the bar in Cambridge, we parked my car by the waterfront in

Boston and walked up a hill toward an expensive restaurant. Perhaps we were celebrating an anniversary — one month together. From the harbor, fog spilled into the street and around our feet. I had on high heels, Italian shoes that made me nearly as tall as Thomas. Behind me, I could hear a foghorn, the soothing hiss of tires on wet streets. It was raining lightly, and it seemed as though we would never make it up the hill to the restaurant, that we were walking as slowly as the fog was moving.

Thomas pressed in on my side. We had been at two bars, and his arm was slung around my shoulder rather more passionately than gracefully.

"You have a birthmark on the small of your back, just to the right of center," he said.

My heels clicked satisfyingly on the sidewalk. "If I have a birthmark," I said, "it's one I've never seen."

"It's shaped like New Jersey," he said.

I looked at him and laughed.

"Marry me," he said.

I pushed him away, as you would a drunk. "You're crazy," I said.

"I love you," he said. "I've loved you since the night I found you in my bed."

"How could you marry a woman who reminded you of New Jersey?"

"You know I've never worked better."

I thought about his working, the dozens of pages, the continuously stained fingers.

"It's all your doing," he said.

"You're wrong," I said. "You were ready to write these poems."

"You let me forgive myself. You gave this to me."

"No I didn't."

Thomas had on a blazer, his only jacket, a navy so dark it was nearly black. His white shirt seemed luminescent under the street lamp, and my eye was drawn to the place where his shirt met his belt buckle. I knew that if I put the flat of my hand there, the fabric of the shirt would be warm to the touch.

"I've only known you for a month," I said.

"We've been together every day. We've slept together every night."

"Is that enough?"

"Yes."

I knew that he was right. I put the flat of my hand against his white shirt at the belt buckle. The shirt was warm.

"You're drunk," I said.

"I'm serious," he said.

He pressed toward me, backing me insistently into an alleyway. Perhaps I made a small and ineffectual protest. In the alley, the tarmac shone from the wet. I was aware of a couple, not so very unlike myself and Thomas, walking arm in arm, just past the narrow opening of the alley. They glanced in at us with frightened faces as they passed. Thomas leaned all of his weight against me, and put his tongue inside my ear. The gesture made me shiver, and I turned my head. He put his mouth then on the side of my neck, licking the skin in long strokes, and suddenly I knew that in that posture he would come — deliberately — to show me that he had become helpless before me, that I was an alchemist. He would make of this an offering of the incontinence of his love. Or was it, I couldn't help but wonder, simply the abundance of his gratitude?

I am trying to remember. I am trying hard to remember what it felt like to feel love.

I enter the building with the tall, arched windows and shut the door behind me. I follow signs upstairs to the library. I knock on an unprepossessing metal door and then open it. The room before me is calm. It has thick ivory paint on the walls, and heavy wooden bookshelves. The feeling of serenity emanates from the windows.

There are two library tables and a desk where the librarian sits. He nods at me as I walk toward him. I am not sure what to say.

"Can I help you with something?" he asks. He is a small man with thinning brown hair and wire glasses. He wears a plaid sport shirt with short, crisp sleeves that stick out from his shoulders like moth's wings.

"I saw the sign out front. I'm looking for material on the murders that took place out at the Isles of Shoals in 1873."

"Smuttynose."

"Yes."

"Well . . . we have the archives."

"The archives?"

"The Isles of Shoals archives," he explains. "They were sent over from the Portsmouth Library, oh, a while ago. They're a mess, though. There's a great deal of material, and not much of it has been cataloged, I'm sorry to say. I could let you see some of it, if you want. We don't lend out materials here."

"That would be —"

"You'd have to pick an area. A subject."

"Old photographs," I say. "If there are any. Of people, of the island. And personal accounts of the time."

"That would be mostly in diaries and letters," he says. "Those that have come back to us."

"Yes. Letters then. And photographs."

"Have a seat over there at the table, and I'll see what I can do. We're very excited to have the archives, but as you can see, we're a bit short-staffed."

I have then an image of Thomas with Adaline and Billie. Each has a vanilla ice-cream cone. The three of them are licking the cones, trying to control the drips.

Thomas said, "I'll go find Adaline." He did not say, "I'll go find Adaline and Billie," or "Adaline and Rich."

The librarian returns with several books and folders of papers. I thank him and pick up one of the books. It is an old and worn volume, the brown silk binding of which has cracked. The pages are yellowed at the edges, and a few are loose. Images swim in front of me, making an array of new covers on the book. I shut my eyes and put the book to my forehead.

I look at an old geography of the Isles of Shoals. I read two guidebooks printed in the early half of the century. I take notes. I open another book and begin to riffle the pages. It is a book of recipes, *The Appledore Cookbook*, published in 1873. The recipes intrigue me: Quaking Pudding, Hash Made from Calf's Head and Pluck, Whitpot Pudding, Hop Yeast. What is pluck? I wonder.

From the folders the library has given me, papers slide out onto the table, and I can see there is no order to them. Some papers are official documents from the town, licenses and such, while others are clearly bills of sale. Still other papers seem to be letters written on a stationery so fragile I am almost afraid to touch them. I look at the letters to decipher the old-fashioned penmanship, and with dismay I realize that the words are foreign. I see the dates: April 17, 1873; November 4, 1868; December 24, 1856; January 5, 1867.

There are a few photographs in the folders. One is a portrait of a family of seven. In the photograph, the father, who has a beard and a full head of hair, is wearing a waist-coat and a thick suit, like a captain of a ship might have. His wife, who has on a black dress with a white lace collar and lots of tiny white buttons, is quite plump and has her hair pulled severely back off her head. Everyone in the photograph, including the five children, appears grim and bug-eyed. This is because the photographer has had to keep the shutter open for at least a minute, during which time no one is allowed to blink. It is easier to maintain a serious expression for sixty seconds than it is a smile.

In one of the folders, various documents seem interspersed with students' papers and what look to be, to judge from the titles, sermons. There is also a faded, flesh-colored box, a box expensive writing paper might once have come in. Inside the box are pages of writing — spidery writing in brown ink. The penmanship is ornate, almost impossible to make out, even if the words were in English, which they are not. The paper is pink at the edges, slightly stained in one corner. A water stain, I think. Or perhaps even a burn. It smells of mildew. I stare at the flowery writing, which when looked at as a whole makes a lovely, calligraphic design, and as I lift the pages out of the box, I discover that a second set of papers, paper-clipped together, is at the bottom of the box. These pages are written in pencil, on white-lined paper, and bear many erasure marks, which have been written over. They

also bear one purple date stamp and several notations:
*Rec'd September 4, 1939, St. Olaf's College Library.
Rec'd 14.2.40, Oslo, forwarded Marit Gullestad. Rec'd
April 7, 1942, Portsmouth Library, Portsmouth, New
Hampshire.*

I look at the first set of papers and the second. I note
the date at the beginning of each document. I study the
signature at the end of the foreign papers and compare it
to the printed name at the end of those written in English.

Maren Christensen Hontvedt.

I read two pages of the penciled translation and set it
on my lap. I look at the date stamp and the notations,
which seem to tell a story of their own: the discovery of a
document written in Norwegian; an attempt to have a
translation made by someone at St. Olaf's College; the
forwarding of that document to a translator in Oslo; the
war intervening; the document and its translation be-
latedly sent to America and then relegated to a long-
neglected folder in the Portsmouth Library. I take a deep
breath and close my eyes.

Maren Hontvedt. The woman who survived the murders.

Maren Hontvedt's Document

TRANSLATED FROM THE NORWEGIAN BY MARIT GULLESTAD

19 September 1899, Laurvig

I F IT SO PLEASE the Lord, I shall, with my soul and heart and sound mind, write the true and actual tale of that incident which continues to haunt my humble footsteps, even in this country of my birth, far from those forbidding, granite islands on which a most unforgivable crime was committed against the persons whom I loved most dearly in all the world. I write this document, not in defense of myself, for what defense have those who still live, and may breathe and eat and partake of the Lord's blessings, against those who have been so cruelly struck down and in such a way as I can hardly bear to recall? There is no defense, and I have no desire to put forth such. Though I must add here that I have found it a constant and continuous trial all these twenty-six years to have been, even by the most unscrupulous manner of persons, implicated in any small way in the horrors of 5 March 1873. These horrors have followed me across the ocean to my beloved Laurvig, which, before I returned a broken and barren woman, was untainted with any scandal, and was, for me, the pure and wondrous landscape of my most treasured childhood memories with my dear family, and which is where I will shortly die. And so I mean with these pages, written in my own hand, while there are some few wits remaining in my decrepit and weakening body, that the truth shall be known. I leave instructions for this document to be sent after my death into the care of John Hontvedt, who was once my husband and still remains so in the eyes of the Lord, and who resides at Sagamore Street in the town of Portsmouth in the state of New Hampshire in America.

The reader will need sometimes to forgive me in this self-imposed trial, for I find I am thinking, upon occasion, of strange and far-away occurrences, and am not altogether in control of my faculties and language, the former as a consequence of being fifty-two years of age and unwell, and the latter owing to my having completed my last years of schooling in an interrupted manner.

I am impatient to write of the events of 5 March 1873 (though I would not visit again that night for anything save the Lord's admonition), but I fear that the occurrences of which I must speak will be incomprehensible to anyone who has not understood what went before. By that I mean not only my own girlhood and womanhood, but also the life of the emigrant to the country of America, in particular the Norwegian emigrant, and most particularly still, the Norwegian emigrant who makes his living by putting his nets into the sea. More is known about those persons who left Norway in the middle of this century because the Norwegian land, even with all its plentiful fjords and fantastical forests, was, in many inhospitable parts of this country, unyielding to the ever-increasing population. Such dearth of land, at that time, refused to permit many households even a modest living in the farming of oats, barley, mangecorn and potatoes. It was these persons who left all they had behind, and who set intrepidly out to sea, and who did not stop on the Atlantic shores, but went instead directly inland to the state of New York, and hence from there into the prairie heartland of the United States of America. These are the emigrants of our Norway who were raised as farmers in the provinces of Stavanger and Bergen and Nedenes, and then abandoned all that they had held dear to begin life anew near the Lake of Michigan, and in the states of Minnesota and Wisconsin and in other states. The life of these emigrants was, I believe and am sorry to have to write, not always as they had imagined it to be, and I have read some of the letters from these wretched persons and have heard of the terrible hardships they had to bear, including, for some, the worst trial of all, the death of those they loved most, including children.

As I have not ever had children, I have been spared this most unthinkable of all losses.

In our village, which was Laurvig, and which was well coasted and had a lovely aspect out to the Laurvigsfjord and to the Skaggerak from many vantage points, some families who made their livings from the sea had gone to America before us. These persons were called "sloopfolk," as they had sailed in sloops in voyages of one to three months, during which some unfortunates perished, and some new life was born. John and I, who had been married but the year, had heard of such folk, though we did not have the acquaintance of any of these persons intimately, until that day in the seventh month of 1867, when a cousin of John's whose name was Torwad Holde, and who is since deceased, set sail for new fishing grounds near to the city of Gloucester, off the coast of the state of Massachusetts in America, fishing grounds that were said to hold forth promise of great riches to any and all who would set their nets there. I must add at this point that I did not believe in such fanciful and hollow promises, and would never have left Laurvig, had not John been, I shall have to say it, *seduced* by the letters of his cousin, Torwad, in particular one letter that I no longer have in my possession but remember in my heart as a consequence of having had to read this letter over and over again to my husband who had not had any schooling because of the necessity of having had to go to sea since the age of eight. I reproduce that letter here as faithfully as I can.

20 September 1867, the Isles of Shoals

My Dear Cousin,

You will be surprised to hear from me in a place different from that where I last wrote to you. I have moved north from the city of Gloucester. Axel Nordahl, who you may remember visited us last year, came to Gloucester to tell myself and Erling Hansen of the fishing settlement of which he was a part at a place called the Isles of Shoals. This is a small grouping of islands nine miles east of Portsmouth, New Hampshire, which is not far north of Gloucester. I am now residing with Nordahl and his good family on the island of Appledore, and I can report that he has a trawler here, and that he has found a bounty of fish such as I have never seen before in any waters. Indeed, I do not think there are any waters on earth that are so plentiful as these in which he has set his nets. A man can put his hand into this sea and fetch up, with his hand only, more fish than his boat might bear. I am firmly of a mind to remain here through the winter with Nordahl and then burden his family no more as I will build my own cottage on the island of Smutty-Nose, which has a strange name and which is also sometimes known as Haley's Island. When spring comes I will have saved enough dollars from my work with Nordahl to begin such a project. This is a better life, Hontvedt, than that which exists in Laurvig, or in Gloucester, where I was lodged with fifty other fishermen of the fleet and where my wages did not exceed one dollar a day.

I beg of you, John, to share this bounty with me. I beg of you to bring your brother, Matthew, who may be as pleased as I am to fish in these fertile waters. I have selected on this island called Smutty-Nose a house for you to lease. It is a good house, strongly built to withstand the Atlantic storms, and I might have taken up residence there myself if I had already had a family. In the spring, if the Lord permits me to find a wife, I shall move from Appledore so that we may all be a family in the Lord's sight.

If you come, as I am hoping, you must go by coastal ferry to Stavanger, and thence to Shields, England. There you will take the rail to Liverpool where you will join a great flood of emigrants who will take passage with you on a packet to Quebec, where ships are landing now, preferring to avoid the

higher tariffs charged in Boston and New York. For your voy-
age, you will want fruit wine to alter the taste of the poor
water, and dried fish. Grind some coffee and put it in a box.
You will also want to bake the flatbrød and pack it in the
round tubs you have seen down at the docks, and also cure
some cheese. If you have a wife and she is with child, then
come before it is her time, as infants do not well survive the
journey. Seven perished on my own passage, owing to the
diphtheria croup which was a contagion on board. I will tell
you in truth, Hontvedt, that the sanitary conditions aboard
these ships are very poor, and it is too bad, but on my journey
I was well disposed to prayer and to thinking of the voyage as
a deliverance. I was seasick all but the last two days, and
though I arrived in America very gaunt and thin, and re-
mained so in Gloucester, now I am fat again, thanks to the
cooking of Nordahl's wife, Adda, who feeds me good porridge
and potato cakes with all the fresh fish you can imagine.

When you are here, we may together purchase a trawler in
the town of Portsmouth. Send me news and greet all my
friends there, my mother, and all soskend.

Your cousin and servant unto death,
Torwad Holde

May God forgive me, but I confess that I have truly
hated the words of Torwad Holde's letter and even the
man himself, and I do so wish that this cursed letter had
never come into our house. It was an evil missive indeed
that stole my husband's common sense, that took us from

our homeland, and that eventuated in that terrible night of 5 March. Would that this letter, with its stories I could not credit, this letter that bore with its envelope strange and frightening stamps, this letter with its tales so magical I knew they must be lies, been dropped into the Atlantic Ocean during its transit from America to Norway.

But I digress. Even with the distance of thirty-one years, it is possible for me to become overwrought, knowing as I do what came later, what was to follow, and how this letter led us to our doom. Yet even in a state of distress, I must admit to understanding that a mere piece of paper can not be the instrument of one's undoing. In John, my husband, there was a yearning for adventure, for more than was his lot in Laurvig, desires I did not share with him, so content was I to be still near my family. And also, I must confess, there had been that summer, in the Skaggerak and even in the Kristianiafjord, a fish plague that had greatly lessened the number of mackerel available to the fisher-folk, and though not a consequence of this, but rather as a result of the importation of fish from Denmark, a simultaneous lowering of the price of herring in Kristiania, which caused my husband, in a more practical manner, to look toward new fishing grounds.

But bringing up a living fish with one's bare hands? Who could be such a blasphemer as to put forth such lies against the laws of nature?

"I will not go to America," I said to Evan on the landing at Laurvig on 10 March 1868.

I believe I spoke in a quavering voice, for I was nearly overcome by a tumult of emotions, chief among them an acute distress at having to leave my brother, Evan Christensen, behind, and not knowing if I would see him or my beloved Norway ever again. The smell of fish from the barrels on the landing was all around us, and we could as well distinguish the salted pork in wooden cases. We had had to step cautiously to the landing, as all about us the rod iron lay for loading onto the ship, and to my eye, this disarray seemed to have been made by a large hand, that is to say by the hand of God, Who had strewn about the pier these long and rusty spokes. I believe that I have so well remembered the sight of this cargo because I did not want to look up that day at the vessel which would carry me away from my home.

I must say that even today I remain quite certain that souls which take root in a particular geography cannot be successfully transplanted. I believe that these roots, these tiny fibrous filaments, will almost inevitably dry and wither in the new soil, or will send the plant into sudden and irretrievable shock.

Evan and I came to a stopping place amidst the terrible noise and chaos. All about us were sons taking leave of their mothers, sisters parting from sisters, husbands from young wives. Is there any other place on earth so filled with sweet torment as that of a ship's landing? For a time, Evan and myself stood together in silence. The water from the bay hurt my eyes, and a gust came upon us and billowed my skirt which had become muddied at the hem on the walk to the landing. I beat my fists against the silk, which was a walnut and was cinched becomingly at the waist, until Evan, who was considerably taller than myself, stayed my hands with his own.

"Hush, Maren, calm yourself," he said to me.

I took my breath in, and was near to crying, and might have but for the example of my brother who was steadfast and of great character and who would not show, for all the earth, the intense emotions that were at riot in his breast. My dress, I have neglected to say, was my wedding dress and had a lovely collar of tatting that my sister, Karen, had made for me. And I should mention as well that Karen had not come to the landing to say her farewells as she had been feeling poorly that morning.

The gusts, such as the one that had whipped up my skirt, turned severe, spiriting caps away and pushing back the wide brims of the bonnets on the women. I could hear the halyards of the sloops slapping hard against their masts, and though the day was fair, that is to say though the sky was a deep and vivid navy, I thought the gusts might presage a gale and that I would be granted a re-prieve of an hour or a day, as the captain, I was certain, would not set sail in such a blow. In this, however, I was mistaken, for John, my husband, who had been searching for me, raised his face and beckoned me toward the ship. I saw, even at a distance, that relief softened his squint, and I know that he had been afraid I might not come to the landing at all. Our passage had been paid already — sixty dollars — but I had, for just a moment, the lovely and calming image of two berths, two flat and tiered berths, sailing empty without us.

Evan, beside me, sensing that the fury had left my arms, released my hands. But though my wretchedness had momentarily abandoned me, my sorrow had not.

"You must go with John," he said to me. "He is your husband."

I pause now as if for breath. It is very difficult for me to write, even three decades later, of my family, who was so cruelly treated by fate.

In our family, Karen was born first and was some twelve years older than myself. She was, it must be said, a plain woman with a melancholy aspect, which I have always understood is sometimes appealing to men, as they do not wish a wife who is so beautiful or lively that she causes in her husband a constant worry, and our Karen was strong, an obedient daughter, and a skilled seamstress as well.

I see us now sitting at my father's table in the simple but clean room that was our living room and dining room and kitchen and where also Karen and I slept behind a curtain, and where we had a stove that gave off a great deal of heat and always made us comfortable (although sometimes, in the winter, the milk froze in the cupboard), and I am struck once again by how extraordinarily different I was from my sister, for whom I had a fond, though I must confess not passionate, regard. Karen had dun eyes that seldom seemed to change their color. She had had the misfortune, from a young age, to have fawn-colored hair, a dull brown that was not tinged with golden highlights nor ever warmed by the sun, and I remember that every day she fixed it in exactly the same manner, which is to say pulled severely behind her ears, with a fringe at her forehead, and rolled and fastened at the back of her head. I am not certain I ever saw Karen with her hair free and loose except for those occasions when I happened to observe her make herself ready for bed. Normally, Karen, who had great difficulty sleeping, was late to bed and early to rise, and I came to think of her as keeping a kind of watch over our household. Karen did have, however, an excellent figure, and was broad in her shoulders and erect in her posture. She was a tall woman, some five inches taller than myself. I was, if not diminutive, then small in my proportions. Like Karen, I too had broad shoulders, but perhaps a less plain face than hers when I was twenty. I did not possess, however, her obedience, nor her excellence as a seamstress. Though I would say otherwise at the time, I took a foolish pride in this when I was a girl, preferring the world of nature and imagination to that of cloth and needle, and I know that in my heart I set myself up as the more fortunate of us two, and I believed at the time that if ever I should have a husband, he would be a man who would be drawn to a woman not solely for her domestic skills, which has always seemed to be the measure of a woman, but also for her conversation.

In our family there was only the one other child besides Karen and me, Evan, my brother, who was two years older than myself, and so it happened that we were raised as one, so close were we in age, and so far from Karen. At that time, there were many deprivations visited upon the fisher-folk. Because of the shortness of the fishing season near to our home, our father, in order to feed his family, had sometimes to leave us for months at a time during the winter, to fish not by himself in his skiff, which he preferred and which better suited his independent nature, but rather to join the fishing fleets that sailed along the west coast and further north after the cod and the herring. When our situation was very bad, or it had been a particularly harsh winter, my mother and sometimes my sister had to hire themselves out for washing and for cooking in the boarding house for sailors on the Storgata in Laurvig.

But I must here dispel the image of the Christensen family in rude circumstances, hungry and in poverty, for

in truth, though we had little in the way of material goods
in my early childhood years, we had our religion, which
was a comfort, and our schooling, when we could make
our way along the coast road into Laurvig, and we had
family ties for which in all my years on this earth I have
never found a replacement.

The cottage in which we lived was humble but of a
very pleasing aspect. It was of wood, painted white, and
with a red-tiled roof, as was the custom. It had a small
porch with a railing in the front, and one window, to the
south, that was made of colored glass. In the rear of our
home was a small shed for storing nets and barrels, and in
front there was a narrow beach where our father, when we
were younger, kept his skiffs.

How many times I have had in my mind the image of
leaving Laurvig, and seeing from the harbor, along the
coast road, our own cottage and others like it, one and a
half stories tall, with such a profusion of blossoms in the
gardens around them. This area in Norway, which is in the
southeastern part of the country, facing to Sweden and
Denmark, has a mild climate and good soil for orchards
and other plants such as myrtle and fuchsia, which were
in abundance then and are now. We had peaches from a
tree in our garden, and though there were months at a time
when I had only the one woolen dress and only one pair
of woolen socks, we had fruit to eat and fresh or dried fish
and the foods that flour and water go together to make,
such as porridge and pancakes and lefse.

I possess so very many wonderful memories of those
days of my extreme youth that sometimes they are more
real to me than the events of last year or even of yesterday.
A child who may grow to adulthood with the sea and the

forest and the orchards at hand may count himself a very lucky child indeed.

Before we had reached the age when we were allowed to go to school, Evan and I had occasion to spend a great deal of time together, and I believe that because of this we each understood that in some indefinable manner our souls, and hence our paths, were to be inextricably linked, and perhaps I knew already that whatever fate might befall the one would surely befall the other. And as regards the outside world, that is to say the world of nature (and the people and spirits and animals who inhabited that tangible world), each of us was for the other a filter. I remember with a clarity that would seem to be extraordinary after so many years (these events having occurred at such a young age) talking with Evan all the long days and into the nights (for is not a day actually longer when one is a child, time being of an illusory and deceptive nature?) as if we were indeed interpreting for each other and for ourselves the mysterious secrets and truths of life itself.

We were bathed together in a copper tub that was brought out once a week and set upon a stand in the kitchen near to the stove. My father bathed first, and then my mother, and then Karen, and lastly, Evan and me together. Evan and I were fearful of our father's nakedness and respectful of our mother's modesty, and so we busied ourselves in another room during the times when our parents used the copper tub. But no such restraints had yet descended upon us as regards our sister, Karen, who would have been, when I was five, seventeen, and who possessed most of the attributes of a grown woman, attributes that both frightened and amazed me, although I cannot say it was with any reverence for her person that

Evan and I often peeked behind the curtain and made rude sounds and in this way tortured our sister, who would scream at us from the tub and, more often than not, end the evening in tears. And thus I suppose I shall have to admit here that Evan and myself, while not cruel or mischievous by nature or necessarily to anyone else in our company, were sometimes moved to torment and tease our sister, because it was, I think, so easy to do and at the same time so enormously, if unforgivably, rewarding.

When our turn for the bath had come, we would have clean water that had been heated by our mother in great pots and then poured into the copper tub, and my brother and myself, who until a late age had no shame between us, would remove our clothing and play in the hot soapy water as if in a pool in the woods, and I remember the candlelight and warmth of this ritual with a fondness that remains with me today.

Each morning of the school year, when we were younger and not needed to be hired out, Evan and I rode together in the wagon of our nearest neighbor, Torjen Helgessen, who went every day into Laurvig to bring his milk and produce to market, and home again each afternoon after the dinner hour. The school day was five hours long, and we had the customary subjects of religion, Bible History, catechism, reading, writing, arithmetic and singing. We had as our texts Pontoppidan's Explanation, Vogt's Bible History and Jensen's Reader. The school was a modern one in many of its aspects. It had two large rooms, one above the other, each filled with wooden desks and a chalkboard that ran the length of one wall. Girls were in the lower room and boys in the upper. Unruly behavior was not allowed, and the students of

Laurvig School received the stick when necessary. My brother had it twice, once for throwing chalk erasers at another student, and once for being rude to Mr. Hjorth, a Pietist and thus an extremely strict and sometimes irritating man, who later died during an Atlantic crossing as a result of the dysentery aboard.

In the springtime, when it was light early in the morning, and this was a pearly light that is not known in America, an oyster light that lasts for hours before the sun is actually up, and so has about it a diffuse and magical quality, Evan and I would wake at daybreak and walk the distance into Laurvig to the school.

I can hardly describe to you the joy of those early morning walks together, and is it not true that in our extreme youth we possess the capacity to see more clearly and absorb more intensely the beauty that lies all before us, and so much more so than in our later youth or in our adulthood, when we have been apprised of sin and its stain and our eyes have become dulled, and we cannot see with the same purity, or love so well?

The coast road hugged at times the very edge of the cliffs and overlooked the Bay, so that on a fine day, to the east of us, there would be the harbor, with its occasional schooners and ferries, and beyond it the sea twitching so blindingly we were almost forced to turn our eyes away.

As we walked, Evan would be wearing his trousers and a shirt without a collar and his jacket and his cap. He wore stockings that Karen or my mother had knit, wonderful stockings in a variety of intricate patterns, and he carried his books and dinner sack, and sometimes also mine, in a leather strap which had been fashioned from a horse's rein. I myself, though just a girl, wore the heavy dresses of the day, that is to say those of domestic and homespun manufacture, and it was always a pleasure in the late spring when our mother allowed me to change the wool dress for a calico that was lighter in weight and in color and made me feel as though I had just bathed after a long and oppressive confinement. At that time, I wore my hair loose along my back, with the sides pulled into a topknot. I may say here that my hair was of a lovely color in my youth, a light and soft brown that picked up the sun in summer, and was sometimes, by August, golden near the front, and I had fine, clear eyes of a light gray color. As I have mentioned, I was not a tall girl, but I did have a good carriage and figure, and though I was never a great beauty, not like Anethe, I trust I was pleasant to look upon, and perhaps even pretty for several years in my late youth, before the true responsibilities of my journey on earth began and altered, as it does in so many women, the character of the face.

I recall one morning when Evan and myself would have been eight and six years of age respectively. We had gone perhaps three quarters of the way to town when my brother quite suddenly put down his books and dinner sack and threw off his jacket and cap as well, and in his shirt and short pants raised his arms and leapt up to seize a branch of an apple tree that had just come fully into bloom, and I suspect that it was the prospect of losing himself in all that white froth of blossoms that propelled Evan higher and higher so that in seconds he was calling to me from the very apex of the tree. *Hallo, Maren, can you see me?* For reasons I cannot accurately describe, I could not bear to be left behind on the ground, and so it was with a frenzy of determination that I tried to repeat

Evan's acrobatics and make a similar climb to the height
of the fruit tree. I discovered, however, that I was encum-
bered by the skirts of my dress, which were weighing me
down and would not permit me to grab hold of the tree
limbs with my legs in a shimmying fashion, such as I had
just witnessed Evan performing. It was, then, with a gesture of irritation and perhaps anger at my sex, that I
stripped myself of my frock, along that most travelled of
public roads into Laurvig, stripped myself down to my
underclothes, which consisted of a sleeveless woolen vest
and a pair of unadorned homespun bloomers, and thus
was able in a matter of minutes to join my brother at the
top of the tree, which gave a long view of the coastline,
and which, when I had reached Evan, filled me with a
sense of freedom and accomplishment that was not often
repeated in my girlhood. I remember that he smiled at me
and said, "Well done," and that shortly after I had reached
Evan's perch, I leaned forward in my careless ebullience
to see north along the Laurvigsfjord, and, in doing so, lost
my balance and nearly fell out of the tree, and almost certainly would have done had not Evan grabbed hold of my
wrist and righted me. And I recall that he did not remove
his hand, but rather stayed with me in that position, his
hand upon my wrist, for a few minutes more, as we could
not bear to disturb that sensation of peace and complete-
ness that had come over us, and so it happened that we
were both late for school on that day and were chastised
by having to remain after school for five days in a row, a
detention neither of us minded or complained about as I
think we both felt the stricture to be pale reprimand for
the thrilling loveliness of the crime. Of course, we had
been fortunate that all the time we had been in the tree no

farmer had come along the road and seen my frock in the dirt, a shocking sight in itself, and which doubtless would have resulted in our capture and quite likely a more severe punishment of a different nature.

At school, Evan was well liked, but though he did join in the games, he did not take extra pains to become popular in the manner of some boys of the town. He was not a boy, or ever a man, who was filled with anger or resentments as some are, and if a wrong was done to him, he needed only to correct it, not exact a punishment for the crime. (Though I am sorry to say that Evan was eventually to learn, as were we all, that there was no righting of the ultimate wrong that was done to him.) In this way, I do not think I have measured up to him in character, for I have often felt myself in the sway of intense emotions that are sinful in their origin, including those of anger and hatred.

Evan was always substantially taller than myself, and for a time was the tallest boy in the Laurvig school. Although he had slightly crooked teeth in the front, he developed a handsome face that I believe resembled our father's, though, of course, I never saw my father as a younger man, and by the time I was old enough for such impressions to register, my father's cheeks were sunken and there were many wrinkles on his face, this as a consequence of the weathering that occurred at sea and was a feature of most fishermen of that time.

When our schooling was finished for the year, we often had the long days together, and this was the very greatest of joys, for the light stayed with us until nearly midnight in the midsummer.

I see us now as if I were looking upon my own self. In

the woods, just west of where our home was situated, there was a little-visited and strange geographic phenomenon known as Hakon's Inlet, a pool of seawater that was nearly black as a consequence of both its extraordinary depth and of the sheer black rock that formed the edges of the pool and rose straight up to a height of thirty feet on all sides, so that this pool was, with the exception of a narrow fissure through which seawater flowed, a tall, dark cylinder. It was said to be twenty fathoms deep, and along its walls were thin ledges that one, with some practice, could navigate to reach the water and thus swim, or fish, or even lower a boat and paddle about. Yellow stone crop grew in the fissure, and it was altogether a most magical place.

At this pool, on a June morning, I see a small girl of eight years of age, who is standing on a ledge, holding her dress above the water, revealing her knees and not caring much, as there had not yet been between herself and her brother any loss of innocence, nor indeed any need for false modesty on the part of either, and beyond her, perched upon a nearby shelf of rock, with a rudimentary fishing pole in his hands, her brother, Evan. He is smiling at her because she has been teasing him in a pleasant manner about the fact that he has grown so tall that his pants rise a good inch above his ankles. He is, upon his rock, the embodiment of all that Norwegian parents might wish in their boys, a tall and strong youth, with the thin pale hair that we have come in this country to favor so, and eyes the color of water. Presently, the boy puts down his fishing pole and takes from his sack a small dark object that he quickly flings out over the water, and which reveals itself to be a net of the finest threads, intricately woven, a gauze, more like, or a web of gossamer, catching the light of the sun's rays that hover and seem to stop just above the surface of the pool. The girl, intrigued, makes her way to the ledge on which the boy is standing and sees that the net is large and comments upon this, whereupon the boy tells her that he has made it deep so that it will sink low into the pool and bring up from its depths all manner of sea creatures. The girl watches with fascination as the boy, who has had a not inconsequential amount of experience with fishing nets, and who has fashioned the present one from threads from his mother's sewing cabinet, expertly spreads the net over the surface of the black water and allows it, with its weighted sinks, to lower itself until only the bobbers at the four corners are visible. Then, with a deft movement of his body, and indicating that the girl should follow him, he hops from ledge to ledge, dragging the gathering net behind him. After a time, he lets the bobbers float closer to the wall of the pool, where he then snags them and slowly brings up the net. He hauls his catch up onto the ledge on which the pair are standing and opens it for their inspection. In the net are wriggling bits and sacs of color the girl has never seen before. Many of these sea creatures have lovely iridescent colorings, but some appear to her grotesque in texture, like mollusks without their shells. Some are translucent shapes that reveal working innards; others are heaving gills flecked with gold or round fat fish with bulging eyes or simple dark slivers the color of lead. Some of the fish the girl recognizes: a sea bass, a codfish, several mackerel.

But the girl is frightened by the grotesque display, and is fearful that the boy has perhaps trespassed in the unnatural world, and has brought up from the black pool living things not meant to be seen or to see the light of day, and, indeed, some small peacock-blue gelatinous spheres begin to pop and perish there upon the ledge.

"Maren, do you see?" the boy asks excitedly, pointing to this fish and to that one, but the girl is both attracted and repulsed by the catch, wanting to tear her head away, yet not able to, when suddenly the boy picks up the four corners of the net and upends the catch into the water, not realizing that the girl's foot is on a part of the net, where-upon the gossamer tears and catches on the girl's bare ankle, and with one swooping movement, she plunges into the water, believing that she might kick the net away whenever she wants to, and then discovers in a panic (that even now I can taste at the back of my throat) that both feet have become entangled in the threads and the skirt of her dress has become weighted with water. In addition, in her fright, she is surrounded by the sealife that had been in the net, some of which swims away, and some of which floats near to her face. She flails with her arms and tries to swim, but cannot find a suitable ledge to hang on to. And Evan, who sees that his sister is in great distress, jumps into the water after her, caring little for his own safety, but greatly concerned for hers. I can hear my voice that is filled with the utmost terror, calling out *Help!*, and then again, *Help!*, and Evan's voice, not yet broken and ma-tured, a melodious voice that was most welcome at the Christmas Hymns each year, calling out, *I'll get you, Maren.* I remember now the strength of his hand under my chin, holding my mouth above the water so that I could breathe, while he splashed about most terribly and took in a great deal of water himself, and was as panicked as I, though he would never say so later. It was only by the greatest good fortune that we drifted, in this agitated state, across the pool, to a ledge a meter above the water and that Evan, by the grace of God and by a strength not commonly known to children of that age, grasped that ledge with his free hand and thus saved us both.

I remember that we lay upon the rocky shelf, clasped in each other's arms, for a long time afterward, and it was only after many minutes in such a position that I was able to stop shivering.

I think now upon that day and imagine another fate. A fisherman coming upon the inlet and seeing two children, locked together in embrace, floating just below the surface of the black water, forever free, forever peaceful, and I wonder now if that might not have been a more desirable end for both of us.

In our cottage by the sea, our mother had hung gay curtains of a red-checked cloth, and on our table, there was always, in season, a small glass milk pitcher of flowers that had come from the garden that surrounded the cottage, and for many years after our mother had died, I could not look at a vessel of flowers on a table without thinking of her. I am troubled now that I have primarily indistinct memories of my mother, whom I loved, but who was drawn in her aspect and often so tired as to be unwell. She was, like myself, a small woman who had a great many physical tasks to attend to, and who was not, I believe, of a sufficient fortitude to withstand these burdens. Also I believe that whatever love she did not reserve for her husband, she felt for her son, and in this she could not help herself.

In the evenings, I might be sent to bed while my mother spoke in low tones to Evan. About these talks,

Evan would only say that they were often stories or homilies about virtues of character and defects of same, and that our mother had shown herself to be not religious in her beliefs, which at that time surprised me, as Evan and I and also Karen were required to spend almost all of Sunday in our church.

As to why I was excluded from these talks, my mother must have felt that either my character had already been formed and therefore such homilies were unnecessary, or that these talks in the night would be lost on a girl who would, by nature and by custom, submit herself to her husband's beliefs and character when she married. I am pleased to say that though marriage often constrained my actions, my character and my beliefs, both of which were molded by influences far stronger than the fisherman who became my husband, remained intact and unchallenged for the duration of my years with John Hontvedt. I will add, however, that an unfortunate result of these private talks between my mother and my brother was that I was hard-pressed to disbelieve the notion that of the two of us, Evan was the more greatly loved, and in some way I could not articulate or account for, the more deserving of this love, and thus my own affection for my brother was not compromised but rather enhanced by this exclusionary affection of which I so desperately wanted to be a part.

My mother sat by the table in the evenings when her presence was not required in town, and sewed or made bread for the next day. When I remember her in this way, I see her as in the thrall of a quiet sorrow, not the dreary if not altogether sour melancholy that Karen was sometimes possessed of, but rather a weight upon her spirit that she bore uncomplainingly and in an unobtrusive manner. Perhaps she was not ever really well and simply never told us this. When our father was home, he would sit near to her, mending his nets or just silently smoking his pipe, and though they seldom spoke, I would sometimes catch him regarding her with admiration, although I don't believe the possibility of romantic love between our mother and our father ever consciously occurred to me until I had occasion to witness our father's demeanor after our mother had died.

When I was thirteen years of age, and Evan just fifteen, our mother perished, giving birth to a stillborn child who was buried with her. It was in the worst winter month of 1860, and the environs of Laurvig, and indeed the entire coast region, had been buried with the snows of that year. On the day that my mother perished, there was, in the early hours of the morning, when she had just begun her labor, a wild blizzard of snow so thick it was impossible to see out the windows. My father, who had not been present for the births of his other three children, as he had been at sea during those occasions, did not feel qualified to attend to such an event, and therefore hastened, even in the terrible storm, to fetch the midwife who lived between our cottage and the town, and might be reached if the sleigh, belonging to our neighbor, Mr. Helgessen, could be fetched and could make the passage. Karen, who might have been able to help our mother, was residing that night at the boarding house for sailors, where it was thought she should stay during the storm. Thus myself and Evan, who were too young to help in this matter, except insofar as we could put ice on our mother's brow, wipe her head and arms when it was necessary, and hold her hand when she would let us, stood beside her listening to her terrible cries. I had had until that moment no experience of child-birth, and I had never seen such torment in any individual. I remember that in the candlelight Evan stood shivering with fear in his nightshirt, believing that our mother's agony was a certain sign that she would die. He began to cry out most awfully, although he wished that he would not, and I became distraught at the sight of Evan's crying, since he had always been a strong and undemonstrative boy, and I believe now that I was more distressed at the sound of his weeping, at least momentarily, than I was at the unspeakable rhythmic cries from our mother, and that I may have left my mother's side to tend to him, holding him with thin arms that barely reached around him, kiss-ing his tear-ruined face to soothe him, to stop his shiver-ing, so that when, startled by the sudden silence, I looked back at our mother, I saw that she was gone. A large pool of blood had soaked the bedclothes from her stomach to her knees, and I dared not lift the sheets for fear of what lay beneath them. I think that possibly I may have closed her eyes. My father could not reach the midwife and was forced to turn back. When he finally returned to our house, nearly dead himself, the event was finished.

I remember his hoarse shout when he entered the cot-tage and saw what lay before him. I remember also that I had not the strength to leave Evan, and that I could not go out into the living room to console my father. When fi-nally our father came into our bedroom, with his face blasted by the sight of his beloved wife taken from him in such a violent manner, he found Evan and myself in our bed, holding each other for comfort.

I would not for all the world speak of such gruesome matters except that I have always wondered if I might not have attended to my mother in some better way and thus perhaps have saved her. And I have wondered as well if my memories of this terrible night, or my actions, have been the cause of my barren state in my own womanhood, as if I had been punished by God for not allowing the birth of my sibling.

I remained, for some months after this event, in an agitated state of mind. Indeed, I grew worse and was overtaken by a mysterious malady. I do not remember all of this time very well, but I was told about it often enough by Karen, who was, during those long and dark days, in despair over our mother's death and my illness. Unable to sleep at night, or if I did sleep, subject to the most excruciatingly horrible dreams, and without any medicines that might be a remedy to me, I became weakened and then ill, and from there slipped into a fever that appeared to all around me to have a psychic rather than physical origin. At least that was the opinion of the doctor who was fetched more than once from Laurvig, and who was at a loss to describe the root cause of my symptoms. I recall that for a time I could not move either my legs or my arms, and it was thought that I might have caught the meningitis, even though there were no other reported cases in our area that season. Because I was so incapacitated, I could not feed myself. Karen, having more than her share to do about the house as a result of my being bedridden, left this chore to Evan, who nursed me uncomplainingly, and I believe that he was in a kind of torment himself, owing to the events that had occurred on the night that our mother had died.

There were entire days when I could not speak and had to be held up in a half-sitting position just to take a sip of

Farris water, which was thought to be therapeutic. I was moved for the duration of my illness to my father's bed near to the stove in the living room, while my father took up residence in the room that I had shared with Evan. My brother made a vigil at my bedside. I believe he sat there not speaking for much of the time, but he may have read to me from the folk tales as well. During this time Evan did not attend school.

I was not always lucid during my illness, but there is one incident I remember with absolute clarity, and which has remained with me in all its wonder and complexity.

I had just awakened from a dream-like state one morning some months into the illness. Karen was outside in the garden, and there were daffodils in a pitcher on the table. It must have been late April or early May following my mother's death. Previously, when I had awakened and was emerging from one of my dreams, I had felt frightened, for the feelings of the illness would flood into me and I would be visited by the strangest waking visions, which seemed very real to me at the time, and were all against the tenets of God. But that morning, though I was again beset with such visions, I did not feel fear, but rather a kind of all-encompassing forgiveness, not only of those around me, but of myself. Thus it happened that in the first seconds of consciousness that morning, I impulsively reached for Evan's hand. He was sitting in a wooden chair, his back very straight, his face solemn. Perhaps he himself had been far away when I awakened, or possibly he had been yearning to go outside on that fine day himself. When I put my hand on his, he flinched, for we had not willfully touched since the night that our mother had perished. In truth, I would have to say that he looked stricken when I first touched him, though I believe that this was a consequence of his worry over my health and his surprise at my awakening.

I remember that he had on a blue shirt that Karen had recently washed and ironed. His hair, which had been combed for the morning, had become even paler over the past year and accentuated the watery blue of his eyes.

His hand did not move in mine, and I did not let him go.

"Maren, are you well?" he asked.

I thought for a moment and then answered, "I feel very well indeed."

He shook his head as though throwing off some unbidden thought, and then looked down at our hands.

"Maren, we must do something," he said.

"Do something?"

"Speak to someone. I don't know . . . I have tried to think."

"I don't know what you mean," I said to him.

Evan appeared to be irritated by this admission.

"But you must do," he said. "I know you do." He looked up quickly and allowed his eyes to meet mine.

I believe that wordlessly, in those few moments, we spoke of many things. His hand grew hot under mine, or perhaps it was simply my own fever, and, just as I could not pull away, neither could he, and for some minutes, perhaps even for many minutes, we remained in that state, and if it is possible to say, in a few moments, even without words, all that has to be said between two individuals, this was done on that day.

After a time (I cannot accurately say how long this oc- currence took place), I sat up, and in a strange manner, yet one which on that day seemed as natural to me as a kiss upon a baby's cheek, I put my lips to the inside of his wrist, which was turned upward to me. I remained in that position, in a state of neither beginning nor ending a kiss, until that moment when we heard a sound at the door and looked up to see that our sister, Karen, had come in from the garden.

I remember the bewildered look that came upon her face, a look of surprise and darkening all at once, so that she frightened me, and a sound escaped my throat, and Evan, leaving me, stood up. Karen said to me, although I think not to Evan, *What is it that you do?* To which question I could no more have made an answer than I could have explained to her the mystery of the sacraments. Evan left the room, and I do not believe that he spoke. Karen came to me and hovered over my bed, examining me, her hair pulled tightly back off her head, her dress with its shell buttons rising to her throat, and I remember thinking to myself that though the wondrous forgiveness I had so recently felt encompassed everyone around me, I did not really like Karen much, and I felt a pity for her I had not consciously realized before. I believe I closed my eyes then and drifted back into that state from which I had only a short time earlier emerged.

Not long after that incident, I recovered my health. Never was anyone so glad to greet the lustrous mornings of that spring, though I was quickly advised by Karen that my childhood was now over and that I would have to assume the responsibilities and demeanor of a young woman. Around that time, perhaps even immediately after my illness, it was decided that I would remain sleeping with Karen in the kitchen behind the curtain, and that our father would permanently take up the bed I had shared with Evan. This was because I had reached, during my illness, the age of fourteen, and that while I had been sick there had been certain changes in my body, which I will not speak of here, which made it necessary for me to move out of a room that Evan slept in.

Our mother having died, and our father out at sea for most of the hours in his day, I was put under the care of our sister, who was dutiful in her watch, but who I do not think was ever suited for the job. Sensing something, I know not what, a reluctance on her part perhaps, I was sometimes a torment to her, and I have often, in the years that have since passed, wished that I might have had her forgiveness for this. To her constrictions I gave protest, thus causing her to put me under her discipline until such time as I did not have so much freedom as before.

I would not like to attribute the loss of my liberty, my uncompromised happiness, to the coming of my woman-hood, and I believe it is merely a coincidence of timing, but I was, nevertheless, plagued with extremely severe monthly pains, which may have had, at their root, the more probable cause of my barrenness.

I must stop now, for these memories are disturbing me, and my eyes are hurting.

WHEN I LOOK at photographs of Billie, I can see that she is there — her whole self, the force of her — from the very beginning. Her infant face is intricately formed — solemn, yet willing to be pleased. Her baby hair is thick and black, which accentuates the navy of her eyes. Even then she has extraordinarily long lashes that charm me to the bottom of my soul and stop passersby on the street. Our friends congratulate me for having produced such a beguiling creature, but inwardly I protest. Was I not merely a custodian — a fat, white cocoon?

In the first several weeks after Billie's birth, Thomas and Billie and I inhabited a blur of deepening concentric circles. At the perimeter was Thomas, who sometimes spun off into the world of students and the university. He bought groceries, wrote at odd hours, and looked upon his daughter as a mystifying and glorious interruption of an ordered life. He carried Billie around in the crook of his arm and talked to her continuously. He introduced her to the world: "This is a chair; this is my table at the diner." He took her — zipped into the front of his leather jacket, her cheek resting against his chest or her head bobbing beneath his chin — on his daily walks through the streets of the city. He seemed, for a time, a less extraordinary man, less preoccupied, more like the cliché of a new father. This perception was reassuring to me, and I think to Thomas as well. He discovered in himself a nurturing streak that was comforting to him, one that he couldn't damage and from which he couldn't distance himself with images and words. For a time, after Billie was born, Thomas drank less. He believed, briefly, in the future. His best work was behind him, but he didn't know that then.

In the middle circle were the three of us, each hovering near the other. We lived, as we had since Thomas and I were married, in the top half of a large, brown-stained, nineteenth-century house on a back street in Cambridge. Henry James once lived next door and e. e. cummings across the street. The neighborhood, thought Thomas, had suitable resonance. I put Billie in a room that used to be my office, and the only pictures I took then were of Billie. Sometimes I slept; sometimes Thomas slept; Billie slept a lot. Thomas and I came together in sudden, bewildered clutches. We ate at odd hours, and we watched late-night television programs we had never seen before. We were a protoplasmic mass that was becoming a family.

And in the center circle — dark and dream-like — was the nest of Billie and myself. I lay on the bed, and I folded my daughter into me like bedclothes. I stood at the window overlooking the back garden and watched her study her hands. I stretched out on the floor and placed my daughter on my stomach and examined her new bright eyes. Her presence was so intensely vivid to me, so all-consuming, that I could not imagine who she would be the next day. I couldn't even remember what she had looked like the day before. Her immediate being pushed out all the other realities, blotted out other pictures. In the end, the only images I would retain of Billie's babyhood were the ones that were in the photographs.

At the Athenaeum, I put the papers back into the flesh-colored box and set it on the library table. I fold my hands on top of it. The librarian has left the room. I am wondering how the material can have been allowed to remain in such a chaotic state. I don't believe the Athenaeum even knows what it has. I suppose I am thinking that I will simply take the document and its translation and then bring them back the following week after I have photocopied them. No one will ever know. Not so very different, I am thinking, from borrowing a book from a lending library.

I put the loose letters, photographs, sermons, and official documents back into the folder and eye it, trying to judge how it looks without the box. I put the three books I have been given on top of the folder to camouflage the loss. I study the pile.

I cannot do it.

I put the box back inside the folder and stand up. *Goodbye,* I say, and then, just as I am leaving, in a somewhat louder voice, *Thanks.* I open the metal door and walk evenly down the stairs.

When I emerge from the Athenaeum, Thomas is not on the sidewalk. I wait ten minutes, then another five.

I walk across the street and stand in a doorway. Twenty minutes elapse, and I begin to wonder if I heard Thomas correctly.

I see them coming from the corner. Thomas and Adaline have Billie between them. They count *one, two, three,* and lift Billie high into the air with their arms, like a rope bridge catching a gust of wind. Billie giggles with the airborne thrill and asks them to do it again — and again. I can see Billie's small brown legs inside her shorts, her feet kicking the air for height. People on the sidewalk move to one side to let them pass. So intent are Thomas and Adaline on their game that they walk by the Athenaeum and don't even see it.

Adaline lets go of Billie's hand. Thomas checks his watch. Adaline scoops Billie up into one arm, and hefts her onto her hip, as I have done a thousand times. Thomas says something to Adaline, and she tilts her head back and laughs soundlessly. Billie pats her hair.

Moving fast, I cross the street before they can turn around. I reenter the Athenaeum and take the stairs two at a time. When I open the door to the reading room, I see that my neat stack of books and folders is exactly as I have left it. The librarian hasn't yet returned. I walk over to the long library table and remove the box from the folder. I put it under my arm.

I nearly slap the door into Thomas, who is looking up at the tall building, trying to ascertain whether he is in the correct place. Billie has climbed down from Adaline's hip, but is still holding her hand.

"Sorry," I say quickly. "I hope you weren't waiting long."

"How'd it go?" he asks. He puts his hands in his pockets.

"Fine," I say, bending to give Billie a kiss. "How about you?"

"We had a good time," Adaline says. She seems slightly flushed. "We found a park with swings, and we had an ice-cream cone." She looks down at Billie as if for confirmation.

"Where's Rich?" I ask.

"He's buying lobsters for supper," Thomas says quickly, again glancing at his watch. "We're supposed to meet him. Right now, as a matter of fact. What's that you've got there?"

"This?" I say, holding out the box. "Just something they lent me at the Athenaeum."

"Useful?"

"I hope so."

We walk four abreast along the sidewalk. I am aware of a settling of spirits, a lessening of exuberance. Adaline is quiet. She holds Billie's hand. That seems odd to me, as if she were unwilling to relinquish the tiny hand, even in my presence.

Rich is standing on the sidewalk and cradling two large paper bags. His eyes are hidden behind dark glasses.

We set off for the dock. The sky is clear, but the breeze is strong.

Rich and Adaline go ahead to prepare the Zodiac and to get the life jacket for Billie. I stand beside my daughter. Her hair whips across her face, and she tries unsuccessfully to hold it with her hands.

Thomas is staring into the harbor.

Thomas, I say.

Billie was six weeks old when she began to cough. I was bathing her in preparation for an appointment with the pediatrician, when I observed her — as I had not been able to when she was dressed — engaged in an awful kind of struggle. Her abdomen deflated at every pull for air, like an oxygen bladder on a pilot's mask. I picked

Billie up and took her into Thomas's study. He glanced up at me, surprised at this rare intrusion. He had his glasses on, and his fingers were stained with navy ink. In front of him were white lined pages with unintelligible words on them.

"Look at this," I said, laying Billie on top of the desk.

Together we watched the alarming phenomenon of the inflating and deflating chest.

"Shit," Thomas said. "Did you call the doctor?"

"I called because of the cough. I have an appointment at ten-thirty."

"I'm calling 911."

"You think —?"

"She can't breathe," said Thomas.

The ambulance driver would not let me travel with Billie. Too much equipment was needed; too much attention. They were working on her even as they closed the door. I thought: What if she dies, and I'm not there?

We followed in our car, Thomas cursing and gesturing at anyone who attempted to cut us off. I had never seen him so angry. The ambulance stopped at the emergency ward of the hospital in which Billie had been born.

"Jesus Christ," said Thomas. "We just got out of here."

In the emergency room, Billie was stripped naked and put into a metal coverless box that later Thomas and I would agree looked like a coffin. Of course, Billie was freezing, and she began to howl. I begged the attending physician to let me pick her up and nurse her to calm her. Surely the crying couldn't be good for the coughing and the breathing? But the young doctor told me that I was now a danger to my daughter, that I could no longer nurse her, that she had to be fed intravenously and pumped with antibiotics. He spoke to me as though I had been given an important assignment and had blown it.

Billie was hooked up to dozens of tubes and wires. She cried until she couldn't catch her breath. I couldn't bear her suffering one second longer, and when the doctor left to see to someone else, I picked her up, wrapping the folds of my quilted jacket around her, not feeding her, but holding her to my breast. Immediately, she stopped crying and rooted around for my nipple. Thomas looked at us with an expression of tenderness and fear I had never seen on his face before.

Billie had pneumonia. For hours, Thomas and I stood beside a plastic box that had become Billie's bed, studying the bank of monitors that controlled and recorded her breathing, her food intake, her heart rate, her blood pressure, her blood gases, and her antibiotics. There was no other universe except this plastic box, and Thomas and I marveled at the other parents in the intensive care unit who returned from forays into the outside world with McDonald's cartons and boxes from Pizza Hut.

"How can they eat?" said Thomas.

That night, Thomas was told that he had a phone call, and he left the room. I stood beside the plastic box and rhythmically recited the Lord's Prayer over and over, even though I am not a religious woman. I found the words soothing. I convinced myself that the words themselves would hold Billie to me, that as long as I kept reciting the prayer, Billie would not die. That the words themselves were a talisman, a charm.

When Thomas came back into the room, I turned automatically to him to ask him who called. His face was haggard — thin and papery around his eyes. He blinked, as though he were emerging from a movie theater into the bright sun.

He named a prize any poet in America might covet. It was for *The Magdalene Poems,* a series of fifty-six poems it had taken my husband eight years to write. We both sat down in orange plastic chairs next to the plastic box. I put my hand on his. I thought immediately of terrible contracts. How could we have been given this wonderful piece of news and have Billie survive as well?

"I can't digest this," Thomas said.

"No."

"We'll celebrate some other time."

"Thomas, if I could be, I'd be thrilled. I will be thrilled."

"I've always worried that you thought I was with you because of the poems. That I was using you. As a kind of muse."

"Not now, Thomas."

"In the beginning."

"Maybe, for a while, in the beginning."

"It's not true."

I shook my head in confusion. "How can this possibly matter?" I asked with the irritation that comes of not wanting to think about anything except the thing that is frightening you.

"It doesn't matter," he said. "It doesn't matter."

But of course it did matter. It did matter.

I learned that night that love is never as ferocious as when you think it is going to leave you. We are not always allowed this knowledge, and so our love sometimes becomes retrospective. But that night Thomas and I believed that our daughter was going to die. As we listened to the beeps and buzzes and hums and clicks of the machines surrounding her, we held hands, unable to touch her. We scrutinized her eyelids and eyelashes, her elbows and her fat calves. We shared a stunning cache of memories, culled in only six weeks. In some ways, we knew our daughter better that night than we ever would again.

Billie recovered in a week and was sent home. She grew and flourished. Eventually we reached the day when she was able to irritate us, when we were able to speak sharply to her. Eventually we reached the day when I was able to leave her and go out to take photographs. Thomas wrote poems and threw them away. He taught classes and gave numerous readings and talked to reporters and began to wonder if the words were running out on him. He drank more heavily. In the mornings, I would sometimes find him in the kitchen in a chair, his elbow resting on the counter. Next to him would be an empty bottle of wine. "This has nothing to do with you," he would say to me, putting a hand on the skirt of my robe. "I love you. This is not your fault."

I have sometimes thought that there are moments when you can see it all — and if not the future, then all that has gone before. They say this is true of the dying — that one can see a life — that the brain can perceive in an instant, or at most a few seconds, all that has gone before. Beginning at birth and ending with the moment of total knowledge so that the moment itself becomes a kind of infinite mirror, reflecting the life again and again and again.

I imagine that moment would be felt as a small billowy shock through the body, the *whoomph* of touching a frayed cord. Not fatal in itself, perhaps, but a surprise, a jolt.

And that is how it comes to me on the dock. I can see the years that Thomas and I have had together, the fragility of that life. The creation of a marriage, of a family, not because it has been ordained or is meant to be, but because we have simply made it happen. We have done this thing, and then that thing, and then that thing, and I have come to think of our years together as a tightly knotted fisherman's net; not perfectly made perhaps, but so well knit I would have said it could never have been unraveled.

During the hours that pass between our return from Portsmouth and dinner, we each go our separate ways. Adaline shuts the door and reads Celia Thaxter in the forward cabin; Thomas dozes in the cockpit while Billie kneels beside him, coloring; Rich retreats into the engine compartment to fix the bilge pump; and I sit on Billie's berth with guidebooks and notes and the transcript spread all around me. I open the flesh-colored box and examine the penciled translation. I know that I will read it soon, but I am not quite ready. I feel furtive in the narrow berth, and vaguely ashamed of myself.

I tell myself that the reason for my theft is simple: I want to know how it was, to find the one underlying detail that will make it all sensible. I want to understand the random act, the consequences of a second's brief abandonment. I am thinking not so much of the actions of a single night as I am of the aftermath of years — and of what there would be to remember.

In the guidebooks, I read that history has only one story to tell about John Hontvedt, Maren's husband, at Smuttynose, apart from all the events attending the murders on March 5, 1873. On a frigid day in 1870, three

years before the murders and two years after Hontvedt arrived in America, John left Smuttynose for fishing
grounds northwest of the island. We are told it was a particularly filthy day, ice forming on mustaches and oilskins, on lines, and even on the deck of Hontvedt's
schooner, which remains nameless. John stood on the
slippery shingle of the small beach at Smuttynose, the
sleet assaulting him from a slanting angle, trying to decide whether or not to row out to the schooner. We can
only guess at what finally compelled Hontvedt to go to
sea on such a day, among the worst the Atlantic had to
offer that year. Was it poverty? Or hunger? Expensive bait
that might rot if it wasn't used? An awful kind of restless-
ness?

After setting sail and losing sight of Smuttynose, John
was surprised by a gale that blew up, creating heavy seas
and blizzard conditions. The snow became so thick on the
sea as the hours wore on that John could not have seen
much beyond the boat itself. Perhaps realizing his mistake, John did try then to turn back toward Smuttynose,
but the swells were so high and the visibility so poor that
he could make no headway. He was instead forced to drift
in an aimless pattern in a darkish, white blindness. The
danger of being swamped or of the schooner being
gouged open on unseen rocks and ledges was very real.

A number of the islanders, chief among them a man
named Ephraim Downs, who lived on Smuttynose himself, and who would later live with his family in the
Hontvedt house after the murders (the landlord refusing
to clean away the bloodstains, he said, because he could
get more money from souvenir hunters than he could
from a higher rent), thought John mad for having set out

that day at all, and watched for him to return. When it became apparent that Hontvedt's schooner must be lost, Downs set out in his own larger ship, aptly named the *White Rover*, to search for the disabled or stranded boat. Downs and his crew scanned the sea for hours until they themselves lost their bearings in the storm. After several hours, they finally caught sight of the smaller boat with Hontvedt aboard. Looping across fourteen-foot swells, Downs managed to collect the stranded seaman. After John was safely aboard the *White Rover*, Hontvedt's schooner drifted away and was never seen again.

For many hours, the *White Rover* rode the waves, the men aboard her becoming frozen and covered with ice until they could no longer move. When the boat finally beached herself — and history doesn't tell us where — the crew, who were able to use neither their legs nor their arms properly, hitched themselves over the prow of the boat and tumbled onto the sand. Several of the men from the *White Rover* had frozen their feet through and later had to have them amputated. John Hontvedt appears to have survived intact.

"Mommy, will you take me swimming?"

Billie tugs at my sleeve and rolls her head back and forth in the crook of my arm. I set my book down and lift her onto my lap. A small bit of crayon wrapping is stuck to her bottom lip, and I pick it off. She smells of shellfish and of sunblock.

"I don't know, Jean," calls Thomas from the cockpit. "It's awfully deep out there. I said she had to ask you. I don't especially want to go in again myself."

"She'll be all right if she wears her life jacket," says Rich, emerging from the engine compartment. "Anyway,

I need a swim. I'm disgusting. If we both take her, she'll be OK."

"Please, Mom."

I look at Rich, whose hands are covered with grease, and then I look at Billie. "Sure," I say. "Why not?"

I am able to get over the side of the boat, but I am pretty sure they will never get me back in. Rich has left the swim ladder, which was being repaired, in his van at the dock. Billie cannonballs into the water and bobs straight up, her hair covering her face. I swim close to my daughter, never more than an arm's length away, while Billie flails her arms, barely keeping her mouth above water. The water is, at first, shockingly cold, but after a few minutes I begin to get used to it. From the waterline, the prow of the sailboat seems massive — that of an ocean liner. In the distance, without my glasses, the islands are indistinct shapes of gray and brown.

I give Billie a shove toward Rich, and she "swims" between her uncle and myself — a wriggly fish with no fear. Her mouth fills with seawater. She swallows it and she seems surprised by the taste. She begs Rich for a ride on his back, and when they swim near to me, Billie slides off and clutches me around my neck. Rich's leg is momentarily slippery against my own, and I grab onto his shoulder to keep from going under.

"Careful, Billie," I say, loosening her grip around my neck. "I don't have a life jacket on like you. You'll sink me."

From the bowsprit, Thomas watches us. He has a glass in his hand. I see him turn away and smile. He says something I cannot hear — it must be to Adaline.

When I let go of Rich, he dives deep into the water. He

comes up about thirty feet away from me and begins to swim hard, his arms beating a rhythm to his kick. Billie and I paddle around each other until I see that she is tiring. Thomas reaches down, and between us we are able to get Billie easily back into the boat. As I anticipated, however, I am not strong enough to haul myself up and over, and there is an embarrassing and awkward pulling on arms and legs before I am able finally to flop into the cockpit. Billie wraps herself in a towel and sits, shivering, next to Adaline. When I stand up and put my glasses on, I see that Rich has swum all the way to Smuttynose and is sitting on the beach.

The Isles of Shoals derives its name not from the shoals surrounding the islands, but rather from the Old English word for *school*. As in schools of fish.

During the American Revolution, the Isles of Shoals were evacuated. Because the Shoalers had been trading with the British, the colonial leaders of New Hampshire and Maine ordered all residents off the islands. On January 5, 1776, eighty houses were dismantled, shipped to the mainland, and reconstructed all along the coast, from Massachusetts to Maine. A number of these houses are still standing.

"Loss. Abandonment. Castration. Chauvinism . . ."

"But think of Tom Moore, the charm."

"Melancholy. It's all melancholic," says Thomas. "Kavanaugh, Frost, MacNeice."

"You're forgetting Yeats. The celebration of the human imagination, the magician."

"Donnelly. Hyde Donnelly. Do you know him? *Gray light thieving, mother's grief / Steals by hedgerows —*"

"You're indicting an entire race," Adaline says lightly.

Thomas takes a long sip of scotch.

A thick, peasanty scent of fish and garlic spreads and settles over the cockpit where Adaline and Thomas and I are sitting. Rich is holding a plate of mussels he has just steamed.

"*I* picked them," Billie says, weaving through Rich's legs. She is trying to retain her pride in the mussels, though I sense she has been somewhat defeated in her attempts actually to like them. Just moments ago, going below to fetch the papers I took from the Athenaeum, I saw the partly chewed remains of a mussel stuffed inside a crumpled napkin. Billie has on clothes she particularly likes — a blue T-shirt with Pocahontas on the front and matching shorts — and I know she regards this small gathering as something of a party. As does Thomas. Billie has brought a sandwich bag of Cheerios, so that she can nibble with us. She comes and snuggles beside me, screwing her head up and inside my arm. Thomas and Adaline sit across from me. Within seconds, I know, Billie will ask me for a Coke.

"*Sons are leaving,*" says Thomas.

Rich sets the mussels on a makeshift table in the center of the cockpit, perches himself on the cabin roof, and dangles his legs over the opening. The air around us seems cleansed. Smuttynose is sharply etched and brushed with a thin wash of gold from a low sun. From the sloop, the gulls above the island are dark check marks in the blue dust. I am thinking that it is, possibly, the most beautiful night of the summer.

I have a photograph of the five of us in the cockpit of the Morgan the evening Rich makes the mussels and Thomas breaks the glass. I take the picture while the light is still orange; and, as a result, all of us look unreasonably tanned and healthy. In the photograph, Billie is sitting on Rich's lap and has just reached over to touch a gold wrist cuff that Adaline has put on a few minutes earlier. Rich is smiling straight at the camera, an open-mouthed smile that shows a lot of teeth, which look salmon-colored in the light. Beside him, Adaline has shaken out her hair so that the camera has caught her with her chin slightly raised. She has on a black sundress with thin straps and a long skirt; her cross gives off a glint of sunlight. The low sun is shining almost painfully into everyone's eyes, which is why Thomas is squinting and has a hand raised to his brow. The only part of his face that is clearly identifiable is his mouth and jawline. As for me, I have engaged the timer so that I have time to insert myself into the picture. I am sitting beside Thomas, but am slightly tilted, as though I am straining to be part of the composition. I have smiled, but my eyes are, at that instant, closed in a blink. Thomas has attempted to put his free arm around me, but the camera has caught him with it raised and crooked in the air.

"How exactly did you get the scar?" Adaline is asking.

"We really need to feed Billie," I say, talking as much to myself as to anyone. It has been an exhausting day, and I haven't thought about Billie's dinner at all. I know that Rich has bought lobsters for the rest of us, but Billie will not eat a lobster.

"Mommy, can I have a Coke?"

"In a car accident," Thomas says. "When I was a kid. The driver was drunk." Rich looks up quickly at Thomas, but Thomas turns his head away.

"Not now, Sweetie. It's almost time for supper."

"We have some tunafish," says Rich. "I'll make her a sandwich."

"You've done enough," I say. "The least I can do is make a sandwich." I start to get up.

"I don't want tunafish," Billie says. "I want a lobster."

"Billie, I don't think . . ." I start to say, but Rich stops me with a small shake of his head.

"Why don't you give the lobster a try?" he asks Billie. "And if you don't like it, we can make the sandwich then."

She closes her mouth and nods. I can see that she is slightly worried now that she has won her small contest. I doubt she really wants a lobster.

"Where are you from?" Adaline asks me. As she crosses her legs, a slit in the skirt of her black dress falls open, revealing a long, suntanned calf. Thomas looks down at Adaline's leg, and then away. I am wearing jeans and a sweatshirt. Thomas has a fresh shirt on, a blue shirt with a thin yellow stripe, and he has shaved.

"Indiana, originally," I say. "My parents are dead. I was born late, when my mother was forty-eight."

"Mommy, what do seagulls eat?"

"Fish, I think," I say to Billie. "They dive in the ocean for fish. If you watch them closely, I'll bet you can see them." Self-consciously, I look toward Smuttynose, at the gulls that loop in the air over the ragged shoreline.

"And you do this?" Adaline asks, gesturing with her hands to include the boat, the island, the harbor.

"When I can," I say.

"But, Mom, where do they sleep?"

"That's a good question," I say, turning to Thomas for help.

"Damned if I know," Thomas says.

"They must sleep on rocks," Adaline offers. "They put their heads under their wings, I think."

"Have you ever seen a seagull sleep?" Billie asks her.

Adaline purses her lips. "I must have done," she says. "But I can't think where."

"On the back of a garbage barge in the middle of Boston Harbor," Rich calls out from the galley.

"The rats of the sea," mutters Thomas.

Billie snuggles deeper into the cavity of my arm and chest and speaks into my rib cage. "Adaline is beautiful," she says shyly, not quite certain it is all right to say such a thing aloud.

"I know she is," I say, looking directly at Adaline, who meets my eyes.

"I love you, Mommy," Billie says.

"I love you, too," I say.

Early reports of the murders were hastily written and full of inaccuracies. The first bulletin from the *Boston Post* read as follows: "Two Girls Murdered on Smutty Nose Island, Isles of Shoals. Particulars of the Horrible Butchery — Escape of the Assassin and Subsequent Arrest in Boston — The Murderer's Object for Committing the Deed — Attempt to Kill a Third Person — Miraculous Escape of His Intended Victim — Terrible Sufferings from the Cold — Appalling Spectacle at the Home of the Murdered Females, Etc., Etc. — [SPECIAL DISPATCH TO THE BOSTON POST] Portsmouth, N.H., March 6. Our citizens were horror-struck soon after noon to-day, when a fisherman named Huntress, whose home is at the Isles of Shoals, by landing his boat at Newcastle, and taking them thence to this city, hastened to inform our police that murder most foul had been done at the Shoals."

According to the same report, a "rough young man named Lewis Wagner" was seen walking down to the wharf the previous night with an ax in hand. The next morning at seven o'clock, while Wagner and "Huntress" were "having breakfast together" in Portsmouth, Wagner told the unfortunate Huntress (who had not yet returned home and did not know of the murders) that something was going to happen to him (Lewis Wagner). Anetta Lawson and Cornelia Christenson were the victims. A third woman, Mrs. Huntress, had escaped. Portsmouth City Marshall Johnson was already on his way to Boston to try to apprehend the fugitive murderer, who had, earlier in the day, been seen boarding a train for Boston.

I go below to help Rich in the galley. He has a lobster pot on a burner on the stove, another on a hibachi on the stern. He is heating bread in the oven, and he has made a salad.

I begin to lay out the table. Rich and I move awkwardly about the cramped space, trying not to bump into each other or reach for the same utensil simultaneously. Through the companionway, I can see Billie lying faceup on the cushion I have vacated. She seems to be studying her fingers with great intensity. Across from her, framed in the rectangle, are Thomas's legs in their trousers, and his hand reaching for the bottle he has set by his right foot. The boat moves rhythmically, and through the west-facing portholes, watery reflections flicker on the bulkheads. I am searching for lobster crackers and picks in the silverware drawer when I hear three achingly familiar words: *Wainscot, redolent, core-stung.*

Adaline's voice is deep and melodious, respectful, forming words and vowels — perfect vowels. She knows the poem well. By heart.

I strain so that I can see Thomas's face. He is looking down at his knees. He doesn't move.

I remember the bar, the way Thomas read the poem. I remember standing at a window and reading it in the streetlight while Thomas slept.

"Thomas," I call. The edge in my voice is audible, even to me.

Billie sits up and leans on her elbows. She seems slightly puzzled. Adaline stops reciting.

Adaline's wrists are lightly crossed at her knee. In one long-fingered hand, she holds a wineglass. I am surprised suddenly to realize that this is the first time I have seen her drinking.

"Thomas, I need you," I repeat, and turn away.

I busy myself in the silverware drawer. He puts his head inside the companionway.

"What is it?" he asks.

"I can't find the nutcrackers, and I don't know what you've done with the wine we're having for dinner." My annoyance — a weaseling, sour note — is unmistakable.

"I've got the wine right here," Rich says quietly next to me. He opens the tiny refrigerator door for me to see.

But it is too late. Thomas has already turned and walked away. He stands, looking out over the water. He holds his glass in one hand; the other he has in the pocket of his trousers. Adaline has twisted her body around, so that she, too, is gazing out over the water, but away from Thomas.

Rich goes above to put the corn into the pot on the hibachi. I see Thomas move aside and hold the lid for Rich. After Rich has dumped the ears into the steaming kettle, he wipes his hands on a dishtowel, and then bends and pours himself a glass of wine from another bottle on the cockpit floor. Thomas and Rich, their backs to me, speak a few words to each other, like husbands who have gone to stand by the grill in the backyard. I lean against the lip of the counter in the galley and sip my wine with concentration.

Billie looks at her father, then at me. She rolls over onto her stomach and puts her hands to the sides of her face, as if she were peering at something very tiny on the cushion. Rich turns around and gestures to Adaline to move over a bit. He sits next to her and rests his fingers on her thigh. He slips them in under the slit of her skirt, under the black cloth.

Thomas, who has made a half turn at that moment and is about to speak, sees Rich touch Adaline. He stands as if transfixed, as if not knowing where to put his body. He takes an awkward step forward. He hits Adaline's wineglass, which she has set down on the floor. The glass falls and shatters.

"Jesus," Thomas says.

Louis Wagner was arrested at eight-thirty on the night after the murders at the home of an acquaintance in Boston by both Portsmouth and Boston police. Wagner seemed stunned by the accusation of the murders and swore that he had not been on Smuttynose since November of the previous year. He said he could not have done such a thing because the Hontvedt women had been good to him. He had heard the train whistle at nine o'clock that morning, and, since he was down on his luck in Portsmouth, he thought it might be a good thing to try Boston.

News that the police were bringing Wagner back to Portsmouth on the ten o'clock train on Friday morning swept through the town, and the train route was lined with angry, screaming mobs. Fearing for their prisoner, the police had the train stopped a quarter mile short of the station to take Wagner off, but the crowd spotted him anyway and began to pelt the prisoner — and the police — with stones and ice chunks. They called out "Lynch him" and "String him up." The Marines were summoned, and the police drew their guns. Wagner spent the night in the Portsmouth jail, but was transferred the next day to Saco, Maine, since Smuttynose is technically not in New Hampshire, but in Maine. Again police were confronted with thousands of demonstrators who once more tried to stone Wagner, who was wounded in the head. One of the men in the mob was Ephraim Downs, the fisherman who had once saved John Hontvedt's life.

The prisoner was arraigned at the South Berwick jail and then kept in the Portland jail. He was transported to Alfred, Maine, when the trial of *The State of Maine* v. *Louis H. F. Wagner* opened on June 16, 1873. Louis Wagner stood accused of delivering ten mortal wounds with an ax to the head of "Anethe M. Christenson" and thereby causing her instant death.

After Rich and I clean up the broken glass, he lifts the lobsters from the pot, and we all sit down at the dining table to eat. Thomas, who has drunk even more than he usually does, struggles clumsily with his lobster, spraying bits of white chitin around the table. Billie, as anticipated, loses her appetite for lobster when she watches me crack the shells and extract with a pick the spotted, pink meat. Adaline does not dip her meat with her fingers into melted butter as do the rest of us, but rather soaks it in a bowl of hot broth and eats it from a fork. She works her way methodically through the bright red carapace, missing not a piece of edible flesh.

Thomas goes above to the deck when he cuts his thumb on a claw. After a time, Rich, who may feel that Thomas needs company, also goes above. Billie, too, leaves us, happy to turn her back on the pile of claws and red detritus that is forming in a stainless steel bowl and is becoming vaguely repulsive. Across the table, I watch with fascination as Adaline pulls tiny bits of meat I'd have overlooked from the body of the lobster. I watch her suck and chew, one by one, each of the lobster's spindly legs, kneading the thin shells with her teeth.

"Did you grow up on a farm?" she asks. "Were your parents farmers?"

"Yes, as a matter of fact, they were," I say. "Where in Ireland did you grow up?"

"Cork," she says. "It's in the south."

"And then you went to university."

"Yes," she says. "Billie is wonderful. You're very lucky to have her."

"Thank you. I do feel lucky to have her. How did you end up in Boston?"

"I was with someone," she says. "When I was in London. He worked in Boston, and I came over to be with him. I've always liked Boston."

"How did you come to know so much about Thomas's poetry?" I ask.

She seems surprised at the question.

"I think I've always read Thomas," she says. "Even at Dublin, I thought he was extraordinary. I suppose, after the prize, everyone reads Thomas now, don't they? That's what a prize does, I should think. It makes everyone read you, surely."

"You've memorized his work."

"Oh, not really."

There is an accusing tone to my voice that seems to put her on the defensive.

"The thing about Thomas is that I think he wants to be read aloud," she says. "One almost has to, to fully understand."

"You know he killed a girl," I say.

Adaline slowly removes a lobster leg from her mouth, holds it between her thumb and finger as she rests her hands on the edge of the table. The blue-checked oilcloth is dotted with bits of flesh and yellow drips of butter that have congealed.

"Thomas killed a girl," she repeats, as though the sentence doesn't scan.

I take a sip of wine. I tear a piece of garlic bread from the loaf. I try to control my hands, which are trembling. I believe I am more shocked at what I have just said than she is. By the way I have said it. By the words I have used.

"I don't understand," she says.

She puts the spindly leg on her plate and wipes her fingers on the napkin in her lap. She holds the crumpled napkin in one hand.

"The car accident," I explain. "Thomas was driving." She still seems not to understand.

"There was a girl with him. In the car. Thomas went off

the road, caught his rear wheel in a ditch, and flipped the car."

Adaline reaches up and, with her finger, absently picks at a piece of lobster between her teeth. I look down and notice I have a spill of lobster water on my jeans.

"How old was she?"

"The same age as he was, seventeen."

"He was drunk?"

"Yes," I say.

I wait.

I see it then, the moment of recognition. I can see her processing the information, reciting lines to herself, suddenly understanding them. Her eyes move to the stove and then back to me.

"*The Magdalene Poems,*" she says quietly.

I nod. "But her name wasn't Magdalene. It was Linda."

Adaline flinches slightly at the word *Linda,* as though the commonness of the girl's name makes it real.

"He loved her," she says.

"Yes," I answer. "Very much. I don't think he's really ever gotten over it. In a way, all of his poems are about the accident, even when they seem not to be."

"But he married you," she says.

"So he did," I say.

Adaline puts her napkin on the table and stands up. She walks a few steps to the doorway of the forward cabin. She has her back to me, her arms crossed over her chest.

Rich bends his head into the cabin. "Jean, you should come out here," he calls. "The light is perfect."

He stops. Adaline is still standing in the doorway with her back to me. She doesn't turn around. Rich glances at me.

"What's up?" he asks.

I uncross my legs under the table. "Not much," I say.

I fold my hands in my lap, stunned by my betrayal. In all the years that I have been with Thomas, I have never told a single person. Nor, to my knowledge, has he. Despite our fears when he won the prize, no one discovered this fact about Thomas's youth, as the records were well sealed. Now, however, I know that Adaline will tell others. She won't be able to keep this information to herself.

I can't have done this, I am thinking.

"Rich, leave this," I say quickly, gesturing toward the mess on the table. "I want to go up. With Thomas. With the light still good. I'll do the dishes later." I push away from the table. Rich comes down the ladder and stands a moment with his hands over his head, holding on to the hatch. He seems puzzled.

Behind me, Adaline goes into the forward cabin. She shuts the door.

The Honorable R. P. Tapley of Saco, Maine, was the lawyer for the defense of Louis H. F. Wagner. George C. Yeaton, Esq. was the county attorney. The Honorable William G. Barrows was the presiding judge. The members of the jury were Isaac Easton of North Berwick, George A. Twambly of Shapleigh, Ivory C. Hatch of Wells, Horace Piper of Newfield, Levi G. Hanson of Biddeford, Nahum Tarbox of Biddeford, Benajah Hall of North Berwick, Charles Whitney of Biddeford, William Bean of Limington, Robert Littlefield of Kennebunk, Isaac Libbey of Parsonfield, and Calvin Stevens of Wells.

Although all of the jury, the lawyers, and the judge were white men of early American — that is to say, English — stock, neither the accused nor the victim, nor the woman who survived, nor even most of the witnesses, was an American citizen.

In the cockpit, Thomas comes to sit beside me. Billie leans against Thomas's legs. My hands begin to shake. I feel an urge to bend forward, to put my head between my knees.

The three of us watch the sun set over Newcastle and Portsmouth, watch the coral light move evenly across Appledore and Star, leaving in its wake a colorless tableau. From below, Rich switches on the running lights.

I want to tell Thomas that I have done something terrible, that I don't know why I did it except that I couldn't, for just that moment, bear Adaline's certainty that she knew Thomas well — perhaps, in a way, even better than myself.

On Star, windows are illuminated, and people walk through pools of deep yellow light.

"You're trembling," Thomas says.

The Magdalene Poems are an examination of the life of a seventeen-year-old girl in the last four seconds of her life, written in the voice of a seventeen-year-old boy who was clearly her lover and who was with her when she died. The poems speak to the unfulfilled promise of love, to the absolute inevitability of that promise remaining unfulfilled. The reader is allowed to imagine the girl as a middle-aged woman married to the man who was the boy, as an elderly widow, and as a promiscuous sixteen-year-old. The girl, whose name is Magdalene, is — as seen from the eyes of the boy — extraordinarily beautiful. She has the long slender body of a dancer, abundant multihued hair that winds into intricate coils at the nape of her neck, and full curved lips of even dimensions with barely any bow at all.

According to the State of Maine, on March 5, 1873, six people lived in the one-and-one-half-story red cottage on Smuttynose, and there were no other inhabitants on the entire island that winter. John and Maren Hontvedt had come in 1868. Karen, Maren's sister, and Matthew, John's brother, had each come separately in 1871. Karen almost immediately entered service at the Laighton's Hotel on Appledore Island, while Matthew joined John on the *Clara Bella,* the latter's fishing schooner. Evan, Maren's brother, and his wife, Anethe, had arrived on the island in October of 1872, five months before the murders.

At daybreak on March 5, Matthew, Evan, and John left Smuttynose and sailed northeast in the schooner to draw their trawls. The Ingerbretson men from Appledore joined them in their own schooner. The plan for the day was to fish in the morning, return for lunch, and then head for Portsmouth to sell their catch and purchase bait. But just before noon, an unexpected and swift-rising wind prevented them from making an easy sail home to Smuttynose. Because they knew they had to have bait, they called over to Emil Ingerbretson and asked him to stop at the island and tell the women that they would not be home until evening. The three women — Maren, Karen, and Anethe — cooked a stew and made bread for the men in preparation for their return after dark.

Louis Wagner, standing at Rollins Wharf in Portsmouth, watched the *Clara Bella* come into the dock. Wagner, who was wearing that day two sweaters, a white dress shirt, and overalls, helped John and Matthew and Evan tie up their boat. Louis told the men that the bait they wanted, which was coming by train from Boston, would be delayed and wouldn't be in until nearly midnight. Louis then asked John for money for something to eat, and John laughed and said that none of the men had brought any money because they had thought they would go home first, and that they would have to eat on credit with Mrs. Johnson, to whose house the bait was to be delivered. Wagner then asked John if he had had any luck with his fishing, and John answered that he had been able to save up six hundred dollars. The three men of Smuttynose said goodbye to Louis, leaving him on the dock, while they went to fetch their dinner.

Baiting the trawls was a time-consuming and slimy business. Each of a thousand hooks had to have its piece of baitfish, a stinking sliver of herring that would have come in barrels from Boston by train, and did in fact arrive much later than expected in Portsmouth that night, preventing the men from returning to Smuttynose at all. Each individual hook had to be separated from the tangle, baited, then coiled into a tub so that the lot could be thrown overboard when the schooner, the next day, had made it to the fishing grounds. To bait the trawls took three men six hours. When the work was finished, it was not uncommon for one or more of the men to have stabbed himself with fishhooks.

Louis Wagner had emigrated from Prussia to the United States seven years earlier. He was twenty-eight years old and was described by those who knew him as being tall and extremely strong, light-haired, and having "steel blue" eyes. Other descriptions of him depict his eyes as soft and mild. Many women thought him handsome. He had worked at the Isles of Shoals off and on, loading and unloading goods, and with John Hontvedt on the *Clara Bella* for two months, September to November of 1872. For seven months of that year (from April to November), Wagner had boarded with the Hontvedts, but he had been crippled much of the time with rheumatism. After leaving the Hontvedts, he signed on as a hand with the *Addison Gilbert*, which subsequently sank, leaving Wagner once again without a job. Just prior to the murders, he had been wandering in and among the boardinghouses, wharves, docks, and taverns of Portsmouth, looking for work. He is quoted as having said, to four different men, on four different occasions, "This won't do anymore. I am bound to have money in three months' time if I have to murder for it." While in Portsmouth, he resided at a boardinghouse for men that belonged to Matthew Johnson and his wife. He owed his landlord money.

According to the prosecution, at seven-thirty on the evening of March 5, Louis Wagner stole a dory, owned by James Burke, that had been left at the end of Pickering Street. Just that day, Burke had replaced the dory's thole pins with new, expensive ones. Wagner intended to row out to the Isles of Shoals, steal the six hundred dollars that John had spoken of, and to row immediately back. This would be a twenty-five-mile row, which, even in the best of circumstances, would be extremely taxing for any man. That day it was high tide at six P.M., low at midnight. There was a three-quarters moon, which set at one A.M. On a favorable tide, it took one hour and forty minutes to row from Pickering Street to the mouth of the Piscataqua River (which flowed through Portsmouth), and one hour and fifteen minutes to row from there to Smuttynose. This is a round-trip, in favorable conditions, of just under six hours. If a man tired, or encountered any obstacles, or if he did not have completely favorable conditions, the row to and from the Isles of Shoals could take as long as nine or ten hours.

County Attorney Yeaton reconstructed Wagner's plan as follows: Maren would be asleep in the southwest bedroom, and Anethe would be upstairs. Wagner would fasten the door that linked Maren's bedroom to the kitchen by sliding a slat from a lobster trap through the latch. Since the money would be in the kitchen in a trunk, he felt there would be no difficulty. Wagner mistakenly assumed that Karen would still be on Appledore. He brought no murder weapon with him.

Wagner, who had the current with him, moved quickly down the river and past Portsmouth. When he reached the Shoals, he circled the island silently to see if, by some chance, the *Clara Bella* had returned. When he was certain there were no men on the island, he rowed himself into Haley's Cove. This was at approximately eleven P.M. He waited until all of the lights in the houses on Appledore and Star had been extinguished.

When the islands were dark, he walked in his rubber boots up to the front door of the cottage, where an ax leaned against the stone step. He entered the kitchen and fastened the door to the bedroom.

The dog, Ringe, began to bark.

Louis turned abruptly. A woman rose from her bed in the darkness and called out, "John, is that you?"

I take Billie below to get her ready for bed. She still finds the head a novelty, particularly the complicated flushing of the toilet. She brushes her teeth and then puts on her pajamas. I settle her into her berth and sit next to her. She has asked for a story, so I read her a picture-book tale of a mother and her daughter gathering blueberries in Maine. Billie lies in a state of rapt attention and holds in her arms a threadbare cocker spaniel she has had since birth.

"Let's say our things," I say, when I have finished the book.

When Billie was a toddler, she learned to talk, as most children do, by repeating what I said to her. As it has happened, this particular bit of repetition, a bedtime litany, has lasted for years.

"Lovely girl," I say.

"Lovely Mom."

"Sleep well."

"Sleep well."

"See you in the morning."

"See you in the morning."

"Don't let the bedbugs bite."

"Don't let the bedbugs bite."

"Sweet dreams."

"Sweet dreams."

"Love you."

"Love you."

"Goodnight."

"Goodnight."

I put my lips against her cheek. She reaches up her arms, letting go of the dog, and hugs me tightly.

"I love you, Mom," she says.

That night, on the damp mattress that serves as a bed, Thomas and I lie facing each other, just a few inches apart. There is enough light so that I can just make out his face. His hair has fallen forward onto his brow, and his eyes seem expressionless — simple dark pools. I have on a nightshirt, a white nightshirt with pink cotton piping. Thomas is still wearing the blue shirt with the thin yellow stripes, and his undershorts.

He reaches up and traces the outline of my mouth with his finger. He grazes my shoulder with the back of his hand. I move slightly toward him. He puts his arm around my waist.

We have a way of making love now, a language of our own, this movement, then that movement, signals, long-practiced, that differ only slightly each time from the times before. His hand sliding on my thigh, my hand reaching down between his legs, a small adjustment to free himself, my palm under his shirt. That night, he slides over me, so that my face is lightly smothered be-tween his chest and his arm.

I freeze.

It is in the cloth, faint but unmistakable, a foreign scent. Not sea air, or lobster, or a sweaty child.

It takes only seconds for a message to pass between two people who have made love a thousand times, two thousand times.

He rolls away from me and lies on his back, his eyes staring at the bulkhead.

I cannot speak. Slowly, I take the air into my lungs and let it out.

Eventually, I become aware of the small twitches in Thomas's body — an arm, a knee — that tell me that he has fallen asleep.

To get a landscape photograph at night, you need a tripod and decent moonlight. Sometime after midnight, when everyone is asleep on the boat, I take the Zodiac over to Smuttynose. I use the paddle, because I do not want to wake Thomas or Rich with the motor. In the distance, the island is outlined by the moon, which casts a long cone of light onto the water. I beach the Zodiac at the place where Louis Wagner left his dory and retrace the steps he would have taken to the house. I stand in the foundation of the house and replay the murders in my mind. I look out over the harbor and try to imagine a life on the island, at night, in the quiet, and with the constant wind. I take two rolls of Velvia 220, seventy-two shots of Smuttynose in the dark.

I HAVE BEEN THINKING this morning upon the subjects of storytelling and truth, and how it is with the utmost trust that we receive the tales of those who would give them to us.

Not long after our mother had died, and I had recovered from my illness, Karen became, as I have said, the mistress of the house, and Evan and I were sent out to work, me to a neighboring farm, and Evan to sea. This was not such an unusual occurrence, not in that area and in that time.

Our father, having grown older and grieving for the loss of his wife, was going to sea fewer days than he had before and not for long journeys as he had done in the past. Thus he did not have a surplus of fish to sell or to dry. All around us at this time, there were other families in failing circumstances, some far worse off than we were, families in which the father had drowned, and the mother and the eldest son had the responsibility of feeding many young children, and also families whose livelihoods had been reduced by the economic troubles of the region and, indeed, of the entire country at that time, and there were many indigent and homeless persons as a result. By contrast, I remember very few occasions when our family actually had no food in the pantry, although I do recall at least one and perhaps two winters when I had only one dress and one pair of socks to see me through to spring, and we could not get wool to spin to make another pair.

The decision to send Evan out to work was, I believe, an easy one for my father, since Evan was a tall and strong boy of sixteen, and there were many youths of the same age in the environs of Laurvig who had been working for some time. It was thought that Evan would make a better wage as a hired mate to someone else than he might by selling the herring and the cod he would catch with my father; but because there was very little fishing work in Laurvig Bay in those years, Evan had to go to Tonsberg, which was twenty kilometers north of Laurvig. There he was told about a man named John Hontvedt, who was looking for a mate and who lived in a house with six other fishermen, one of them his brother, Matthew. From that day forward, which was 12 October 1860, until such time as Evan and John entered into partnership, Evan worked with John Hontvedt on his fishing sloop, the *Malla Fladen,* and lived in that house for six days a week.

As for myself, I stayed one more year at school, and then was hired out to the Johannsen farm. This was a grave time in my father's life, and I believe the decision to send his youngest child out to work was a wrenching one for him to make. Karen could no longer go to the boarding house as she was needed at home, and since I was only fourteen and my father did not think it suitable for me to work in similar circumstances, he inquired about work for me elsewhere, where the conditions might be more gentle. As it happened, it was Karen who was advised of the position with Knud Johannsen, who was a recent widower himself, and she urged my father to send me there.

Knud Johannsen's dairy farm lay six kilometers back from the sea, an uphill climb on my way to work in the morning and, of course, a downhill slope in the evening, which was just as well, since I usually was so very tired then that I needed gravity to propel me forward to our cottage. My hours at the Johannsen farm were long and difficult, but generally, not unpleasant. During the time of my employ at that household, which lasted two years and eight months, Evan and I did not have many opportunities to see each other, and almost never alone, and this was a sorrow to me. Because of Evan's hard work and prosperity, however, our family's fortunes did gradually increase, so that I was allowed to discontinue my work for Mr. Johannsen and re-enroll in school, where I stayed for one year and seven months, entering a course of preparation for further study, though sadly I was not ever to go on to university. It was my good fortune, while in school, however, to put my whole heart and mind into my studies and thus command the attention of Professor Neils Jessen, the headmaster, who then took upon himself the bettering of my language skills so that I subsequently found pleasure in the study of rhetoric and composition. I trust that while I was lacking in certain rudimentary prerequisites for this challenging task at hand, I acquitted myself passably well, as Professor Jessen spent many hours with me after school in hopes that I might be the first female student from the Laurvig School to attend the university in Kristiania.

As it happened, however, I was not able to go on to university, owing to a lack of sufficient funds, even though my brother regularly sent to us large portions of his wages, and so I applied for and was given a position as clerk at the Fritzoe ironworks, which I held for two years. And then, in the winter of 1865, John Hontvedt and his brother, Matthew, moved to Laurvig, and shortly after that, the direction of my life changed quite dramatically.

A house in the Jorgine Road had become vacant and was to be leased at a low price, and Evan had spoken highly of the area to John these several years. Because of his hard work and cleverness, John Hontvedt had done well for himself in the fishing trade, and with him Evan had earned enough money to put some by. The two men, with Matthew Hontvedt, thus entered into a partnership aboard a sloop which they purchased and which was called the *Agnes C. Nedland.*

John Hontvedt was not a particularly tall man, not when compared to our father and to Evan, both of whom were well over six feet, but John gave the impression of strength and of size nevertheless. He had brown hair of a cinnamon tint that he wore thick and long, combed across his brow, and he had as well eyes that hinted at a gentleness of spirit. They were hazel, I believe, or possibly gray, I cannot remember now. His face was not narrow, as was Evan's, but rather square in shape, and he had a handsome jaw. I suspect he had been thin as a boy, but as a man, his body, like his face, had filled out. His chest was round and formed like a fish barrel. He had no fat on him at that time.

Hontvedt had a habit of standing with his hands hooked around his belt, and of hitching his trousers sometimes when he spoke. When he sat, he crossed his legs at the knees, as some women do, but he was never feminine in any other of his gestures. Occasionally, when he was tense or anxious, he would hold his elbow with one hand, and swing the free arm in an exaggerated manner, an odd gesture, I always thought, and one I came to think of as belonging exclusively to John. He had lost one finger of his left hand as a consequence of having severed it in a winch.

I believe our father was, at the time I met John Hontvedt, apprehensive for his two daughters. Certainly this was true as concerns his responsibilities toward Karen, who, at thirty-three, had lost her youth and seemed destined to remain a maid. It was a shame upon a father, then as now, if he could not marry off his daughters, and I shudder to think of all the young women who have been so unsuitably given away, only to live out lives of utter misery simply to assuage the public strain of their fathers.

I will not accuse our father of such base desires, however, for, in truth, I do not think this was so, but I believe that he was, after having watched his eldest daughter turn herself into a spinster, anxious to see me well married. Also, I must add here that my father had not recently met a man in these parts who was of so good a fisherstock and who had prospered so well as John. And I believe my father had reason to be grateful to John Hontvedt for his having taken on our Evan, and in that way gradually changing the fortunes of our family.

One evening, after Hontvedt had been to our table for dinner, he suggested that he and I go out walking together.

I had not actually wanted to go walking at all, and certainly not with John Hontvedt, but I did not see how I could refuse such a request, particularly as it had been made in front of my father. It was a mild night in early October, with long shadows that caused the landscape to take on a heightened clarity. We walked in the direction of the coast road, toward town, John with his hands in the pockets of his trousers, mine folded at my waist, as was proper for a young woman then. John took up the burden of the conversation, talking, as I recall, with great ease and volubility, although I cannot remember anything of what he said. I confess it was often this way between us, as I frequently allowed my thoughts to wander whilst he spoke, and, oddly enough, he seldom seemed to notice these absences of mine. That evening, when after a time I did begin to attend to what he was saying, I noticed that we were quite far from the cottage. We were standing on a headland that looked out over Laurvigsfjord. The ground was covered with gorse that had gone aflame with the setting sun, and the blue of the water below us had reached that deep solid sapphirine that comes only late in the evenings. We were admiring this view, and perhaps John was addressing me, when I noticed that he had moved closer to me than was strictly comfortable. Nearly as soon as I had this observation, he put his hand lightly at the back of my waist. This was a gesture that could not be misunderstood. It was, I believe I am correct in saying, a somewhat possessive gesture, and I was then in no doubt as to its intent. I think I may have moved slightly away from him, but John, who was dogged in his pursuits, moved along with me, so that he had no need to remove his hand. As we stood there, I recall that his fingers began to inch even further, so that he was able to circle my waist. I thought that if I did not speak to him at that moment he

might take my passivity as an invitation for further inti-
macies, which I did not want, so I moved abruptly away
from him then.

"Maren," he said, "there are things about which I must
speak to you."

"I am feeling quite tired, John. I think we should go
back to the cottage."

"You know," said John, "that I have given some
thought to emigrating to America. I have been much impressed with reports of the American customs and views,
particularly the idea that there is no class distinction. That
a man pays only a little tax on the land he actually owns,
and is not filling the pockets of the idle, who do no work
at all."

"But would you leave all that you know behind and go
to a country in which if you do not have money you must
remain where you are on the coast?" I asked. "I have
heard tales of the large sums that are necessary to travel to
the interior, and even there the land is already being
twice-sold so that the original owners reap enormous
profits, and cheap land can no longer be had by newly arrived immigrants. I have also heard that commodities are
very expensive there. A barrel of salt costs nearly fifty
orts! And coffee is forty skillings a pound!"

"Since I would want to remain on the coast," he answered, "I do not see the worry about having money to
travel inland. But I do understand your point, Maren. One
must have a stake with which to begin a new life, for a
house and supplies and transportation and so on."

"Would you truly settle there, on the coast of America?" I asked.

"I might if I had found a wife," John answered.

At the word *wife,* John looked at me, and my eyes turned toward his, even before I had understood the suggestion in his declaration. It was the first time such a thought had clearly presented itself to me, and I confess I was at first quite shocked.

"I'm sorry, Maren," he said. "You seem distressed, and this was not at all my intention. Indeed, my intention was quite the opposite. In all my days on earth, I have never met a sweeter woman than you, Maren."

"Really, John, I am feeling quite faint."

"Whether I should go to America or remain in Norway, I am of an age now, and happily of sufficient means, that I may think of taking a wife. I trust that I may be worthy enough in my character to ask . . ."

I have never appreciated women who resort to histrionics or who show themselves to be so delicate in their constitutions that they cannot withstand the intense images that words may sometimes conjure forth, but I must acknowledge that at that moment, standing on the headland, I was so sorely exercised in my futile attempts to convince my companion to cease his conversation and escort me back to the cottage that I was tempted to feign a swoon and collapse in the gorse at his feet. Instead, however, I spoke to John rather sharply. "I insist that we return or I shall be ill, John," I said, and in this way I was able, for a time, to stave off what seemed to me to be an inevitable request.

It was only the next day that my father himself broached the subject. Evan had gone off to bed, and Karen was visiting the privy in the back, so that my father and I were alone. He wished, he said, to see me settled with a family. He did not want me to be dependent upon himself, as he did not think he had many years left. I cried out at this declaration, not only because I did not like to think upon my father's death, but also because I was cross at having twice in one week the necessity to fend off the prospect of marrying John Hontvedt. My father, brushing aside my protests with his hand, spoke of John's character, his healthy financial situation, and, finally, though I thought his priorities misplaced, of Hontvedt's apparent affection for me, which might, in time, he said, develop into a deep and lasting love. I was greatly vexed by having to think upon these matters, but I hasten to tell you that in Norway at that time, it was seldom the place of a young daughter to criticize her father, and so it was that I had to hear my father out at length on the subject of my eventual marriage. Dutifully, I said that I was grateful for his concerns, but that it was too soon in my life to take such a large and grave step, and that it would only be with the utmost care and consideration that I would do so.

I thought the matter at an end, or at least held in abeyance for a time, when, due to an impulsive gesture on my part, which I was later deeply to regret, I myself caused the subject to be brought up again, and finally resolved.

It was some four weeks later, in mid-November, and the weather was quite bitterly cold, but in the late afternoons a strange and wondrous phenomenon would occur on the bay. Because the water was considerably warmer than the air above it, great swirls of mist would rise from the sea, like steam lifting from a bath. These swirls, due to the light and angle of the sun at that time of year, would take on a lovely salmon color that was breathtaking to behold. So it was that the bay, which was normally thick with fisher-traffic in and out of the harbor, had that Sunday an entirely magical quality that I do not believe was reproduced anywhere else on earth. It was a natural occurrence that Evan and myself had sometimes observed on our journeys as children along the coast road, and it had never failed to halt our progress as we stood in rapt worship of such a simple, yet magnificent, accident of nature. That afternoon, I asked Evan if he would like to accompany me out to the cliffs, where we might better observe the bay. I thought this would be a good opportunity for Evan and myself to speak with each other apart from the others, which we rarely had occasion to do. Evan was at first reluctant, since I believe that he was particularly exhausted from his arduous week (for a fisherman's work is invariably made more difficult in cold temperatures), but I persisted in my invitation, and I daresay I talked him into it.

We walked for some distance without speaking. My brother seemed rather preoccupied that afternoon, and I was somewhat at a loss as to how to begin our conversation. As Evan walked beside me, I could not help myself from making a close observation of him. Already it was apparent that, at the age of twenty-two, the sun and the sea had begun to take their toll, as he had tiny lines around his eyes and mouth and on his forehead. His brow seemed to have knit itself together in a permanent manner, and I thought this the result of a constant squint on the water. His skin was weathered, with that texture seamen get that resembles nothing so much as fine paper. The blisters and rope burns on his hands had long since turned to calluses, but I could see the scars of many hook tears on his fingers. Additionally, I observed that Evan had attained, during his absence, his full growth, and I may say here that he towered over me. He was not, as I may have mentioned earlier, built broad in the shoulders, as John was, but rather was sinewy in his structure, though he gave off the appearance of great strength. I think that partly this was due as well to his character, which was extremely reserved and not given to much foolishness.

After a time, we passed a few pleasantries between us, but spoke of nothing that might be of a difficult nature, at least not immediately. I had dressed that day in my heavy woolen cloak, and my face was wrapped in a long scarf of a fine pale blue, the wool of which I had sent for from Kristiania.

"Do you remember," I asked when we had reached the cliffs and were gazing out at the bay, from which rose what appeared to be a miasmic wall of coral and rose and pink, "all the walks we used to take along this very coast road?"

He looked surprised for a minute, and then he said, "Yes, I do, Maren."

"And the day you climbed the tree, and I took off all my clothes and went up after you?"

"It seems so long ago."

"And how you saved me at Hakon's Inlet?"

"You would have saved yourself."

"No, I'd have drowned. I'm sure of it."

"It wasn't a very safe place to play," he said. "If I saw children there now, I'd chase them off."

"We never thought about safety."

"No, we didn't."

"Those were such good times," I said.

Evan was silent for a moment. I assumed that he was,

like myself, contenting himself with the fond memories of our childhood, when suddenly a great sigh erupted from him, and he turned himself away from me.

"Evan, what is it?" I asked.

He didn't answer me. I was about to ask him again what the matter was, but I was silenced by the sight of tears that had, at that moment, sprung to his eyes. He shook his head violently, so that his hair swung about. Indeed, he was shaking his head in the rough manner of men who wish literally to throw out of their heads the thoughts that lodge there. I was so frightened and appalled by this sudden show of emotion and of intense hatred toward himself that I fear I cried out in the most desperate way and flung myself to my knees, for I have never been able to bear signs of grief or of sorrow on the face of my brother — and indeed, these signs triggered in me memories of the night our mother perished, a night on which Evan, and thus myself, had nearly lost our senses.

When next I was aware of my brother, he was tugging on my sleeve and trying to get me to stand up.

"Don't be so dramatic, Maren," he said curtly. "You'll freeze to death." He brushed tiny pebbles from my cloak.

And then, without any further words between us, Evan began to walk along the coast path south in the direction of the cottage. It was apparent, from his gait, that he did not intend I should follow him.

I had never been abandoned by Evan in so horrid a manner, and although I did soon recover myself and think how distraught my brother must have been to have wept in front of me and how truly sorry I was for his troubled nature, I felt bereft there on the cliffs and also, I must say, quite angry.

I walked home with a furious step and, at a critical juncture in the road, I took a turn that I have forever regretted. At the Jorgine Road, I walked east, toward John Hontvedt's cottage.

My legs and hands were trembling as I climbed the porch steps of Hontvedt's house, from the earlier disturbances on the cliffs or simply the inappropriateness of my visit I cannot say, but as you may imagine, John Hontvedt was exceedingly surprised to see me. After his initial shock, however, he could not hide his pleasure.

I allowed John Hontvedt to make me a cup of tea and to serve this to me in his front parlor, along with biscuits that he had purchased in town. He had not fully dressed, and had no collar on, and in his haste to prepare the tea, did not put one on. Perhaps it was only the absence of the collar and the sight of his braces, but I felt as though the entire encounter were an improper one. Indeed, I could not easily have explained my presence in John Hontvedt's house to anyone were someone to come upon us. What was I doing unchaperoned in a single man's living quarters on a Sunday afternoon? Possibly it was in an effort to answer that query, even to myself, that I spoke to John.

"Do you remember that on our walk of several weeks ago you were speaking of some matters?" I asked.

He put down his mug of tea. "Yes, I do." I believe I had surprised Hontvedt in the act of trimming his beard, as it had an odd, misshapen appearance.

"And I insisted that you stop speaking of them?" I asked.

"Yes."

"I have thought about the matters which you brought up, and it seems to me that these are subjects we might at some later date continue to discuss. That is, we may explore them further."

"Oh, Maren —"

"This is not to say at all that I find the idea acceptable at the moment. I am merely stating that I will allow further discussion."

"You cannot imagine —"

"You understand, of course, that it is really too soon for me to think of leaving my father's house. . . ."

To my horror, John Hontvedt left his seat altogether and placed himself at my feet. I made a motion with my hands to make him rise, but he seized both of my hands in his.

"Maren, I shall not disappoint you!" he cried. "I shall make you the happiest woman in all of Norway."

"No, John, you have misunderstood. . . ."

He reached forward to embrace me. I believe he underestimated his strength and his ardor, for when he put his arms around me, he nearly squeezed the breath out of my body. In the next minute, he was covering my face and my hands with kisses and had leaned his entire torso onto my lap. I tried to stand up, but could not move in this embrace. I became frightened then, frightened of being overtaken by someone stronger than myself, and also quite hollow with the first sensations of a decision so wrong as to threaten to poison my entire soul.

"John!" I cried out. "Please stop!"

John then stood up, and he said that he would walk me to the cottage. I protested, as I did not want Karen or my father to see Hontvedt in such an excited state, nor did I want this excitement to carry over into any possible conversation between Father and John.

"I shall make you very happy, Maren," he said.

"Thank you," I said, although I sincerely doubted that he could do this.

And thus it was that John Hontvedt and myself came to be engaged.

Hontvedt and I were married on 22 December 1867, just after the winter solstice. I wore the walnut silk I have mentioned in these pages, as well as a fringed bonnet with braided ties that fastened behind the ears and under the chin. Professor Jessen, who remained my friend, lent Hontvedt and myself his house in Laurvig for a small wedding party after the ceremony at Laurvig Church. I confess I was not so gay on this occasion as I might have been, as I was somewhat fearful of the heavy responsibilities that lay before me as the wife of John Hontvedt, and also because my brother, Evan, did not come to my wedding, owing to the fact that he was home ill with a bronchial infection, and this was a distress both to John and myself.

After the reception, at which John drank a good deal of aquavit, which Professor Jessen had been kind enough to provide for us, I was forced to leave the others, as was my duty, and to go away with John, to his house, where we were to spend our first night together. I should say here that our initial occasion as man and wife was not entirely successful, owing in part to John's state of inebriation, which I had reason, in the event, to be grateful for, and also to some confusion, when John cried out, although there was only, I am relieved to say, myself to hear, that I had deceived him. Since I had not given any thought to these technicalities, nor had I been properly educated in that aspect of marriage, having only Karen, who, of course, cannot have had any experience herself, to instruct me, I was alarmed by John's cries, but fortunately, as I have indicated, the drink then overwhelmed him, and though I anticipated some discussion on this subject the next morning, it was never again raised, and I am not certain to this day if John Hontvedt ever retained any consciousness of the particular occurrences of our wedding night, his memory having been expunged, so to speak, by the aquavit.

Torwad Holde's hateful letter came to us shortly after the wedding. All that long winter, in the darkness, newly married, I was engaged in numerous preparations for the Atlantic crossing. John wanted to set sail in the early spring as it would allow us several months of mild weather during which to establish ourselves in a fishing community, find lodgings and lay by enough food to see us through the following winter.

Though I had no inclination myself to take this voyage, I knew the value of having stores, as I had read many America letters which attested to the necessity of bringing one's own provisions, and in sufficient quantity, on the crossings. Sometimes Karen assisted me in this work, but not often, as I was no longer living in my father's house. All that long winter, in the darkness, newly married, I made clothes for John and myself of wool, and of colored gingham when I could come by it. John built for us barrels and chests, into which I put salted fish, herring, sour milk, beer, rye rusks, whey cheese, peas, cereal, potatoes and sugar. In other chests, I packed tallow candles, soap, a frying pan, a coffee burner, kettles, a flatiron, a tin funnel with matches, many linens and so on. Indeed, I believe I so occupied myself in the preparations for our journey that I was able to put from my mind, until those last moments on the dock with Evan, the nearly unthinkable fact of the voyage itself, which would mean my departure from Norway forever. To this end, I had not made any farewells, either to my family or to my few friends, believing that to do so might weaken whatever small resolve I had in regards to my duty, which was to accompany my husband on this sojourn.

Our sailing vessel, which was sloop-rigged, contained, belowdecks, forty bunks, each of which was to be sleeping quarters, as well as storage, for two persons. So that John and I, for thirty-nine days, shared a narrow pallet with many of our provisions, and owing to the fact that I dared not remove my outer garments in that crowded room, and also to the dreadful pitching and rolling of that ship, I hardly slept at all during those interminable nights. Instead I lay in the blackness of that hold listening to various persons praying and crying and being sick, with no hope of release until North America was reached, or the ship sank, and there were nights of such wretchedness that, God forgive me, I sometimes wished for the latter.

We were not treated badly by the crew, as I have heard was the case on some Atlantic crossings, particularly aboard those vessels that were owned by the English, but water was strictly rationed, and so much so that it was a trial to most of us to manage on just one quart a day, although John and I did have the beer to drink when our thirst was almost intolerable. I had the seasickness from the second day out, and I may say here that I believe there is no physical torment, which then permits recovery, greater than the seasickness, which causes one to feel ill at one's very soul. So wretched was this affliction that I was unable to eat, and might have grown seriously ill as a consequence of this. I must, however, despite the misery of those days, count myself among the lucky, for there were those on board who contracted the ship's fever and the cholera, and it is a wonder of God that these dreadful contagions did not spread to us all. During the fourth week of our voyage, which was the worst in regards to illness on board, there were many burials at sea, the most trying of which was the burial of a small boy, who had contracted the ship's fever, which is also called typhus, and who was so thin at the time of his death that, though he had boarded the ship fat enough, he had to be buried with sand in his casket, so that the poor child might sink to the depths, and not stay afloat behind the ship, which would truly have been an unendurable torment to the mother, who was already in despair. I believe this was the lowest moment of our journey, and that there was not one person on board, who was still conscious and sensible, who was not sorely affected by this tragedy.

I am told that on the voyage, those who were not ill engaged in knitting and sewing, and some playing of the flute and violin, and I think that John, as he remained in robust health the entire trip, may have participated in the music-making and singing that sometimes spontaneously erupted out of the tedium of the crossing. We lost fourteen persons to illness during the journey, and one woman from Stavern gave birth to twins. I have always thought this a grotesquely unacceptable ratio of deaths to births, and had I paid more attention to the stories of fatal diseases on board these ships, I might have been able to persuade John Hontvedt not to make the crossing at all. But this is idle speculation, as we did make the journey, did reach Quebec, where we were quarantined for two days, and did travel further south to the town of Portland in the state of Maine, and thence to Portsmouth in the state of New Hampshire, where we were met by Torwad Holde, who took us, in his schooner, to the island of Smutty Nose, where I was to reside for five years.

In having undertaken to write this document, I find I must, unhappily, revisit moments of the past, which, like the Atlantic Crossing, are dispiriting to recall. And as I am in ill health at the time of this writing, it is a twice-difficult task I have set for myself. But I believe that it is only with great perseverance that one is able to discover for oneself, and therefore set before another, a complete and truthful story.

I had been forewarned that we would be living on an island, but I do not think that anyone could adequately have prepared me for the nature of that particular island, or, indeed, of the entire archipelago, which was called the Isles of Shoals and lay 18 kilometers east of the American coast, north of Gloucester. As it was a hazy day on our first trip from Portsmouth to the islands, we did not spy the Shoals altogether until we were nearly upon them, and when we did, I became faint with disbelief. Never had I seen such a sad and desolate place! Lumps of rock that had barely managed to rise above the water line, the islands seemed to me then, and did so always after that day, an uninhabitable location for any human being. There was not one tree and only the most austere of empty, wooden-frame dwellings. Smutty Nose, in particular, looked so shallow and barren that I turned to John and implored him, "This is not it! Surely this is not it!"

John, who was, at that moment, struggling to conquer

his own considerable shock, was unable to answer me. Though Torwad Holde, who was, the reader may recall, the author of the infamous letter that had brought us to America (and to whom I was perhaps not as cordial as I might have been), yelled out with some enthusiasm, "Yes, Mrs. Hontvedt, these are the Isles of Shoals. Are they not wonderful?"

After we had made anchor in the tiny harbor, and I, trembling, had been helped onto the island of Smutty Nose, I felt a deep sinking as well as the beginnings of fear in my breast. How could I live on this inhospitable ledge in the middle of the Atlantic Ocean, with nothing around me but seawater, with the nearest shore not even within sight that day? How could I accept that this was the place where I should spend the rest of my life, and upon which shortly I was to be abandoned by all human company, with the exception of John Hontvedt? I clung to my husband, which I was not in the habit of doing, and begged him, I am ashamed to say, right in the presence of Torwad Holde, to take us back to Portsmouth instantly, where we might at least find a house that was settled on the soil, and where there might be about us flowers and fruit trees such as we had known in Laurvig. John, embarrassed for me and disentangling himself from my embrace, went to help Torwad Holde carry our provisions into the cottage that stood on that island with the forlorn look of a child who has been abandoned or not ever loved. Although it was spring, there were no inhabitants in any of the other buildings on the island, and there were no blossoms in the crevices of the rocks. The soil, when I bent down to feel it, was not even three inches deep. What beautiful thing could possibly grow in such a wasteland?

Around me I could hear no human sounds, apart from the grunts and sighs of John and Torwad Holde as they went to and fro with their burdens. There was, however, the steady irritating whine of the wind, for it was a cold day in early May, not at all spring-like. I walked slowly eastward, as if in a trance, as if, having committed no crime, I had been sentenced to a life in exile in the bleakest of penal colonies. I gazed out to the horizon line, imagining that my beloved Norway lay in my line of sight. We seemed to have travelled half the earth! And for what purpose?

After a time, when I could bear it, I entered the wooden-frame house that would be my home for five years. It was sided with clapboards, and was of an entirely unadorned style I was not familiar with. It had, I imagine, originally been built for at least two families, as there were two separate dwellings within the one, each with its own front door on the northwestern side of the house. The house had been painted a dull red, and there were no shutters on the windows. A single chimney, such as might accommodate a stove, had been put into the house. Inside of each apartment, there were three small rooms downstairs and one small room up a short stairway. The stove was put into the largest room of the first apartment, and henceforth we used that room as our kitchen and living room, and, in winter, as our bedroom as well. As it was then 9 May, however, John put our bed in the southwestern corner of that apartment. I believe that the previous tenants, doubtless a fisher-family such as we, had been in rather poor financial circumstances, as the walls were papered with newsprint that had yellowed, and, in some places, torn. No curtains hung on the windows, and there was no

evidence of any painting or of any effort to make a cheer-
ful abode. The entire interior was bleak, and, if I may say
so, quite gloomy, as there was, in the kitchen, only one
small window at the end of the room. As the house held
the smell of mildew as well, I thought it could not have
been occupied for some time.

John brought a chair into the house, and I sat on it. He
touched me on the shoulder, but did not speak, and then
he went out again.

I sat, in an attitude of prayer, with my hands folded in
my lap, though I could not pray, as I thought then that
God had abandoned me. I knew that I would not be able
to leave the island, that our arrival at this place was irrev-
ocable, as was my marriage to Hontvedt, and I had, I remember, to bite my cheek to keep from breaking into
tears that once started might continue forever.

But perhaps God did not abandon me after all on that
day, for as I sat there, paralyzed with the weakest of sins,
which is despair, I believe it was God's hand that caused
me then to realize that I must somehow survive my ordeal
so that I would one day be reunited with my brother. I
stood up and walked to the window and looked out over
the rock. I vowed then to keep as still and as silent as possible so that the strong emotions that threatened to con-
sume me might come under my control, in much the same
way that a drowning man, clinging to a life raft, will know
that he cannot afford to wail or cry out or beat his breast,
and that it is only with the utmost reserve and care and patience that he will be able to remain afloat until he is
saved. It would not do, I also knew, to bemoan constantly
my great loss to my husband, for John would quickly tire
of that lament, and would feel, in addition, a personal sor-

row that would inhibit his own ability to embrace the life he had chosen. I turned away from the window and examined again the interior of the cottage. I would make a home here, I told myself. I would not look eastward again.

IN AFRICA, WHEN I was on assignment there, some Masai whom I met thought that if I took a photograph of them, and if I went away with that photograph, I would have stolen their soul. I have sometimes wondered if this can be done with a place, and when I look now at the pictures of Smuttynose, I ask myself if I have captured the soul of the island. For I believe that Smuttynose has a soul, distinct from that of Appledore or Londoner's, or any other place on earth. That soul is, of course, composed of the stories we have attached to a particular piece of geography, as well as of the cumulative moments of those who have lived on and visited the small island. And I believe the soul of Smuttynose is also to be found in its rock and tufted vetch, its beggar's-ticks and pilewort, its cinquefoil brought from Norway. It lives as well in the petrels that float on the air and the skate that beach themselves — white and slimy and bloated — on the island's dark beach.

In 1846, Thomas Laighton built a hotel on Smuttynose known as the Mid-Ocean House. This hotel was a thin, wooden-frame, clapboard structure, not much bigger than a simple house. It was built on pilings and had a wrap-around porch on three sides. Over the tin roof of the porch hung a hand-painted sign from a third-story window. The sign was imperfectly lettered and read, simply, MID-OCEAN HOUSE.

From photos of the hotel, there is little evidence of landscaping around the building; sand and rock and sea-grass border the pilings under the porch. But history tells us that the hotel, in its heyday, boasted a garden, several fruit trees, and a bowling green. Nathaniel Hawthorne, Henry David Thoreau, Edward Everett Hale, and Richard Henry Dana were guests at the Mid-Ocean. In one archival photograph, three unidentified people are relax-ing on the porch. One man is wearing a suit with a white straw hat; a woman has on a high-necked, long-sleeved black dress, with a black silk bonnet, a costume that seems better suited for a Victorian funeral than for a holi-day on Smuttynose. A second woman, who appears to be stout, and who has her hair rolled at the back, has on a white blouse, a long black skirt, and over it an apron. One imagines her to have been the cook. The Mid-Ocean House burned in 1911. In March of 1873, the hotel was unoccupied because the season didn't begin until June.

I wonder now: Did Maren ever go to the Mid-Ocean Hotel? Might John, on a pleasant summer evening, have walked his wife the hundred yards, across the rocks with the wildflowers snagged and blowing, to the hotel porch, and had a cup of tea and a piece of American cake — a bowl of quaking pudding? Whitpot? Would they have sat, straight-backed, in the old woven rockers, damp and loos-ened already from the sea air, and looked out to a view they knew already by heart? Might this view — this panorama of rocky islands and spray and some pleasure boats coming now from the mainland — have looked different to them than it did from the windows of the red house? Did Maren wear a dress brought from Norway, and were they, as they sat on the wooden porch in the slight breeze from the water, objects of curiosity? Their shoes, their speech, their not-perfect manners giving them away? Might they have sat beside Childe Hassam at his easel or Celia Thaxter with her notebook and passed a pleasantry, a nod, a slight bow? Might John once have reached over to the armrest of his wife's chair and touched her hand? Did he love her?

Or was the hotel a building they could not enter except as servants — John, in his oilskins, bringing lobsters to the cook? Maren, in her homespun, her boots and hands cracked, washing linens, sweeping floorboards? Did they, in their turn, regard the guests as curiosities, American rich who provided Shoalers with extra monies in the summer season? Pale natives who were often seasick out from Portsmouth?

I like to think of Hawthorne on Smuttynose, taking the sea air, as had been prescribed. Would he have come by steamer from Boston, have brought a boater and a white suit for the sun? Would he have been inspired by the desolation of the Shoals, tempted to bathe in the extraordinarily deep waters that separated Smuttynose from Appledore or Star? Might he have been invigorated by the conversation of the intellectuals and artists Celia Thaxter had gathered around her — Charles Dickens and John Greenleaf Whittier, William Morris Hunt, a kind of colony, a salon. Did he eat the blueberry grunt, the fish soup, the pluck that was put before him? And who put it there? Is it possible that a Norwegian immigrant hovered over him? Did this woman ask a question of Nathaniel Hawthorne, a pleasant question, having no idea who he was, another guest is all, in her charming but broken English? *Tings. Togedder. Brotter.*

It is almost impossible now, looking across to Smuttynose, to imagine Hawthorne on that island. There is no trace of the Mid-Ocean Hotel. It has passed into recorded memory, historical fact, with no life except in sentences and on photographic emulsion. If all the sentences and photographs about the hotel were to be swept into the sea that surrounds Smuttynose, the Mid-Ocean — Hawthorne's stay there, an immigrant's abbreviated pleasantries — would cease to exist.

No one can know a story's precise reality.

On October 2, 1867, a boxing match was held at Smuttynose. Because gambling was illegal in the 1860s, isolated locations, without much interference from the police, were in demand. The Isles of Shoals, and Smuttynose in particular, appeared to be ideal for this purpose. Two fighters went at it for an hour and a half in the front yard of the Charles Johnson house, previously known as "the red house," and subsequently to be known as the Hontvedt house. The spectators came by boat. Another fight was planned, but was canceled when bad weather prevented any observers from reaching the island and made the contestants seasick.

At dawn on the morning of the second day at the Isles of Shoals, I am awakened by unwanted and familiar sounds. I slip out of the bed, with its damp-roughened sheets, and begin to make a pot of coffee in the galley. When I run the water, I cannot hear the movements in the forward cabin. I am waiting for the coffee to drip through the filter, my arms crossed over my chest, a sense of wet seeping through my socks, when I reach up and pop open the hatch for just a sliver of fresh air. I see immediately that the sky is a darkened red, as though there has been a fire on the shore. I open the hatch fully and climb up through the companionway in my robe. A band of smoky crimson arches over all the islands, a north-south ribbon that seems to stretch from Portland all the way to Boston. The red is deep in the center, becoming dustier toward the edges. Beneath the swath of red, gulls catch the light of the slanted sun and seem momentarily imbued with a glow of color all their own. I am somewhat concerned — the way you are when nature goes off her routines — yet I want to go below, to wake Billie, to show her this phenomenon of sunlight on water particles in the air. But Billie is already there, behind me.

"I've cut my foot, Mommy" is what she says.

I turn in the cockpit. Her face is sticky and puffed with sleep, her mouth beginning to twist with the first messages of pain. She has on her summer baseball pajamas, shorts and a T-shirt — *Red Sox,* they say. Her feet are white and tiny and bare, and from her right foot the blood is spreading. She moves slightly toward me and makes a smudge on the white abraded surface of the cockpit floor. A small stray shard from last night's broken glass must have fallen below the ladder of the companionway. My opening the hatch this morning has woken Billie, who then walked into the small triangle under the ladder to retrieve one of Blackbeard's treasures, the key chain.

I go below to get towels and hydrogen peroxide and bandages from the first-aid kit, and after I have washed and dressed the cut and am holding Billie in my arms, I look up and realize there is no trace, nothing left at all, of the red band in the sky.

Rich comes up onto the deck, puts his hands to his waist, and examines the color and texture of the sky, which is not altogether clear, not as it was the day before. To the east, just below the morning sun, a thin layer of cloud sits on the horizon like an unraveling roll of discolored cotton wool. Rich, who looks mildly concerned, goes below to listen to the radio. When he returns to the deck, he brings with him a mug of coffee. He sits opposite Billie and me in the cockpit.

"How did it happen?"

"She cut it on a piece of glass."

"She's all right?"

"I think so. The bleeding seems to have stopped."

"NOAA says there's a cold front coming through later today. But NOAA is not to be entirely trusted."

Rich moves his head so that he can see beyond me. There is a gentle chop, but the harbor still seems well protected. Across the way, there is activity aboard a ketch anchored near us. Rich nods at a woman in a white polo shirt and khaki shorts.

"Looks like they're leaving," he says.

"So soon? They just got in last night."

A sudden breeze blows the skirt of my robe open, and I fold it closed over my knees. I do not really like to be seen in the morning. I have a sense of not being entirely covered, not yet protected. Rich has on a clean white T-shirt and a faded navy-blue bathing suit. He is barefoot and has recently showered. The top of his head is wet, and he doesn't have a beard. I wonder where Adaline is.

"I don't know," he says, speculating out loud about the storm. "It isn't clear how bad it will be, or even if it will definitely be here by tonight."

I shift Billie on my lap. I look over toward Smuttynose. Rich must see the hesitation on my face.

"You need to go over to the island again," he says.

"I should."

"I'll take you."

"I can take myself," I say quickly. "I did it last night." This surprises him.

"After everyone was asleep. I wanted night shots."

Rich studies me over the rim of his coffee. "You should have woken me," he says. "It isn't safe to go off like that by yourself. At night, especially."

"Was it scary, Mommy?"

"No. Actually, it was very beautiful. The moon was out and was so bright I could see my way without a flashlight."

Rich is silent. I pick up my own mug from the deck. The coffee is cold. Billie sits up suddenly, jogging my arm. The coffee spills onto the sleeve of my white robe.

"Mommy, can I go over with you tonight? To the island when it's dark? Maybe there will be ghosts there."

"Not tonight," says Rich. "No one's going over there tonight. We may be having a storm later. It wouldn't be safe."

"Oh," she says, dropping her shoulders in disappointment.

"I've got landscape shots from the water," I say, tallying up my meager inventory. "And night shots, and I've done Maren's Rock. But I need shots from the island it-

self, looking out to Appledore and Star, and to the east,
out to sea. And also some detail shots."

"Like what?"

"Scrub pine. Rose hips. A window of the Haley house,
the footprint of the Hontvedt house. I should have done
this yesterday when I had the chance. I'm sorry."

"It's all right," he says. "We have time."

"Me too!" says Billie excitedly.

Rich shakes his head. "You stay here with your dad
and Adaline." He reaches over and pulls my daughter
from my lap. He whirls her around and tickles her at her
waist. She begins to laugh with that unique helplessness
that borders on hysteria. She tries to wriggle away from
his grasp and screams to me to help her. "Mommy, save
me! Save me!" But when Rich suddenly stops, she turns
to him with an appreciative sigh and folds herself into
his lap.

"Whew," she says. "That was a good tickle."

George E. Ingerbretson, a Norwegian immigrant who
lived at Hog Island Point on Appledore Island, was called
to the stand. He, like many who were summoned, spoke
in a halting and imperfect English that was not always
easy to transcribe. He was asked by the county attorney
what he observed between seven and eight o'clock on the
morning of March 6, 1873. He replied that he had two
small boys and that they had come into his house and
said, "They are halooing over to Smutty Nose." He was
then asked what he saw when he got to the island.

"I saw one bloody axe; it was lying on a stone in front
of the door, John Hontvet's kitchen door. The handle was
broken. I went around the house. I saw a piece knocked
off the window. Then I stopped. I saw John was coming. I

did not look into the window. I only saw the bloody axe and blood around."

After John Hontvedt arrived, along with several other men, Ingerbretson went inside the house.

"Evan Christensen went just ahead of me; he opened the door. Evan is the husband of Anethe."

"Who else went with you at that time?" Yeaton asked.

"John Hontvet and Louis Nelson and James Lee, no one else. John's brother, Matthew, was with us. I do not know whether he went into the house or not."

"State what you saw."

"It was Anethe, lying on her back, head to the door. It looked to me as though she was hauled into the house by the feet. I saw the marks."

"Of what?"

"From the south-east corner of the house into the door."

"Traces of what?"

"Of blood."

"Was there any other body there?"

"Yes. Then we went out and went into another room in the northward side, north-east of the house. We came in and there was some blood around, and in the bed-room we found another dead body."

"Whose body was that?"

"That was Karen Christensen."

"Did you notice any wounds upon the body of Anethe?"

"Yes; there are some scars on the head."

"What part of the head were they?"

"In the ear most, just about the right ear. She had some scar in her face there."

"Scar on top of the head?"

"We did not look much after that time."

Yeaton then asked Ingerbretson some questions about the well that belonged to the house and its distance from the house, and whether he had disturbed any of the bodies. Ingerbretson said that he had not. Yeaton asked the fisherman if he had seen any tracks, and Ingerbretson said no, he had not seen any tracks. Before Yeaton dismissed the witness, he asked if, when he had arrived on Smuttynose that morning, there was any living person on that island.

"Yes," the fisherman replied.

"Who was it?"

"Mrs. Hontvet and a little dog."

"State condition in which you found her."

"In an overbad condition. She was in her night-dress crying and halooing, and blood all over her clothes, Mrs. Hontvet's clothes. I got her into the boat."

"Do you know whether her feet were frozen?"

"Yes. I searched her feet right off and they were stiff. I carried her over to my house."

Before a shoot, I will prepare the cameras — check my film and the batteries, clean the lenses — and I begin these tasks in the cockpit. Billie has gone below to wake Thomas. I can hear them talking and laughing, playing on the bed, although the wind, with its constant white noise, steals their words.

Adaline emerges from the companionway. She smiles and says, "Good morning." Her legs are bare, and she is holding a towel around her, as if she had just stepped from the shower, although she is not wet. Her hair is spread all along her back in knots and tangles. I can see a small bit of red beneath the towel, so I know that she has on her bathing suit, and I wonder for a moment why she has the towel around her. How strange we women are in the mornings, I am thinking, this modesty, this not wanting to be seen. Adaline turns her back to me and puts her foot up on the cockpit bench, inspecting her toes.

"I hear Billie got a cut," she says.

"Yes. She did."

"Bad?"

"Not too."

"I'm going for a swim."

She lets the towel drop to the cockpit floor. She keeps her back to me, and I notice things I have not before. The plate-shallow curve of her inner thigh. The elongated waist. The patch of hair she has missed just above the inside of her right knee. I think about what her skin would feel like. This is painful curiosity. She steps up to the back of the stern, positions herself for a dive. She skims the water like a gull.

She does not come up sputtering or exclaiming from the cold, as I might have done, but rather spins in a lovely barrel roll and swims with an economy of strokes, her feet barely moving at all. I see wisps of red amid the chop. She swims for about ten minutes, away from the boat and back. When she is done, she climbs up over the stern with ease, refusing my outstretched hand. She sits opposite me in the cockpit and picks up the towel to dry herself. She is slightly winded, which is somehow reassuring.

"You kept your maiden name," she says.

"Jean Janes had an infelicitous ring to it," I explain. I notice that the water beads up on her skin.

"It wasn't for professional reasons then?"

"Not exactly."

She sets the towel down beside her and begins to brush out her hair.

"Did I hear Rich say there might be a storm?" she asks.

"We may have to leave before this afternoon." The thought of leaving the harbor fills me with swift, sharp regret, as if I had left something significant unfinished.

"Where are we going?"

"I don't know. Portsmouth possibly. Or Annisquam."

She bends her head to her knees, letting her hair fall forward to the floor. She brushes upward from the nape of her neck. She throws her head back and begins to brush from the sides of her face. In my camera bag is a Polaroid camera I use in test shots. Often, when I have a scene I like, I take a Polaroid first, so that I can examine the composition and the light and make adjustments if necessary before shooting the real thing. I take the Polaroid out of my camera bag and aim it at Adaline. I quickly snap a picture. She blinks at the click. I rip the film out and hold it in my hand, waiting for the image to appear. In the photograph, Adaline is holding a brush to her head. Her hair, which has dried in the sun, has streaked itself a light blond, or perhaps it is a photographic deception. Her skin looks dark by contrast, deeply tanned. I hold the picture out to her.

She takes it in her hand and examines it.

"A mere negative of my former self," she says and smiles.

In Haley's Cove, a pier supported a long warehouse and fish processing plant. The men of Smuttynose invented the process of drying fish called dunning. Large vessels would tie up inside the pier to load and offload goods and fish, which were then stored in the building known as the Long House. The area that comprises the pier, the Long House, Captain Haley's House, and the footprint of the Hontvedt cottage is not much bigger than a modest suburban backyard.

Dunfish sold for three or four times the price of regularly prepared fish. So many fish were harvested by Shoalers that in 1822 the national price of fish was quoted not from Boston but from the Isles of Shoals.

When Thomas comes up the ladder, he brings with him the smell of bacon and pancakes.

"Billie and I made breakfast," he says. "Adaline's setting the table."

I am rereading one of the guidebooks to see if I have overlooked a landmark, an artifact that I should not miss when I go across to Smuttynose to finish the shoot. In my lap is Maren Hontvedt's document and its translation, as well as a thin pamphlet, one of the accounts of the murders.

"What's that?" he asks. A conciliatory gesture. Interest in my work.

"This?" I ask, holding up the guidebook.

"No, that."

I lay my hand on the papers with the brown ink, as if protecting them. "It's the thing I got from the Athenaeum."

"Really. Can I see it?"

Without looking precisely at him, I hand the papers to Thomas. I can feel the color and the heat coming into the back of my neck.

"It's not in English," he says.

"There's a translation."

"This is an original document," he says with some surprise. "I'm amazed they let you have it."

There is a silence.

"They didn't," I say. I push my hair behind my ears.

"They didn't," he repeats.

"I knew they wouldn't give it to me, so I took it. I'll give it back."

"What is it?"

"It's a memoir. By Maren Hontvedt."

"Who is?"

"The woman who survived the murders."

"It's dated 1899."

"I know."

He hands the papers back to me, and I look up at him for the first time. His hair has been combed off his forehead with his fingers and lies in thinning rows, an already harvested crop. His eyes are bloodshot, and his skin, in the harsh, flat light, looks blotchy.

"You don't need this stuff for your assignment," he says.

"No."

He is about to turn and go back down to the galley, but he hesitates a moment on the steps. "What's going on with you?" he asks.

I shade my brow with my hand. "What's going on with you?" I ask.

At the Shoals, men have always fished for haddock and for hake, for porgies and for shad. In 1614, Captain John Smith first mapped the islands and called them Smythe's Isles, and he wrote that they were "a heape together."

Halyards slap against the mast, an insistent beat we can hear at the double bed–cum–dining table in the center of the cabin. Thomas and Billie have made pancakes — kidney shaped, oil glistened, and piled high upon a white platter. There is also bacon, which Adaline declines. She chooses toast and orange juice instead. I watch her, nearly naked, lift her mug of decaffeinated coffee to her lips and blow across the rim. I am not sure that I could now sit at a breakfast table in my bathing suit, though I must have done so as a younger woman.

Are we, as we age, I wonder, repaid for all our thoughtless gestures?

Billie, next to me, still has on her Red Sox pajamas. She smells of sleep. She is proud of her misshapen pancakes, and eats six of them. I think it is the one certain way to get Billie — any child? — to eat a meal. Have her cook it herself.

I have on my robe. Rich his bathing suit. Thomas the shirt he slept in. Is it our dishabille that creates the tension — a tension so pronounced I find it hard to swallow? Rich wears the weather report on his face, and we seem excessively focused on the food and on Billie, in the manner of adults who have not found an easy entrée into the conversation. Or who are suddenly wary of conversation: "These are wonderful, Billie. I can see the bear now." "What kind of coffee is this? It has an almond flavor." "I love bacon. Honestly, is there anything better on a camping trip than a bacon sandwich?"

Sometimes I watch the way that Thomas watches me. And if he catches me at this, he slips his eyes away so gracefully that I am not sure he has seen me. Is this simply the familiarity of bodies? I wonder. I no longer know with any certainty what he is thinking.

"Do you keep a journal?" Adaline asks Thomas.

I am surprised by the question. Will she dare a reprise of Pearse?

Thomas shakes his head. "Who has so many words that he can afford to spend them on letters and journals?" he asks.

Rich nods. "Tom's a terrible letter writer."

I haven't heard the nickname in years.

"His literary executor will have it easy," Rich adds. "There won't be anything there."

"Except the work," I say quietly. "There's a lot of the work."

"A lot of false starts," says Thomas. "Especially lately."

I look over at Thomas, and I wonder if what I see is the same face I knew fifteen years ago. Does it seem the same to me? Is the skin the same? Or is the expression now so different than it was then that the muscles have become realigned, the face itself unrecognizable?

"Is it definite that man did it?"

Adaline's question startles all of us. It takes me a second to catch up. "Louis Wagner?" I ask.

"Do they know for sure?"

"Some think yes," I answer slowly, "and some think no. At the time, Wagner protested his innocence. But the crime created a tremendous amount of hysteria. There were riots and lynch mobs, and they had to hurry the trial."

Adaline nods.

"Even now, there are doubts," I add. "He hadn't much of a motive for the murders themselves, for example, and that row from Portsmouth to Smuttynose would have been brutal. He'd have had to row almost thirty miles in the dark. And it was the first week in March."

"It doesn't seem possible," says Rich. "I couldn't do it. I'm not even sure I could do it on a flat surface."

"Also, I've read parts of the trial transcript," I say, "and I can't figure out why the prosecution didn't do a better job. Maren Hontvedt's clothes were blood-soaked, but the defense didn't really pursue this. And the coroner was very careless with the murder weapon — they let the sea spray wash off all the fingerprints and blood on the journey back to Portsmouth."

"Surely, they had fingerprinting techniques then," says Rich.

"On the other hand," I say, "Wagner seems to have no alibi for that night, and the next morning he's reported to have told people he committed murder."

"Jean doesn't always get to pick her assignments," Thomas says. He sounds apologetic.

"A crime of passion," says Rich.

"A crime of passion?" Adaline narrows her eyes. "In the end, a crime of passion is just sordid, isn't it? At heart. We think a crime of passion has a morality all its own — people have thought so for years. History is full of judgments that forgive crimes of passion. But it doesn't have a morality, not really. It's pure selfishness. Simply having what you want."

"I think it's the knife that makes it seem like a crime of passion," says Thomas. "It was a knife, wasn't it?"

"An ax."

"Same thing. It's the intimacy. With a gun, you can kill a person at a distance. But with a knife, you have to touch the victim — more than touch. Manhandle. Subdue. It would seem to require, at least for the several seconds it takes to complete the deed, a sustained frenzy or passion."

"Or a lucrative contract," says Rich.

"But even then," argues Thomas, "there would have to be something in the act — the handling of the victim, the feel of the knife against the flesh — that attracted the killer to that particular method."

"Thomas," I say, nodding at Billie.

"Mommy, take a picture of the pancakes," she says. "Before they're all gone?"

I reach behind me into my camera bag and bring out the Polaroid. I shoot the platter with the pancakes that are left, and then rip the film out and give it to Billie to hold. She's a pro at this, and holds the corner casually.

"The Masai," I say idly, "believe that if you take a photograph of a person, you have stolen his soul. You have to pay them for the picture."

"The soul is for sale then?" asks Adaline.

"Oh, I think the Masai are shrewder than that."

"See, Adaline? Look!" Billie stands on the bench to hand Adaline the Polaroid. As she does, she cracks her head on the sharp corner of an overhanging cabinet. The color leaves Billie's face, and her mouth falls open, but I can see that in this company my daughter is determined not to cry.

I reach over and fold her into me. The photograph flutters onto the table. She presses her face into my chest, and I feel her breath through the opening of my robe. Adaline picks up the Polaroid. "Lovely picture, Billie," she says.

I kiss Billie's forehead, and she pulls away from me, turning in her seat, trying bravely to smile. Adaline hands the picture to Billie.

"Very game," says Adaline to me.

"Thanks."

"I envy you."

I look quickly up at her and catch her eyes. Does she mean Billie? Or does she mean having my daughter with me? Or does she mean Billie and Thomas — the whole package?

"Sometimes I imagine I have caught a likeness of a person's soul," I say carefully. "Occasionally, you can see it. Or what you imagine is the true character of that person. But of course, it's only a likeness, and that likeness is only an image, on the paper."

"But you can fool with images," she says. "Didn't I read that somewhere? Can't you change the image?"

"You can now," I say. "You can do it almost flawlessly with computers."

"So you could, theoretically, create another character, another soul."

"This is assuming that you believed the camera could capture the soul in the first place," I say.

"This is assuming that you believed in the soul at all," says Thomas. "That what you saw was not simply an arrangement of organic particles."

"But surely you believe in the soul," Adaline says quickly, almost defensively. "You of all people."

Thomas is silent.

"It's in the poems," she says.

I have a series of photographs of Billie and Thomas together, taken shortly after we have eaten the pancakes. I have dressed and am getting my gear together in preparation for the boat ride over to Smuttynose. I take out the Hasselblad, which I have loaded with black-and-white. I do four quick shots — click, click, click, click — of Thomas and Billie, who have lingered at the table. In the first, Billie is standing on the padded bench, inspecting Thomas's teeth, counting them, I think. In the second, she has bent her body so that she is butting her head into Thomas's stomach; Thomas, too, is slightly bent, and has wrapped his arms over her back. In the third picture, they both have their elbows propped upon the table and are facing each other, talking. The conversation must be serious; you can see that in the tilt of Billie's head, the pursing of her mouth. In the fourth picture, Thomas has one hand tucked inside the open collar of his shirt, scratching his shoulder. He is facing me, but he won't look at me or at the camera. Billie has turned her head away from Thomas, as though someone has just called to her from the forward cabin.

The head sea is apparent the moment we round the breakwater. Small waves hit the Zodiac and send their spray into and over the inflatable boat. With one hand on the tiller, Rich tosses me a poncho, which I use to protect my camera bags from the salt water. When I look up again, I find I can hardly see for the spray. My face and hair and glasses are soaked, as in a rain, and foolishly, I have worn shorts, so that my legs are wet and cold and covered with goosebumps.

Rich turns the Zodiac around. He has wanted to observe the ocean on the unprotected side of the island, and he has seen enough. He maneuvers back into the harbor and puts the Zodiac up onto the narrow dark beach of Smuttynose, a beach I left only the night before. I dry my glasses on the inside of my sweatshirt and inspect my camera bags for any signs of wet.

"How do you want to work this?" he asks as he is tying up the boat. His T-shirt has turned a translucent peach.

"You want me to go with you and hold things? Or do you want me to wait here?"

"Wait here," I say. "Sit in the sun and get dry. Rich, I'm really sorry about this. You must be freezing."

"I'm fine," he says. "I've been wet before. You do what you have to do." He smiles. "I know this is hard to believe," he says, "but I'm actually having a good time. The truth is" — he gestures to indicate the expanse of the ocean and seems to laugh at himself — "I usually have to go to a lot of trouble to be able to do this on my days off."

"I'll try not to be long. Thirty, forty minutes at the most. And if you do get cold," I say, "give a shout, and we'll get out of here. This isn't worth getting sick over."

I bend to collect my camera bags. When I stand up, Rich is wrestling with his wet T-shirt. He takes it off and wipes the top of his head with it, and then squeezes it out. I watch him walk over to a rock that is in the sun, or what is left of the sun, and lay the T-shirt carefully out to dry. When I was in Africa, I observed the women there drying their clothes in a similar manner — by laying them flat on top of long grasses over a wide field, so that often you would come upon a landscape of bright cloth. Rich glances over at me. Perhaps because he has almost no hair on his head, the thick dark chest hair that spreads across his breast draws the eye. I turn around and walk to the interior of Smuttynose.

The defense waived its right to cross-examine Ingerbretson, at which point the prosecution then called Evan Christensen to the stand. Christensen was asked to identify himself and to talk about his relationship to Smuttynose.

"In March last, I lived at the Shoals, Smutty Nose, in John Hontvet's family; I had lived there about five months. Anethe Christensen was my wife. I was born in Norway. Anethe was born in Norway. I came to this country with her after I married her."

Yeaton asked Christensen what he was doing the day of the murders. Christensen answered: "During the night my wife was killed I was in Portsmouth. I arrived at Portsmouth about four o'clock the night before."

"Who was with you when you arrived at Portsmouth about four o'clock that night?"

"John Hontvet and Matthew Hontvet. I was at work for John in the fishing business."

"Was anyone else with you that night?"

"No, sir."

"Where did you spend the night at Portsmouth?"

"I was on board till twelve o'clock; after that went up to Johnson's house and baited trolls."

"Baited trolls the rest of the night?"

"Yes, till six or seven o'clock in the morning. John Hontvet was with me when I baited trolls."

"When did you first hear of this matter at Smutty Nose?"

"Heard it from Appledore Island."

"Where were you then?"

"On board Hontvet's schooner."

"Who were with you at that time?"

"Matthew Hontvet and John Hontvet; it was between eight and nine o'clock in the morning."

"Did you go ashore?"

"Yes; got a boat and went ashore on Appledore Island."

"Where did you go from Appledore Island?"

"I went first up to Ingerbretson's house. After I left there I went to Smutty Nose. When I got to Smutty Nose, I went right up to the house and right in."

"What did you see there?"

"I saw my wife lying on the floor."

"Dead or alive?"

"Dead."

"What did you do?"

"Went right back out again."

The light is flat and muffled, colors indistinct. Thin, dull cloud has slipped over the sun, still rising in the east. I am annoyed with myself for having wasted too much time the day before shooting Maren's Rock. I walk to the spot where the Hontvedt house once stood. The air has a chill in it, or perhaps it is only that I am chilled because my sweatshirt and shorts are wet. I am grateful that Rich knew not to bring Billie.

I stand in the footprint of the house, surveying its markers. There is little here that will make an outstanding photograph; its purpose will be merely documentary. Unless, that is, I can convey the foundation's claustrophobia.

I know that it is always true that the dimensions of a house, seen from above, will look deceptively small. Space appears to increase in size with walls and furniture and windows. Yet even so, I am having difficulty imagining six grown men and women — Maren, John, Evan, Anethe, Matthew, and, for seven months, Louis Wagner — living in a space not much bigger than the single room Thomas had in Cambridge when I met him. All those passions, I think, on such a small piece of land.

I find what I think must have been one of the two front doors of the house and stand at its threshold, looking out toward Appledore, as Maren must have done a thousand times in the five years she lived on the island. I take my cameras and lenses from their separate pouches, check the light meter, and shoot a series of black-and-white stills to make a panorama of that view. Directly west of me is Gosport Harbor and, beyond that, ten miles of water to the New Hampshire coast. To my north is Appledore; to my south is Star. Behind me, that is to say east of me, is the Atlantic. I back away from the threshold and stand in the foundation's center. Beneath me, the floor of that old house has long given way to thistle and wood sage. I find a small patch of bare ground and sit down. Above me, the clouds are growing oilier, as though a film were being washed across the sky. My sweatshirt sticks to my back, and I shiver.

I dig under the brush to feel the dirt. I bring the soil up and massage it with my fingers. In the place where I am sitting, two women died. One was young, one was not. One was beautiful, the other not. I imagine I can hear Maren's voice.

THE MORNING AFTER we arrived on the island of Smutty Nose, John went off with a man named Ingerbretson to Portsmouth to secure more provisions and also to see about a schooner that might be for sale. In order to make a living on Smutty Nose, around which we were told was an abundance of mackerel, cod, flounder, haddock, and menhaden, John would have to have his own boat plus full gear for fishing. This would be a great expense, and would largely exhaust John's savings, but it was clear to him that no profit, nor even a livelihood, could be earned without such expenditures.

While John was gone, I stripped the walls of the yellowed and ugly newsprint, rolling the papers into logs and burning them on the stove for warmth. At first, the house was colder than it had been, but I knew that shortly John would begin to build wooden walls, behind which he would place goat's tick for insulation. I also found a roll of blue gingham in my stores, which I hastily fashioned into curtains. When these efforts were completed, I examined our remaining provisions for foodstuffs that might make a meal, as I knew that John would be hungry when he returned. All that day I busied myself so that I did not have time for any thoughts about people or a home left behind. I have found, in the course of my adult life, that the best cure for melancholy is industry, and it was only when John and I were imprisoned in the cottage for long weeks at a time during the winter months that I fell victim to that malady and could not control myself or my thoughts and words, so that I was a worry not only to John Hontvedt but also to myself. That day, however, my first day on the island of Smutty Nose, was one of determined busy-ness, and when my husband returned from his sail into Portsmouth, I saw that the changes I had made had pleased him, and he had a smile upon his face, which, for the first time since we had left Norway, replaced the concern that he nearly always had for my well-being.

Our daily life on Smutty Nose was, for the most part, unremarkable in many of its aspects. John and I would wake early, and I would immediately remake the fire that had gone out during the night. John, who would have baited his trawls the evening before, would gather his oil pants and underclothes from the hooks that were in the kitchen, and once dressed would sit down at the table on which I would put in front of him large bowls of porridge and of coffee. We did not speak much, unless there was some unusual piece of information that needed to be imparted, or unless I was in need of some provisions, which I would inform John about. Early on, we had lost the habit of speech with each other, as I think must happen with other husbands and wives who dare not speak for fear of asking the wrong question, or of revealing a festering hurt or a love for another person which might be ruinous to the partnership they had formed.

John would then go down to the beach and from there row out in his dory to his schooner. On good drying days, when he had left the harbor, I would wash the clothes and lay them out on the rocks in the sun. I would bake the flatbrød and prepare the mid-day meal. I would have the task of cleaning the fish John had caught for drying or eating. I made clothes from bolts of cloth I had brought with me or John had managed in Portsmouth. I spun wool with a spinning wheel John had bought in Portsmouth, and knit various articles of clothing for both myself and for John. When I had finished these chores, and if the day were clear, I would go outside with the dog John had given me, which I had named Ringe, and walk the perimeter of the island, throwing sticks for Ringe into the water so that he might fetch them back to me. In time, John built me a hen coop and purchased in Portsmouth four hens, which were good layers, providing me with fresh eggs.

When John arrived in the evenings, I would take from him his soiled oil clothes and undergarments, and he would have a wash at the sink. I would have prepared a light meal for him. By then, he would have put on dry underclothes, and would sit near to the fire. We had both taken up the habit of smoking a pipe, as it soothed us to do so. John's face was weathering, and he was growing many lines in his skin.

Sometime during the evening, usually when I was sitting near to the fire as well, he would put a hand on my knee, and that would be a signal to me that he wished me to join him in bed. Regardless of the cold, he would remove his garments altogether, and I believe that I saw my husband in a state of undress every night of our married life, as he always lit the candle on the table by our bed. As for me, I would have preferred that our marital relations be conducted in the dark, but John would not have this. I usually kept on my nightdress, or if it were very cold, all my garments. Except for one or two occasions when I was bathing, I am not sure John Hontvedt ever saw me in my natural condition. I had, after a time, lost my physical revulsion toward my husband, and tolerated these nightly relations well enough, but I cannot say there was ever any pleasure in the event — particularly so as it became more and more obvious to me that there was something wrong with me that was preventing me from conceiving a child.

Though our daily life on Smutty Nose was one of habit and routine, I would not be correctly portraying life on the Isles of Shoals if I omitted to say that the winters there were exceedingly harsh. Of that seasonal desolation, I can barely write. I am not certain that it is possible to convey the despair that descends upon one who has been subjected to the ceaseless cold and wet, with storms out of the northeast that on occasion smashed fishing boats upon the rocks and washed away the houses of the Shoalers, causing many to die at sea and on land, and imprisoning those who survived in dark and cheerless rooms for so many days on end that it was a wonder we did not all lose our minds. It has been said that the fishermen who lived on those islands at that time were possessed of an extraordinary courage, but I think that this courage, if we would call it so, is merely the instinct to fasten one's body onto a stationary object and hold on, and have as well the luck not to have one's roof blown into the ocean. I remember weeks when John could not go to sea, nor could anyone come across to Smutty Nose, and when the weather was so dangerous that we two sat for hours huddled by the stove in the kitchen, into which we had moved our bed, and the windows and door of which we had sealed from the elements. We had no words to speak to each other, and everything around us was silent except for the wind that would not stop and made the house shudder. Also, the air inside the room became quite poisonous due to the smoke of the stove and of our pipes, and I recall that I almost always had the headache.

Many fisher-families experience lives of isolation, but ours was made all the greater because of the unique geographical properties of an island in the North Atlantic Ocean, which properties then convey themselves to the soul. There was no day, for example, that the foremost element in one's life was not the weather. There might be clear days with heavy seas, cloudy days with light seas, hazy days when one could not see the mainland, days of fog so dense that I could not find the well, nor make my way accurately to the beach, days of such ferocious storms and winds that entire houses were washed in an instant into the sea, and one could not leave one's dwelling for fear of meeting a similar fate, and days upon days of a noxious wind that made the panes of glass beat against their wooden frames and never ceased its whistle in and around the cottage. So important was the state of the elements that every morning one thought of nothing else except of how to survive what God and nature had brought forth, or, on the rare days of clear skies and no wind, of warm sun and exhilarating air, of how thankful one was for such a heady reprieve.

Because of the necessity for John to go out to sea seven days a week in season, and the equally strong necessity to remain shut in for so many weeks at a time in winter, we did not have many friends or even acquaintances on those islands. To be sure, the Ingerbretsons had befriended us, and it was with this family that we celebrated 17 May and Christmas Eve, sharing together the fattigmann, which, if I may say so, achieved a delicate and crispy texture in my hands, even with my crude implements, and also the lute-fisk, a fish which was soaked in lye for several days and then poached to a delicate texture. But as the Ingerbret-sons resided on Appledore and not on Smutty Nose, I had little occasion to spend time with the women in these households as I might have done were there no water bar-riers between us. In this way, I was often alone on the is-land for long stretches at a time.

At this point in my tale, I must hasten to explain to the reader that life on Smutty Nose was not entirely bereft of pleasant moments. As even the barest tree on the darkest hour in winter has a beauty all its own, I eventually came to see that Smutty Nose was not without its own peculiar charms, particularly on those days when the weather would be fine, that is to say, sharp and tingling, with sil-ver glints in the granite, every crevice visible, the water all around us a vivid aquamarine. On those occasions, which in my mind are relatively few in number, I might sit upon a ledge and read one of the books I had been lent in Portsmouth, or I might walk about the island playing with my dog, or I might pick some of the wild growth that sur-vived in the rocks and make a bouquet of sorts for my table.

In the five years I was on Smutty Nose, I ventured into Portsmouth four times. I had, at first, a great deal of trou-ble with the English language, and sometimes it was a trial to make myself understood or to comprehend what was being said to me. I have observed that such a lack of facility with a language tends to make others think of one as not very intelligent and certainly not very well educated. And this used to be a great annoyance to me, as I could converse quite well, and even, I may say, fluently and with some style, in my native tongue, but I was rendered nearly imbecilic when required to express my needs in English.

And here I must say a further word about the American inability to pronounce any Norwegian at all, even, or especially, Norwegian names that were not familiar to them. So that many of the immigrants were forced to change the spelling of their names to make them more easily understood. Thus John, over time, changed his surname to Hontvet, omitting the combination of the *dt*, which Americans found queer in the writing of it and nearly impossible to enunciate correctly. And I also acquiesced to the entering of myself on the church roll at Gosport as Mary S. Hontvet, rather than as Maren, as the Pastor wrote it that way initially, and it was some time before I discovered the mistake. In addition, I observed that after the events of 5 March 1873, the spelling of Evan's name was changed to Ivan in the American newspapers.

Putting aside the language difficulties, I did grow to have some fondness for Portsmouth. To go from the silence of Smutty Nose to the agitation and bustle of Portsmouth was always unsettling, but I could not help but be intrigued by the dresses and bonnets on the women, which I would keep in my mind when I returned to the island. We would visit the pharmacy for tonics and nostrums, and the public market for provisions, and there were always many curious sights in that city, though I confess I was appalled at the lack of cleanliness on the streets, and by the condition of the streets themselves, as they were not graded and were full of ruts and mud and so on. At that time, the main industry of Portsmouth was its ship yard, and always in the background, there was the din of the ironworks. In addition, there were many sailors on the streets, as the Port attracted ships of various nationalities. On three of my trips into Portsmouth, we spent the night with the Johnson family, Norwegians who had come before us, and with them engaged in lively conversation through the night, which was always a joy for me, as there was seldom any conversation of any duration on the island. On these occasions, I was especially pleased to receive news from Norway, and even once from the area near Laurvig, since the Norwegian families in Portsmouth were the recipients of many letters in America. More often than not, these letters were read aloud at table, and discussed at length. We always went to Portsmouth in the summer, owing to the fact that John did not like to take the risk of ferrying me during the winters and chance hitting one of the numerous ice floes that would sometimes block the passage between the mainland and the Shoals.

I did, in that time, receive three letters from Karen telling of our father (and full of vague complaints about her health and the housework), but, curiously, with few mentions of Evan, who himself did not write to us until the second year of my stay at Smutty Nose, and then to tell us of our father's death from old age. In March of 1871, we had a fourth letter from Karen, saying she would join us in America in May.

Karen's letter was a great surprise to John and me. We could not imagine what motivation my sister had for leaving Norway, as she had been quite parsimonious in her letter regarding her reasons for emigrating. She wrote only that as our father had died, she was no longer obliged to stay in that house.

To prepare for my sister's arrival, John purchased a bed in Portsmouth and put it in the upstairs bedroom. I made curtains for that room, and sewed a quilt, which was of a star pattern and took all the scraps I had from my provisions. As I did not have much time in which to finish it, I worked on the quilt all the long days and into the nights until my fingers were numb at their tips, but when the quilt was done, I was glad of the result, for the room now had a cheer which had been entirely absent before.

I remember well the morning of 4 May, when I stood on the beach at Smutty Nose and watched John bring my sister to the island in the dory. He had gone into Portsmouth the day before to wait for the arrival of Karen's ship, and I had seen them coming across from Portsmouth in John's schooner. It was a clear day but exceedingly cold, and I confess that I was apprehensive about Karen's arrival. Though it may strike the reader as odd, I was not eager to change the habits that John and I had shared for three years, nor to admit another person, or, in particular, my sister, about whom I felt somewhat ambivalent.

As Karen drew closer, I examined her appearance. Though I knew she was thirty-seven, she seemed a much older woman than when I had left her, even somewhat stooped. Her face had narrowed, and her hair had gone gray in the front, and her lips, which had thinned, had turned themselves down at the corners. She was wearing a black silk dress with a flat bodice and with high buttons to the collar, around which was a ruffle of fawn lace. She had on, I could see, her best boots, which were revealed to me as she fussed with her skirts upon emerging from the skiff.

Perhaps I should say a word here about my own appearance. I was not in the habit of wearing my best dresses on the island, as I had learned early on that the silk and the cotton were poor protection against the wind and sea air. Therefore, I had taken to wearing only the most tightly woven homespun cloth, and over that, at all times, various shawls that I had knit myself. Also I kept a woolen cap upon my head to protect myself from the fevers that so decimated the island population in the winter and even in the early spring. And, in addition, if it were very windy, I would wear a woolen muffler about my neck. I had not lost my figure altogether, but I had grown somewhat more plump in my stay on the island, which greatly pleased my husband. When I did not have to wear my woolen cap, I preferred to roll my hair on the sides and in the back, and keep some fringe in the front. The only distressing aspect of my appearance, I will say here, was that my face, as a consequence of the island sun and rain and storms, was weathering somewhat like John's, and I had lost the good complexion of my girlhood. I was twenty-five at the time.

Karen stepped from the dory and clasped her hands to her bosom. She looked wildly about her, doubtless stunned, as I had been, by the appearance of her new home. I went closer to Karen and kissed her, but she stood frozen in the sand, and her cheeks were dry and chilly. I told her that she was welcome, and she said stonily that she would never have come to such a place had she not been obliged to endure the greatest shame that ever can befall a woman. I was intensely curious as to the nature of this shame, and asked her there on the beach, but she waved me off and said that she was in need of coffee and bread, as she had been horribly sick on the boat and had not yet fully recovered.

I took her into the house, while John carried her trunk and spinning wheel and the mahogany sewing cabinet that had belonged to my mother. Karen went directly to the table and sat down and removed her bonnet and heaved a great sigh. I could see that in addition to graying, her hair was thinning at the sides and at the top, and this I attributed to the shock of having had our father die, as any death of a loved one may cause the bereaved to age suddenly.

I put on the table a bowl of coffee and a meal which I had prepared in advance. Before she ate, however, she studied the room.

"I was not given to understand from your letters, Maren, that you and John were in such unfortunate circumstances," she said with a distinct tone of disappointment.

"We have managed," I said. "John has made the walls tight and the room as warm as he can."

"But Maren!" she exclaimed. "To have no good furniture, or wallpaper, or pictures on the walls. . . ."

"It wasn't possible to bring such things on the boat," I said, "and we have had no money yet for luxuries."

She scowled. "Your curtains are hastily made," she observed. "America, I see, has not cured your bad habits. I have always said that nothing which will be done well can be done in haste. Dear Sister, they are not even lined."

I remained silent. I did not wish to quarrel with Karen so soon after her arrival.

"And you have not oiled your floorcloth. And what a curious pattern. I have never seen anything quite like it. What is this I have before me?" She had taken something up in her fork, and now put it down again and studied it.

"It is called dunfish, but it is cod," I said.

"Cod!" she exclaimed. "But it is the color of mahogany!"

"Yes," I said. "The people here have the most ingenious way of preserving and drying fish for shipping elsewhere. It is called dunning and keeps —"

"I cannot eat this," she said, pushing away the plate. "My appetite is still not keen. Do you have any honey for the bread? I might be able to get the bread down if you have honey."

"I do not," I said.

"But I see that you have grown fat nevertheless," she said, examining me intently.

I was silent and uncomfortable with such a compliment. Karen sighed again and took a sip from her bowl of coffee. Immediately she screwed up her mouth in pain, and put her hand to the side of her face.

"What is it?" I asked.

"The toothache," she said. "I have been plagued with holes in my teeth for these several years now, and have had no good dentistry for them."

"We must take you into Portsmouth," I said.

"And will you have the money for the dentist," she asked sharply, "if you have no money for wallpaper? When I was at home, I had money from Evan, though there were no decent dentists to be found near Laurvig, I am sorry to say."

Across the table from her, I picked up my own bowl and took a sip of the coffee. "And how is our brother?" I asked.

Karen lifted up her head and fastened her eyes upon mine, and as she did so I began to color and to curse myself for this weakness in my constitution. "He did not write to you?" Karen asked sweetly.

"We have had the one letter," I said. My forehead was now hot and wet. I stood and went to the stove.

"One letter? In all this time? I am quite surprised. I have always thought our brother bore you a special affection. But I suppose our Evan was never one for dwelling much in the past. . . ."

"I expect that Evan has been too busy to write," I said quickly, wishing now to put an end to the subject.

"But not too busy to be a comfort to me, you will be glad to hear," said Karen.

"A comfort?" I asked.

"Oh, most decidedly so." She opened her mouth and rubbed a back tooth. As she did, I could see that many of her teeth were blackened and rotted, and (I hope I will not offend the sensibilities of the reader by revealing this) I could as well detect a terrible smell emanating from that orifice. "Full of the most stimulating conversation in the evenings," she went on. "Do you know that we went together to Kristiania by train over the Easter holiday last year? It was tremendously exciting, Maren. Evan took me to the theater and to supper and we stayed at a hotel. And he spent one afternoon at the University, and spoke to some of the professors there quite seriously of admitting himself to a course of study."

"Evan did?"

"Oh, yes. He has prospered wonderfully and has been able to put some money by. And I do think that now I am gone, he will go to Kristiania, at least for a term, to see how he fares. And doubtless he will meet there some young woman who will turn his head. It's time he settled down, our Evan. Don't you think so, Maren?"

I tried to calm my hands by stirring the soup that was on the stove. "You don't think that Evan will come to America too?" I asked as casually as I could.

"America!" Karen exclaimed. "Whyever for? A man who prospers so well in his own country and has no need to escape will never think of emigrating to another country. No, Maren, I should think not. It was of course difficult for me to have to leave him. . . ."

"Why exactly did you leave?" I asked, turning to her sharply. I was feeling quite cross with Karen at this point.

"We may talk about that at some other time."

Karen turned her head away, and appeared once again to be examining the cottage. "You cannot keep your windows clean?"

"The sea spray," I said. "It is continual."

"At home, I like to use the vinegar."

"I would like to know what has brought you here," I said, interrupting her. "Of course, you are entirely welcome, whatever the reasons, but I do think John and I have a right to know. I hope it is not some dread illness."

"No, nothing like that."

Karen stood up and walked to the window. She folded her arms across her breast and appeared to contemplate the northwest view for some time. Then, with a sigh of, I believe, resignation, she began to tell her story. There had been a man in Laurvig by the name of Knut Eng, she said, who was a widower of fifty-four years, who had courted Karen for seven months with the implicit promise of an engagement not long in the future as they were neither of them young, and then suddenly, after a particularly silly quarrel between them, had broken off their relations, and there was no longer any talk of marriage. So abrupt and shaming was this cessation of his affections, and so widespread the gossip surrounding the affair, that Karen found she could no longer walk with any confidence into town or attend services at our church. Thus the thought of voyaging to America to join John and myself suddenly became appealing to her.

I felt sorry for her loss, though I could not help but think that Karen had most likely done her part to alienate her suitor. Nor was it altogether flattering to know that my sister had come to us only because she was embarrassed to have been spurned. But as it was our custom to welcome all visitors, and particularly those who were family, I tried to make her comfortable and showed her to the upstairs bedroom so that she might have privacy. She found the room uncheerful, and had the poor manners to say so, and, in addition, appeared not to see the star quilt at all. But I forgave her, as she was still in a state of irritation and tiredness owing to her sea-journey.

"What was the nature of the quarrel?" I asked her when she was settled and sitting on the bed.

"I had observed that he was growing more and more stout as the months progressed," she said, "and one afternoon I told him so."

"Oh," I said. I confess I had then to suppress a smile, and I turned away from my sister so that she could not see this effort. "I am sorry that this has happened to you," I said. "I trust you will be able to put all your sadness behind you now that you are in a new world."

"And do you suppose," she asked, "that there is any life for Karen Christensen here on this dreadful island?"

"I am sure there must be," I said.

"Then you, Maren, are possessed of an optimism I cannot share."

And with that, she made a fluttering motion with her hand, a motion I knew well, which dismissed me from her bedroom.

For a time, Karen was my companion during the days when John was at sea, though I cannot say that this was an easy or comfortable companionship, as Karen had grown sorry for herself, and as a result, had become somewhat tedious and dull. She would sit at her spinning wheel and sing the very saddest of tunes, whilst I went about my domestic chores in her presence. I did not like constantly to ask for information about Evan, as Karen had a curious way of regarding me when I did, which always made the blood come into my face, and so I would sometimes have to sit for hours in her company to catch one casual word of my brother, which she gave only sparingly. Sometimes I believe she deliberately withheld information about Evan, and at other times I could see that she was pleased to reveal a confidence I hadn't shared with my brother. These are harsh things to say about one's sibling, but I believe them to be true. When one night I could bear it no longer, and I blurted out to her that I believed in my heart that Evan would eventually join John and me in America, she laughed for a long time and said that Evan had barely mentioned my name in the three years I had been apart from him, and it was her opinion that though one remains attached to a family member forever, he had quite forgotten me.

I was so enraged by this utterance, which she knew wounded me deeply, I went to my room and did not emerge that day or the next day, and finally was persuaded to come into the kitchen by John, who declared that he would not tolerate discord in his house and that my sister and I must make peace between us. In truth, I was embarrassed and eager to put the entire incident, which had not shown me in my best light, behind me.

Karen and I did not have many quarrels like this, however, as she left Smutty Nose within the month. It shortly became apparent that my sister must have money for her teeth, and since there was not work on Smutty Nose, and since I did not really need any help in my domestic routine, nor did we have any extra funds to spare for her, John rowed her across to Appledore, where she was interviewed and hired as a servant to Eliza Laighton, and installed for the summer in a garret room in the hotel the Laighton family occupied and managed. In the winter, she was a personal servant to Eliza.

We were to see Karen at regular intervals during the next two years, primarily on Sundays, when John would take the dory to collect her on her afternoon off so that she might have a meal with us. I did not notice that domestic service improved her disposition much. Indeed, I would say that as the months passed, she seemed to sink further into melancholy, and it was a wonder to me how she was able to maintain her position there at all.

Despite Karen's departure, John and I were almost never to be alone again on the island, as Matthew, John's brother, came to us soon after Karen had gone into service. Matthew was quiet and undemanding and used the northeast apartment for his sleeping quarters. He was a great help to John on the boat. And on 12 April 1872, John brought home a man to board with us, as my husband needed extra monies in order to save up for a new fishing boat. This man was called Louis Wagner.

I think now, in retrospect, I was struck most by Louis Wagner's eyes, which were a metallic blue, and were as well quite canny, and it was difficult to ignore them or to turn one's head away from them, or, indeed, even to feel comfortable in their gaze. Wagner, who was an immigrant from Prussia and had about him an arrogance that I have always associated with Prussians, was large and strongly built. He had coarse hair of a sort that lightens in the elements, so that it was sometimes difficult to say whether he was fair-haired or brown-haired, but his beard was most striking, a vivid copper color under any circumstances, and shiny copper in the sun. Louis's skin was extraordinarily white, which I found surprising in a man of the sea, and his English was poor. But I will confess that he had the most contagious of smiles and quite excellent teeth, and that when he was in good humor and sat at table and told his stories, he had a kind of charm that was sometimes a relief from the silence of Matthew and John.

Louis was lodged in the northeast apartment with Matthew. In the beginning, when Louis was a mate on John's boat, I hardly saw our new boarder, as Louis ate his meals quickly and then repaired almost immediately to his bed, owing to the fatigue the long hours caused in him.

But shortly after he had arrived, Mr. Wagner got the rheumatism, which he said had plagued him chronically nearly all his adult life, and he was rendered so crippled by this ailment that he was forced to stay behind and take to his bed, and in this way I got to know Louis rather better than I might have.

I had not really ever had the experience of nursing another to health, and at first I found the duties awkward and uncomfortable. As Louis could not in the beginning rise from his bed without considerable pain, I was compelled to bring him in his meals, collect his tray when he was done, and clean his room.

One morning, after Louis had been confined to his bed for several weeks, I was surprised in my lounge by a knocking at the outer door. When I opened it, Louis was standing on the stoop in a state of some disarray, his shirt-tails outside of his trousers and his collar missing, but still it was the first time he had been upright in many days, and I was glad to see this. I begged him to come in and sit down at the table, while I prepared some hot coffee for him.

He made his way limpingly to the chair and sat upon it with a great sigh. When he had been well, I had observed him hoisting the dory from the water as if it were a child's plaything; now he seemed barely capable of lifting his arm from the table. He had lost considerable weight, and his hair was disheveled and in need of a wash. Despite his appearance, however, he seemed that day pleased with himself, and he smiled when I brought to him the bowl of coffee.

"I am in debt to you for your kindness," he said after he had taken a swallow.

"It's nothing," I said to him in English, as I always did, since neither of us could speak the other's language. "We hope only to make you well again."

"And that I will be, if I remain in your hands."

"We are all concerned for your health," I said. "My husband and his brother."

"But you are the nurse. I am a great burden to you."

"Oh, no," I said, hastening to assure him that he was welcome. But he shook his head.

"In this country, I have been nothing but a burden. I've had no luck and have not made my mark. I owe money to everyone, and I see no real prospects of a job."

"You have work with my husband," I pointed out.

"But I'm not working now, am I? I'm sick. I can't even pay my rent to you."

"Don't be thinking of that now. You should be thinking of getting well," I said.

"Yes?" he asked, suddenly brightening. "Do you think you will make me well, Mrs. Hontvedt?"

"I will try . . . ," I said, somewhat embarrassed. "But you are hungry. Let me feed you now."

"Yes, Mrs. Hontvedt. Please feed me."

I turned to him as he said this, and he was smiling, and I thought for a moment he might be mocking me, but then I dismissed the notion. I had been waiting for the soup to come to the boil when he had knocked, and now I stirred it and poured some into a bowl. I had in addition the flat-brød that I had baked earlier in the day. The soup was a fish chowder and had, if I may say so, a wonderful aroma, so much so, in fact, that I was compelled to pour myself a bowl.

Louis sipped from his bowl with an inelegant sucking

sound, and I thought that he had probably not ever been much on manners. I observed, as he drank, that his copper beard badly needed trimming, and that while I had been fairly diligent with his laundry, his lying in bed so many hours of the day had stained his shirt around the neck and under the arms. I was thinking that perhaps, if I could find some proper cloth, I would make him a new shirt while he was recovering.

"You are a good cook," he said, looking up from the soup.

"Thank you," I said, "but fish soup is easy, is it not?"

"I can't cook myself," he said. He put his spoon down. "You are lonely here?"

To my surprise, I blushed. I was so rarely ever asked questions of a personal nature.

"No," I said. "I have my dog, Ringe."

"Your dog," he said, observing me. "Is he enough?"

"Well, I have my husband . . ."

"But he is gone all the day."

"And I have work. There is always a great deal to do here. You have seen this."

"Too much work makes for a dull life," he said, and again smiled to reveal his teeth. He brushed his hair, which had grown long and somewhat greasy and over-hung his forehead, with his fingers. "Do you have a pipe?" he asked.

I was, for the moment, confused by this request. I didn't know whether John would like me to share his to-bacco with this boarder, but I didn't quite know how to refuse Louis Wagner.

"My husband sometimes smokes in the evenings," I said.

Louis tilted his head at me. "But he is not here during the day, is he?"

"There are pipes," I said uncertainly.

Louis simply smiled at me and waited.

After a time, uncomfortable under his scrutiny, I went to the box where John kept the pipes, handed one to Louis, and watched as he filled it with tobacco. Outside it was a fair day, with a calm sea. The sun highlighted the salt on the windows so that it looked like ice crystals.

I had never smoked a pipe without my husband, and never at such an early hour in the morning, but I confess that as I sat there observing Louis, my own yearning for a smoke grew, so that after a time, I got out my own pipe and, as Louis had just done, filled it with tobacco. I suppose I had been quite nervous altogether, for the first long draw on my pipe tasted wonderfully marvelous and calmed my hands.

Louis seemed amused that I was smoking with him. "In Prussia," he said, "women do not smoke."

"I am a married woman," I said. "My husband has taught me to smoke."

"And what other things has your husband taught you?" Louis asked quickly with a smile.

I hasten to say that I did not like this rejoinder and so did not answer him, but Louis seemed determined to tease me out of my somber demeanor, and so said to me, "You look too young to be a married woman."

"Then you have seen not too many married women," I said.

"I don't have enough money for a proper woman."

I colored at my understanding of the possible meaning of this utterance and turned my head away.

"John Hontvedt is very lucky to have such a beautiful wife," he said, persisting in this inappropriate speech.

"You are being silly," I said, "and I will not listen to such talk."

"But it's true," he said. "I've been looking at the women in this country for eleven years, and none are so beautiful as you."

I am ashamed to admit, so many years later, that at that moment I was at least partially flattered by this talk. I knew that Louis Wagner was flirting with me, and that it was improper for him to do so, but though I could scold him, I could not quite bring myself to banish him from my apartment. After all, I told myself, he meant no harm. And to be truthful, I had never in my life had a man call me beautiful. I don't believe that my husband ever said such a thing. I don't think, in fact, that he ever even called me pretty. I was not thinking at the time that any of these attentions were in any way dangerous.

"I have made some konfektkake," I said, wishing to change the subject. "Can I give you a piece?"

"What is the konfektkake?" he asked.

"It's a Norwegian sweet," I said. "I think you will like it."

I put before our boarder a plate of chocolate cake. Louis damped his pipe and laid it on the table. After he had taken his first bite of cake, I could see immediately that he had a great liking for it, and he ate steadily until nearly all of it was gone. I was thinking that I had ought to eat the remaining two pieces, as I would not be able to explain to my husband that evening what had happened to the rest, and so I did. Louis wiped the icing from his mouth with the sleeve of his shirt.

"I think that you are seducing me with all this smoke and konfektkake," he said, grinning and pronouncing the Norwegian badly.

I was shocked by his words. I stood up. "You must go now," I said quickly.

"Oh, but Mrs. Hontvedt, do not send me away. We are having such a nice time. And I am only teasing you. I can see you have not been teased much lately. Am I correct?"

"Please go now," I repeated.

He got up slowly from his chair, but in doing so, arranged himself so that he was standing even closer to me than he had been before. I did not like actually to back away from him, and besides, I would have had to press against the stove, which I could not do for fear of burning myself, and so it was that he reached out and put his fingers to my cheek, very gently, and to my everlasting shame, unbidden tears sprang quite suddenly to my eyes, tears so numerous that I was unable to hide them.

"Mrs. Hontvedt," he said in an astonished voice.

I reached up and tore his hand away from my cheek. There was no reply I could have made to him that even I myself could have understood, and as I did not think that he would leave the room, I grabbed my cloak from the hook and ran from the cottage altogether.

Once begun, the tears would not stop, and so I walked nearly blindly to the end of the island and put my hands into fists and shook them angrily at the sea.

I did not tell my husband of Louis Wagner's visit to me, as, in truth, there was not much to tell, but John shortly could see for himself that his boarder was improving in strength. I never did, after that first morning, invite Wagner into my apartment when I was alone, but I saw him often enough, as I continued to nurse him, and then later, morning and evening, when he took his meals with us. Indeed, after he was fully recovered, Wagner took to sitting by the stove in the evenings, so that there would be Wagner and myself and John and Matthew, and sometimes the men would talk, but most often, they would smoke in silence. I am happy to report that I never again lost my composure with Louis Wagner, although I must say he continued to place me under his scrutiny, and if he no longer dared to tease me with words, I did think, from time to time, that he mocked me with his eyes.

There was only one other occasion when I was seriously to wonder at Louis Wagner's intentions and, indeed, his sanity. On a late summer afternoon, while Louis was still recuperating, I heard through the wall that separated our apartment from his room the most dreadful banging about and muttering, and I suddenly became extremely frightened.

"Louis?" I called, and then again, "Louis?"

But I had no reply, and still the commotion in the next room continued. Quite concerned, I ran outside the house and looked in at the window of our boarder's room, which, I am sorry to say, I had not yet adorned with curtains. There I saw a most astounding sight. Louis Wagner, in a fit of uncommon distress, was thrashing and flailing about, upturning objects on the shelf, creating a chaos with the bedclothes, and all the time expressing a terrible rage on his face and in a series of unintelligible sounds. I was too terrified to call to him lest he turn his fury on me, but I was also apprehensive for his own well-being. And then, seemingly as suddenly as he had begun, Louis Wagner stopped his wild behavior and flopped himself back upon his bed and began that sort of hysterical laughing that is accompanied by tears, and after a time, he threw his arm across his eyes, and I think he fell asleep. Reassured that his fit, whatever its origin, had ended, I went back to my kitchen and pondered this unusual and unnatural outburst.

Gradually, as I have said, Louis Wagner recovered his health and was able to return to work for John. Several times, after Louis was up and about, John went, as accustomed, to fetch Karen from Appledore, and on these occasions, which were always on Sunday afternoons, Louis would be dressed in his best shirt, and I must say, that when his hair was washed and combed, he made a rather fine appearance. Karen, perhaps thinking that Wagner might be a possible suitor, was considerably warmer with him than she was with me, and I observed that her melancholy seemed to leave her altogether. She made some effort to fix her face, but this effort was largely unsuccessful in the way that trying to reshape a molded bit of rubber will be a futile enterprise, as the elasticity of the rubber itself will cause the object immediately to resume its original shape. One time Karen actually said to me that she thought Louis Wagner a handsome man and that he seemed to be favoring her with some attention, but as I had actually been there on every occasion they had been together, and had observed Wagner's demeanor toward my sister, which was cordial, but not overly so, I privately thought that Karen must be in the thrall of those peculiar fantasies that visit spinsters in their desperation.

On one such Sunday afternoon as I am describing, Karen came into our house with John. It was, I believe, early in September, and the weather was mild, but quite dreary, as the sun hadn't broken through the cloud in several days. Everything on the island that day was covered with a fine mist, and I fancied I could see the dew on John's hair as well when he brought my sister to us.

But my attention was most drawn to the expression on Karen's face, which seemed a mixture of secret confidence and of pleasure, and was so fixed upon me that I could not turn away from her. She came directly toward me and smiled, and I was quite at a loss as to what she meant to convey to me, and when I asked her outright what seemed to be pleasing her so, she said only that I must be patient, and that perhaps I would find out in good time. Her withholding of her secret made me, I confess, cross with her, and I vowed to put my sister and her machinations out of my mind, but so determined was Karen to whet my curiosity that it was nearly impossible to turn away from her or to avoid her glance. She then proceeded to preside, in her rather silly fashion, over the entire Sunday dinner, speaking of the personages who had been to visit Celia Thaxter, who was Eliza Laighton's mother and a poetess of some repute, of the work on the Jacob Poor Hotel, and of a small altercation she herself had had with her employer, and, in short, speaking of nearly everything but the one thing she wished me to know.

As I am not possessed of extraordinary reserves of patience, and as she meant to keep me guessing an entire week more by not revealing anything else that afternoon, I found that I could not hold my tongue when she was preparing to leave and was putting on her cloak.

"Tell me what your secret is, Karen, or I shall die of curiosity," I said, knowing that this was precisely the begging sentence my sister had wanted to hear from me.

"Oh, it is nothing, Maren," she said airily. "Simply that I have had a letter from Evan."

"Evan," I said, catching my breath. "And did you bring this letter with you?"

"I am so sorry, Maren, but I have forgotten it, and have left it back in my room."

"Then tell me what Evan has written to you."

She looked at me and smiled in a condescending manner. "Only that he is coming in October."

"Evan?"

"He is sailing in two weeks and will be here toward the middle of the month. He says he wishes to stay with you and John, here on Smutty Nose, for a time until he can settle himself."

Evan! Coming to America! I confess I must have betrayed my excitement by clutching John by the arm. "Do you hear Karen?" I asked. "Evan will be coming. And in only a month's time." I bent and picked up my dog, Ringe, who, having sensed a mood of enthusiasm in the room, was leaping about wildly.

I may truly say here that the next weeks were the most pleasant I ever had on Smutty Nose. Even Karen I was able to tolerate with some equanimity, though, irritatingly, she forgot each week to bring Evan's letter to me. I doubt I have ever been as industrious as I was in those early autumn days, scrubbing the upstairs bedroom clean, making curtains and a floorcloth, and as the time grew closer for Evan's arrival, baking many of the delicacies I knew he loved in Norway and probably thought never to have again: the rommegot, the krumcake, and the skillingsbolle. John, I believe, was quite happy to see me so content and purposeful, and I think he did not mind at all that soon we would have another mouth to feed. If the thought of my brother's arrival could cause such happiness in his wife, a happiness that was infectious and conveyed itself to all, so that there was on Smutty Nose an atmosphere of the greatest gaiety and anticipation, then my husband would accept its cause gladly. Even the weather seemed to cooperate, bestowing upon us a succession of clear days with a lively but manageable sea, so that just to walk outside that cottage and breathe in the air seemed nearly intoxicating.

Because I had taken on so many projects and had so little time in which to accomplish them, I was quite beside myself on the last day of all, and most eager to finish the floorcloth for the room that we had made up for him, so that while I might have been watching all day from the window for the first sight of Evan in the schooner and then on the dory, I was instead on my knees. Thus it was that I did not even know of my brother's arrival on Smutty Nose until I heard my husband halloo from the beach.

Actually, it was quite an evil day, with a gale from the northeast sweeping across the island so that one had to bend nearly double to make any progress. Nevertheless, I ran from the cottage down to the beach. I saw a knot of people, and in this knot, a glint of silvery-blond hair.

"Evan!" I cried, running to greet him. I went directly to my brother, seeing his face clearly in what was otherwise a blur of persons and of landscape, and with my arms caught him round the neck. I bent his head down toward me and pressed his face to my own. Evan raised an arm and shouted loudly, "Halloo to America!" and everyone

about us laughed. I saw that John was standing just behind Evan, and that John was smiling broadly, as I believe
he truly loved me and was glad of my good fortune.

And so it was that in the midst of these giddy saluta-
tions, my arms still clutched to my brother, I slowly
turned my head and my eyes rested upon an unfamiliar
face. It was the face of a woman, quite a beautiful woman,
clear of complexion and green-eyed. Her hair was thick
and not the silvery blond of my brother, but a color that
seemed warmed by the sun, and I remember thinking how
odd it was that she had not worn it pinned up upon her
head, particularly as it was blowing in a wild manner all
about her person, so that she, from time to time, had to
clutch at it in order to see anything at all. Her face was
lovely, and her skin shone, even in the dull light of the
cloud. Gradually my brother loosened himself from my
embrace and introduced me.

"This is Anethe," he said. "This is my wife, Anethe."

I SIT IN THE FOUNDATION of the house an unreasonably long time, using up the precious minutes I have left in which to finish the assignment. When I stand up, my legs are stiff, and I am still shivering badly. I cannot take off my wet sweatshirt, since I have no other clothes with me, and I don't think there are any in the Zodiac. I gather my cameras together and begin to shoot, in the flat light, the detail shots I have described to Rich. I move methodically about the island, hunching into the wind when I am not actually shooting. I take pictures of the graves of the Spanish sailors, the ground on which the Mid-Ocean Hotel once stood, the door of the Haley house. I use six rolls of Velvia 220. I shoot with a tripod and a macro lens. I don't know exactly how much time elapses, but I am anticipating Rich's impatience when I round the island and return to the beach. So I am surprised when he isn't there.

I sit down on the sand and try to shield my legs with my arms. When that proves unsatisfactory, I roll over onto my stomach. The sand, I discover, has held the sun's warmth, and it feels good against my bare legs, even through the cotton of my shorts and sweatshirt. I take off my glasses and set them aside. Like a small sea creature, I try to burrow deeper into the sand, shielding my face with the sides of my hands. I find that by doing this, and by breathing evenly, I can almost control the shivering.

I do not hear Rich as he approaches. The first indication I have that he is near me is a thin trickle of sand, as from a sand timer, from my ankle to my knee and along the back of my thigh. First one leg, and then another.

When I do not turn over or respond, I feel the slight pressure of fingers on my back. He kneels in the sand beside me.

"Are you all right?"

"No."

"You're soaked."

I don't answer.

"What's wrong?" he asks.

I have sand on my forehead. I turn my head slightly, away from him. I can see the oily wet on the small dark rocks of the beach, a crab at eye level scurrying along the crusty surface and then disappearing into a hole. There is a constant susurrus of the wind, fainter on the ground, but ceaseless still. I think that if I had to live on the island, I would go mad from the wind.

Rich begins to rub my back to warm me, to stop the shivering. "Let me get you into the dinghy. And onto the boat. You need a hot shower."

"I can't move."

"I'll help."

"I don't want to move."

I am thinking that this is true. I do not ever want to move again. I do not want to go back to the boat, to look at the faces of Thomas and Adaline, to wonder what they have been doing, or not doing, what has been said between them. What lines of poetry might have been quoted. Or not quoted. I know that Billie is on the boat, and that because of her I will have to go back, will shortly want to go back. I will have to participate in the sail to Portsmouth or to Annisquam or find a way to survive another night in the harbor. I understand that I will have to be a participant on this cruise — a cruise for which I am responsible. I know that I will have to repack the cameras, finish the log, go home and develop the film, and hope that I have something to send into the magazine. I know that I will have to return to our house in Cambridge, that Thomas and I will go on in our marriage, as we have, in our way, and that I will continue to love him.

At this moment, it doesn't seem possible that I am capable of any of it.

I want only to dig into the sand, to feel the sand around me for warmth, to be left alone.

"You're crying," Rich says.

"No, I'm not."

I sit up and wipe my nose on the sleeve of my sweatshirt. The entire front of my body is coated with a thin layer of sand. There is sand in my hair, on my upper lip. I wrap my arms around my legs as tightly as I can. Without my glasses I cannot see the sloop or anyone on it. Even the Zodiac, only twenty feet away, is an orange blur. A shape I take to be a gull swoops down upon the beach and lurches along the pebbles. There is comfort in not being able to see the shapes of things, the details.

I bury my face in my knees. I lick my upper lip with my tongue and bring the sand into my mouth. Rich puts his hand at the back of my neck, the way you do with a child when the child is being sick to her stomach. His hand is warm.

It seems to me that we remain in that position, neither of us speaking or moving, for an unreasonably long time.

Finally I sit back and look at my brother-in-law. I can see him clearly, but not much beyond. He seems puzzled, as though he is not entirely sure what is going to happen next.

"Do you remember the wedding?" I ask.

He removes his hand from my neck with what I sense as a complicated mixture of regret and relief. "Of course I remember the wedding."

"You were only twenty-two."

"You were only twenty-four."

"You wouldn't wear a suit, and you had a ponytail. You wouldn't kiss me after the wedding, and I thought it was because you were cross that you'd been asked to wear a suit."

"You had on a black dress. I remember thinking it was a great thing to wear to your own wedding. You had no jewelry. He didn't give you a ring."

"He didn't believe in that sort of thing," I say.

"Still."

"You and I went swimming that morning."

"With Dad. Thomas stayed home and worked. On his wedding day."

"It's his way. . . ."

"I know, I know."

"I thought at the time that Thomas was making an extraordinary commitment in marrying me. That it was almost brutally hard for him to do."

"My parents were thrilled."

"Thrilled?"

"That he'd got you. You were so solid."

"Thank you."

"No, I mean you were rooted, grounded. They were tremendously relieved he had found you."

"I wasn't going to cause him any trouble."

"You weren't going to let him cause trouble to himself."

"No one can prevent that."

"You've tried."

"Thomas isn't doing well," I say.

"You're not doing well."

"We're not doing well."

I shake my head and stretch my legs out in front of me. "Rich, I swear I think marriage is the most mysterious covenant in the universe. I'm convinced that no two are alike. More than that, I'm convinced that no marriage is like it was just the day before. Time is the significant dimension — even more significant than love. You can't ask a person what his marriage is like because it will be a different marriage tomorrow. We go in waves."

"You and Thomas."

"We have periods when I think our coming together was a kind of accident, that we're wedded because of a string of facts. And then, maybe the next day, or even that night, Thomas and I will be so close I won't be able to remember the words to a fight we had two hours earlier. The fact of the fight, the concept of an accident, will be gone — it won't even seem plausible. You called him Tom."

"Earlier. I did. I don't know why."

I look up toward the sloop I cannot see. My horizon of beach and rocks and water is a dull watercolor blur.

"What do you think is going on out there?" I ask.

Rich turns away from me. "Jean, don't do this to yourself."

"Is it that obvious?"

"It's painful to watch."

I stand up abruptly and walk away from the water. I walk fast, meaning to shake Rich, to shake them all. I want refuge — from the cold, from the island, most of all from the sight of the sloop in the harbor. I walk toward the Hontvedt house. From where I have so recently come.

But Rich is right behind me. He follows me over the rocks, through the thick brush. When I stop, he stands beside me.

"This is where the women were murdered," I say quickly.

"Jean."

"It's so small. They lived here in the winter. I don't know how they did it. I look at this island, and I try to imagine it. The confinement, the claustrophobia. I keep trying to imagine the murders."

"Listen —"

"There aren't even any trees here. Did you know that until recently children who were raised on the island never saw a tree or a car until they were teenagers?"

"Jean, stop."

"I love Thomas."

"I know you do."

"But it's been hard."

"He makes you worry."

I look at Rich, surprised at this insight. "Yes, he does. He makes me worry. Why did you shave your hair?"

He smiles and rubs his head.

"Do you love Adaline?" I ask.

Rich looks out toward the boat. I think that he, too, is wondering.

"It's a sexual thing?" I ask.

He tilts his head, considering. "She's very attractive," he says. "But it's a bit more than that. She's . . . intriguing."

"And we're not intriguing," I say. "We're just good."

"We're not that good," he says, and he smiles. He has perfect teeth.

I put my hand on his arm.

He is stunned. I can feel that, the small jolt through the body. But he does not pull away.

"Jean," he says.

I lean forward and put my mouth on the skin of his arm. Did I misread the trickle of sand on the backs of my legs?

When I look up, I can see that Rich is bewildered. I realize this is the first time I have ever seen him lose his composure.

"Why?" he asks.

I study him. I shake my head. *Deliberately,* I could say. Or, *To do it before Thomas does it to me.* Or, *Before I have absolute proof he has done it to me.* Or, simply, *Because I want this, and it's wrong.*

Without touching me with his hands, he bends to kiss me. The kiss is frightening — both foreign and familiar.

I lift my sweatshirt up over my head. Oddly, I am no longer cold, and I have long since stopped shivering.

I can hear his breathing, controlled breathing, as if he had been running.

I feel the top of his head, that smooth map.

He kisses my neck. Around us, gulls and crabs swoop and scurry in confusion, alarmed by this disturbance in the natural order of the universe. I taste his shoulder. I put my teeth there lightly.

He holds me at my waist, and I can feel his hands trembling.

"I can't do this," he says into the side of my head. "I want to." He traces a circle on my back. "I want to," he repeats, "but I can't."

And as suddenly as it opened, a door shuts. For good. I lean my head against his chest and sigh.

"I don't know what came over me," I say.

He holds me tightly. "Shhhh," he says.

We stand in that posture, the clouds moving fast overhead. There is, I think, an intimacy between us, an intimacy I will not know again. A perfect, terrible intimacy — without guilt, without worry, without a future.

Calvin L. Hayes, a member of the coroner's jury who participated in the inquest held over the bodies of Anethe Christensen and Karen Christensen, took the stand for the prosecution and explained in some detail what he had observed: "We arrived on the island between eight and half-past eight P.M. We landed and proceeded to the house formerly occupied by John C. Hontvet. Upon entering the house there is first a small entry from which opens a kitchen. When we entered the kitchen we found the furniture strewn all over the floor, the clock lying on the lounge face down; clock was not going. I did not look at the face

of the clock; it fell evidently from a small bracket just
over the lounge in the corner. The body of Anethe Christensen lay in the middle of the kitchen floor, the head
towards the door through which we entered. Around the
throat was tied a scarf or shawl, some colored woolen garment, and over the body some article of clothing was
thrown loosely. The head was, as you might say, all battered to pieces, covered with wounds, and in the vicinity
of the right ear two or three cuts broke through the skull
so that the brains could be seen running through them.
There was a bed-room opening from the kitchen; in that
was a bed and trunk, the trunk opened, the contents scat-
tered over the floor. The body of Anethe was placed upon
a board upon a table, and an examination made by the
physicians who were present. We then proceeded to the
other part of the house. The arrangement of the other end
of the house was similar to the end into which we first
went. We went into an entry, from there into a room that
corresponded to the kitchen, out of which another bed-
room opened. In that bed-room, face down, we found the
body of Karen Christensen. The windowsill of the first
bed-room I spoke of was broken off, window in the south-
west end of house. The body of Karen Christensen had a
white handkerchief knotted tightly around the neck, tied
at the back of the neck, so tightly that the tongue was pro-
truding from the mouth. Upon the inside of the sill of the
window on the south-west end of the house, was a mark
as though made with the pole of an axe, and on the outside
of the window-sill, the part that was broken off, there was
another mark as though made with some round instrument, as the handle of an axe. The head of Karen Chris-

tensen was covered with wounds, but not so bad as the first one. Only one I think broke the skull. I found an axe there."

Hayes produced the murder weapon.

He continued: "I took the axe from the island. It has been in my custody since. I found the axe lying by the side of the first door we entered; it does not now resemble its condition then at all; it was besmeared with blood and covered with matter entirely. In coming from the island the sea was very rough, and the spray washed nearly all the blood off."

After Calvin Hayes testified, Dr. John W. Parsons, the physician who performed the autopsy of Anethe, took the stand.

"The examination was made on March 8," he began, "in the city of Portsmouth, at the rooms of the undertakers, Gerrish & Adams. I found upon examination one flesh wound upon the right side of the forehead upon the upper part. The left ear was cut through nearly separating it from the head, and this wound extending down behind the ear an inch or two; flesh wound merely. There was a flesh wound on the left side of the head just above and in front of the ear, under which there was a compound fracture of the skull. There was a flesh wound in front of the right ear, and another almost separating the right ear from the head, and extending down behind it. There were two flesh wounds upon the upper part of the right side of the head, above the ear. There was a small flesh wound upon the left side of the head above the large wound spoken of. There were a few other minor scratches, and wounds about the scalp, but that is all worthy of notice."

Dr. Parsons then stated that, in his opinion, a very

heavy instrument had to have made the blows, and that, yes, it could have been an ax.

Rich makes me put my sweatshirt on and leads me back down to the beach. I notice that he is careful to let go of my hand at the exact point the sloop comes into view. We search in the sand for my glasses, and I clean them off. I retrieve my camera bag and lift it onto my shoulder. The sky has darkened and casts a dispiriting light.

"I've never been unfaithful," I say.

Rich scrutinizes my face. "I'd be very surprised to hear you had been."

"Thank you for —"

"Don't," he says sharply. "I'm not sure you understand. Back there I wanted to. Believe me, I wanted to. I've been angry with Thomas for a long time. Angry at his carelessness. Angry at the way he takes you for granted. But it's more than that. I've" — he searches for the word — "admired you since the day I first met you."

"Admired?" I ask, smiling.

"I don't dare use any other words," he says. "Not now."

"It's all right," I say with a small laugh. "Feel free. I can take it."

Rich crosses his arms over his chest and gazes out over the expanse of Smuttynose. I think I see, in Rich's profile, something of Thomas. The long space between the upper lip and the nose. The slant of the brow.

"Rich," I say, touching his arm lightly. "I'm only kidding."

His face, when he turns back to me, seems momentarily defeated. Sad.

"I think you're beautiful," he says.

Fat drops of rain begin to fall around us, making saucer

shapes in the sand. Rich looks down at his feet, then wipes the top of his head.

"The rain is coming," he says. "We'd better go."

Early in the trial, Maren Hontvedt, the only eyewitness to the murders, took the stand. She gave her name as Mary S. Hontvet, using the name and spelling she had adopted in America. She said that she was the wife of John C. Hontvet and was the sister of Karen Christensen. Evan Christensen, she stated, was her brother.

Yeaton began to question her.

"How long before this matter at Smutty Nose did you live there?" Yeaton asked.

"Five years," Maren answered. "I was at home day before the murder."

"Was your husband there that day?"

"He left in the morning, about day-light with my brother, and his brother. Evan is husband of Anethe."

"After he had left that morning, when did you next see your husband?"

"I saw him the next morning after, cannot tell, but about ten o'clock."

"At nine o'clock that night, who were present at your house before you went to bed?"

"I, Karen, and Anethe. There were no other persons upon that island at that time."

"What time did you go to bed that night?"

"Ten o'clock. I slept in the western part of the house in the bed-room. I and Anethe slept together that night."

"About ten o'clock you went to bed."

"About ten. Karen stayed there that night; she slept on a lounge in the kitchen. The lounge upon which Karen slept was in the easterly corner of the kitchen, corner standing up that way, and my bed-room that way." Maren pointed with her hands for the benefit of the court.

Yeaton then asked her how the door between the kitchen and the bedroom had been left that night.

"Left open," Maren said.

"How were the curtains?"

"I did not haul them down, it was a pleasant night, so I left them open."

"I speak now of the curtains to the kitchen."

"Yes."

"How was the outside door to that part of the house, fastened or not?"

"No, sir, it was not fastened. The lock was broke for some time, broke last summer and we did not fix it, it was unfastened. Karen was undressed, bed made; we made a bed up."

"Was there a clock in that room?"

"Yes, clock standing right over the lounge in the corner."

"If you were disturbed that night or awoke, state the first thing that awoke you, so far as you know, what took place."

There was an objection here by Tapley for the defense, and some talk among the lawyers and the court. Finally, Maren was allowed to answer.

"'John scared me, John scared me,' she says."

"Are you able to determine in any way about what time during the night that was?"

"We woke up. I know about his going and striking her with a chair."

"About what time was it?"

"The clock has fallen down in the lounge, and stopped at seven minutes past one."

"After you heard Karen cry out, John scared me, what next took place?"

"John killed me, John killed me, she halooed out a good many times. When he commenced striking her with a chair she halooed out, John killed me, John killed me."

"What did you do?"

"As soon as I heard her haloo out, John killed me, I jumped up out of bed, and tried to open my bed-room door. I tried to get it open but could not, it was fastened."

"Go on."

"He kept on striking her there, and I tried to get the door open, but I could not, the door was fastened. She fell down on the floor underneath the table, then the door was left open for me to go in."

"What next?"

"When I got the door open I looked out and saw a fellow standing right alongside of the window. I saw it was a great tall man. He grabbed a chair with both hands, a chair standing alongside of him. I hurried up to take Karen, my sister, and held one hand on to the door, and took her with my other arm, and carried her in as quick as I could. When I was standing there, he struck me twice, and I held on to the door. I told my sister Karen to hold on to the door, when I opened the window and we were trying to get out."

"Which window was that?"

"My bed-room window, and she said no, I can't do it, I am too tired. She laid on the floor with her knees, and hanging her arms upon the bed. I told Anethe to come up and open the window, and to run out and to take some clothes on her, to run and hide herself away."

"Where was Anethe when you told her that?"

"In my bed-room."

"Well."

"She opened the window."

"Who opened the window?"

"Anethe opened the window, and left the window open and run out. I told her to run out."

"Where did she run out?"

"Out of the window, jumped out of the window."

"Go on."

"I told her to run, and she said I can't run. I said you haloo, might somebody hear from the other islands. She said, I cannot haloo. When I was standing there at the door, he was trying to get in three times, knocked at the door three times when I was standing at the door."

"What door?"

"My bed-room door. When he found he could not get in that way, he went outside, and Anethe saw him on the corner of the house. She next halooed, Louis, Louis, Louis, a good many times, and I jumped to the window and looked out, and when he got a little further I saw him out the window, and he stopped a moment out there."

"How far from the window was he when he stopped?"

"He was not far from the window; he could have laid his elbow right that way on the window." Maren then illustrated this gesture for the court.

Yeaton asked: "Who was that man?"

"Louis Wagner."

"Go on. What else took place?"

"And he turned around again, and when Anethe saw

him coming from the corner of the house, back again with a big axe, she halooed out, Louis, Louis, again, good many times she halooed out, Louis, till he struck her. He struck her with a great big axe."

"Did you see that part of her person the blow took effect?"

"He hit her on the head. He struck her once, and she fell down. After she fell down, he struck her twice."

"Well."

"And back he went on the corner again, and I jumped out, and told my sister to come, but she said, I am so tired I can't go."

"Which sister was that?"

"Karen. I told Karen to come; she said, I am so tired I can't."

"You jumped out where?"

"Out through my bed-room window, and I ran down to the hen-house where I had my hens, and opened the door and thought of hiding away in the cellar. I saw the little dog coming, and I was afraid to hide away there because he would look around, and I was afraid the dog would bark, and out I went again. I thought I would run down to the landing-place, and see if he had dory there, and I would take the dory and draw to some island. I looked down the dock, but I did not find any boat there, so I went around. I got a little ways out from the house, and I saw he had a light in the house."

"Go on, and state what you saw or heard."

"He had hauled the window curtains down too. I did not haul them down, but he had them hauled down before I got into the kitchen. I forgot to state that. I went down on the island, ran a little ways, and heard my sister haloo again. I heard her so plain I thought she was outside of the house. I ran to find rocks to hid myself away underneath the rocks on the island."

"How long did you remain there among the rocks?"

"The moon was most down, and I staid till after sunrise, about half an hour after sunrise."

"What relation are you to Anethe and Karen?"

"Anethe married my brother, and Karen was my own sister."

Beyond the harbor, the sky blackens and hangs in sheets. The sun, which is still in the southeast, lights up all the boats in the harbor and the buildings on Star with a luminescence against the backdrop that is breathtaking. We can actually see the front moving.

The rain hits Rich's face and washes over his brow, his eyes, his mouth. Drops hang on the tip of his nose and then fall in rivulets down his chin. He has to narrow his eyes into slits, and, as he holds the tiller, I wonder how he can see at all. The T-shirt he has so recently dried drags on his chest from the weight of the water.

I sit with my feet anchoring the poncho over the cameras. I have taken my glasses off, and I am trying to shield my eyes with my hands. All at once, there is a green wall beside us, the hull of the boat. Rich touches my knee. I shake my head.

A figure looms above us, and a hand reaches down.

"Give me the cameras first," Thomas shouts. "I'll take them in."

23 September 1899

W HEN I FINALLY UNDERSTOOD, on the beach, that Evan had brought a wife with him to America, I was at such a loss for words that I was unable to express anything further there on the shore, and it wasn't until some time afterwards that I had the strength to make a proper greeting to the woman, who, I must say, was possessed of such an astonishing beauty it was an effort to draw one's eyes away from her. It was a beauty the chief components of which are vibrant youth as well as lovely aesthetic form, and I could not help but observe, even in those first few moments, that my brother was most infatuated with his new bride, and that he was, except for perhaps three or four occasions in his childhood, more ebullient than I had ever seen him. He had worn that day a leather jerkin and cap, over which he had his yellow oilskin jacket, and he stood with an umbrella close to the young woman like a man servant who does not want one foul drop of rain to fall upon his mistress, with the obvious difference being that Evan was the mistress's husband and was unable to refrain from putting his hands on her in one way or another nearly all the time they remained on the beach and in my kitchen that afternoon. I had the distinct impression that Evan believed that if he did not stay near to his wife she might suddenly vanish.

Anethe was tall for a woman, perhaps only a hand's length shorter than our Evan, and after she removed her cloak in our entryway, I saw that she had an admirable figure, that is to say, she was slim-waisted but not flat-chested, and her figure was most fetchingly shown to advantage in a prettily made, high-necked, lace blouse. She had fine Nordic features (high cheekbones, clear skin, and dusty gray-green eyes with pale eyelashes), altogether an open and guileless face nearly always set in a pleasing attitude. In fact, I doubt I have ever known anyone who smiled as much as that young woman, so much so that I began to wonder if her mouth mustn't hurt from the effort, and I can hardly ever remember seeing Anethe's face in repose, except for a few occasions when she was sleeping. If her comeliness was of the sort that is lacking in enigma and mystery, qualities which I believe are necessary for true classical beauty, her mien suggested an uncommon light and, even more, a sunny disposition I have seen only in young girls. Of course, Anethe was considerably more than a girl when she came to us, being already twenty-four, but she seemed innocent, if not altogether naive. In Laurvig, she had been the youngest daughter of a shipwright and had been watched over keenly by this father, who, I was told, was loath to let her go, even at an age when young women are in serious danger of becoming spinsters if they do not marry. Also, I thought that Anethe's father must have instilled in his daughter a passionate desire to please, since her entire being, her face, her posture and her words, seemed dedicated to this effort.

My brother's wife had as well, I must add here, a remarkable head of hair, and I can attest to the fact that when she took out her combs and unbraided her plaits, this hair reached all the way to the back of her calves.

With Evan close to her side, Anethe, smiling all the while, recounted for us (with myself translating into English for our boarder, so that, in essence, for me, these tales were somewhat tediously twice-told) the particulars of their marriage vows, of their wedding trip to Kristiania, and of the crossing itself, which the newlyweds seemed to have weathered in fine fashion. In fact, so great was their enthusiasm for this adventure to America, though I trust they would have retained a desire for any sojourn so long as it allowed them to be together, that they often interrupted each other or spoke simultaneously or finished the other's sentences, a practice that began to wear upon me as the afternoon progressed, in the same way that one might come to be irritated by the overworked and frequent repetition of a once-charming trait in a young child. Also, I think it is not necessary to say that I was extremely vexed at my sister, Karen, who was not present that afternoon, but who had deliberately withheld important information from me, for what reasons I cannot think, except to cause me the most acute humiliation. At times, sitting there in my lounge, next to the stove, serving Evan and Anethe and Louis Wagner and John and Matthew the sweets I had made expressly for this occasion, thinking to please with delicacies from our Norway my brother, who, I am sorry to report, ate almost nothing that day, and observing Louis Wagner, who was, from a distance I suspect

he would have breached in an instant if he thought he had
so much as a chance, practically as entranced by Anethe's
melodious voice and lustrous skin as was her husband, I
was nearly overtaken by a rage so powerful at my sister I
felt myself quiver in my very soul and had immediately to
ask the Lord for forgiveness for the terrible thoughts
against her person I was entertaining. I knew that shortly
she would come to my house, as she did on most Sundays
and certainly would this coming Sunday since it would be
her first visit in America with Evan and his new wife, and
I thought that I would speak to her most severely about
the malign game she had played with me, and of its consequences. If I had been able to, without revealing my in-
nermost feelings and casting some shame upon myself, I
would have banished Karen altogether from Smutty
Nose, or at least until such a time as she might confess her
wicked machinations. Altogether, it was an afternoon of
mixed emotions, and more mixed still when Evan and
Anethe repaired to their sleeping quarters above the
lounge. They went up to their bedroom to lay down their
trunks and to change their clothes, and, ostensibly, to rest,
but it was quite shamefully apparent, from the sounds emanating from that room just above my head, that resting
was the furthest thing from their minds, and so difficult
was it to sit there below them listening to the noise of
their relations in the presence of my husband, his brother
and our boarder, all of whom pretended to hear nothing
and to take great interest in the cake which I had cut and
served to them, that though it was an evil day outside, I
put on my cloak and left that house, and had I had anywhere else on earth to go, I can assure you that I would
have done so.

On Sunday, when Karen came, I said no word about my surprise at Evan's marriage, as I did not want to give my sister the satisfaction of seeing in me the very emotion she had apparently taken such pains to elicit. Indeed, I was most gracious during that particular Sunday dinner, and I like to think I confounded our Karen by openly rejoicing in Anethe's arrival to our islands, and in pointing out to Karen the comely attributes and domestic skills of the young wife, and if Karen studied me oddly and tried several times to ensnare me in my own trickery by coaxing Anethe or Evan to tell of moments the two had shared in Norway during their courtship, I trust that a certain smugness, with which Karen had entered our house that day, began to fade and dissipate as the afternoon wore on. Of course, I had had to tell some untruths, as Anethe was a most appalling seamstress and cook and was almost entirely lacking in any knowledge of housewifery whatsoever. And I think it is probably not incorrect to say that young women with beauty are seldom possessed of great domestic ability, primarily because this quality is often unnecessary in order to attract eligible men into marriage. I often wonder how many of these men, in the second or third month of their wedded life, confronted with disorder in the household and weeks of ill-prepared meals, begin to speculate about the brilliance of their choice. Our Evan, of course, was spared this disillusionment, as I remained in charge of the housekeeping and of the meals, and suffered Anethe as but a poor assistant, more in need of instruction than of praise.

For five months on that island, I lived with Evan and Anethe, and with my husband and his brother and, for part of that time, our boarder as well. In October and early

November, when the men would leave for the day, Anethe would come down to the stove in her nightdress, and after she had had her bowl of coffee, she would dress and share the chores with me, but oddly I felt lonelier with her there than I had without her, and there were many days that I wished her gone or never come, and I felt badly about this, as there was nothing offensive in Anethe's disposition or in her person, certainly nothing that warranted such a desire. She was given to storytelling and even sometimes to teasing, and for hours at a stretch, while we spun or sewed or cooked, she would talk of Evan, all the while laughing, joking, and sharing the little intimate secrets that women sometimes tell each other, although I have never felt compelled to do so. I heard many times and could relate to you now the smallest details of their courtship and of their wedding, and of the long walks they took along the coast road and in the forest. Occasionally Anethe would attempt to glean from me anecdotes from my own time with Evan, but I was not so generous and could spare no stories, as they were still close to my bosom, and moreover, my poor narratives would have lacked lustre in the telling, as it was understood that in Evan's life Anethe had taken precedence, and so how could anything I relate be but a poor second cousin to the more legitimate? When the men came in the late afternoon, Anethe would run down to the cove to find Evan, and the two would play with each other as they stumbled up the path to the house. Even in the snow she did this.

It wasn't until the fourth week after Evan and Anethe had come to us that I found myself in a room alone with my brother. John and Matthew and Louis had gone into Portsmouth for provisions, but Evan had stayed behind to mend some nets. He could speak no English, and I think he was reluctant to make himself uncomfortable in that way in that city. Anethe, I recall, was still upstairs in her room. She was not an early riser and had no need to be except to bid her husband farewell in the mornings, for it was usually myself who rose before daybreak and fired up the stove and made the meal for the men, and gave them whatever clothes they might need. On this particular morning, however, Evan, too, had risen late, and had not yet had his breakfast. I was pleased to prepare it for him, although he protested and said he did not deserve it as he had been unforgivably lazy. He said this in a good-natured manner, and it was understood that he was joking. This was, as you may imagine, an altogether new side of my brother I was seeing, for before this time, he had nearly always been a pensive and thoughtful man. I began to think that his marriage had altered his very chemistry, or had, in some way, brought forth joy and hope from where they had lain buried inside him all those years.

Evan took off his jacket, as he had been down to the cove to see the men off, and he sat at the table. He was wearing a blue cotton shirt without a collar, and had exchanged that day his overalls for a pair of woolen trousers with suspenders. Over the last several years, his body had filled out some, so that I was most impressed with the length and breadth of his back, which seemed strong. Also his face, which before had shown the beginnings of the sunken cheeks which was certainly a family trait if not a national one, had filled out as well. These changes combined to give an impression of contentment and of a man who now daydreamed when once he had brooded. His hair, I noticed, had grown long in the back, and I wondered if I should offer to cut it, or if this task belonged now to Anethe. Indeed, it was difficult to know just exactly what the nature of the attachment between Evan and myself was, apart from our history, and though I wished to discuss in some oblique manner this question, I was content, for the moment, simply to be serving my brother at table.

I set before him a plate of bread and geitost, and sat down with him.

"Do you think John will be long in Portsmouth?" I asked.

"The tide is favorable, and the wind as well. They must have bait and set the trawls, and fill out the list you have given them, but I think they will be home before dark. And anyway, there is a moon tonight, so there is no danger either way."

"Why didn't you go with them? Isn't Portsmouth vastly more interesting than this poor island?"

He laughed. "This poor island has everything I need and ever wanted," he said. "My wife is here." He took a mouthful of biscuit. "And my sister," he added with a nod. "And I do not need the distraction of the city at the moment. I am content to sit here and mend the nets and think about my good fortune instead."

"You and Anethe are settling in well then?"

"Yes, Maren, you have seen this."

"She is very agreeable," I said. "And she is pleasant to look upon. But she has a lot to learn about keeping a house. I suppose she will learn that here."

"She can't fail with such a good teacher," Evan said, stabbing his spoon in my direction. I winced, for I thought sometimes that his new jocularity was overbearing and not really suited to him, however happy he had become.

"Maren, you have turned yourself into a first-rate cook," he said. "If I do not watch myself, I will grow fat from your cooking."

"You are already fat from your happiness," I said to him.

He laughed a kind of self-congratulatory laugh. "That is overweight I would not mind carrying," he said, "but you are growing fat as well, and with luck you may grow fatter still." I think my brother may actually have winked at me.

I got up at once and went to the stove.

"I mean that you will one day give us all some good news," he said amiably.

Still I said nothing.

"Maren, what is it?" he asked. "Have I said something wrong?"

I struggled for a moment over the wisdom of answering my brother, but I had waited for so long to speak with him, and I did not see when I would easily have another opportunity.

"I cannot have a child," I said, turning, and looking at him steadily.

He looked away toward the south window, through which one could see across the harbor and over to Star. I did not know if he was simply taken aback, or if he was chastising himself for so carelessly bringing up a painful subject. I saw, when he turned his head, that the silver-blond hair was thinning at the crown. He looked up. "Are you sure of this, Maren? Have you been to a doctor?"

"I have no need of doctors. Four years have been proof enough. And, truth to tell, I am not so surprised. It is something I have suspected all my life, or at least since . . ."

I hesitated.

"Since our mother died," I said quietly.

Evan put down his spoon, and brought his hand up to the lower half of his face.

"You remember," I said.

He did not answer me.

"You remember," I said, in a slightly more distinct voice.

"I remember," he replied.

"And I have thought," I said quickly, "that my illness after that time and the simultaneous onset of my womanhood . . ."

He began to rub the underside of his chin with his forefinger.

"That is to say, the beginning of my monthly curse . . ."

He suddenly took his napkin from his lap and put it on the table. "These are not matters of which we should speak, Maren," he said, interrupting me. "I am sorry to have brought up such a private subject. It is entirely my fault. But I do want to say to you that there can be no possible cause and effect between the events of that time and the state of your" — he hesitated at the word — "womb. This is a subject for doctors and for your husband at the very least. Also, I think that sometimes such difficulties may result from a state of mind as well as a state of bodily health."

"Are you saying I am barren because I have wished it so?" I asked sharply, for I was more than a little piqued at this glib remark on a matter he can have known so very little about.

"No, no, Maren," he said hastily. "No, no, I have no authority to say such things. It's just that I . . ." He paused. "Your marriage to John is a happy one?"

"We have managed," I said.

"I mean," he said, with a small, awkward flutter of his hand, "in the matter of a child . . ."

"Do you mean, does my husband put his seed into me with regularity?" I asked, shocking him, for he colored instantly and darkly.

He stood up in a state of confusion, and I was immediately remorseful and angry with myself for causing him this discomfort. I went to him and put my arms about his neck. He separated my hands from behind his neck and held my arms by their wrists, and I leaned against his chest.

My eyes filled with tears. Perhaps it was the proximity of his familiar body and the smell of him that allowed me to weep. "You have gone on," I cried. "You have gone on, but I . . . I cannot go on, and sometimes I think I will go mad."

His smell was in the fabric of his shirt. I pressed my face into the cloth and inhaled deeply. It was a wonderful smell, the smell of ironed cotton and a man's sweat.

He pulled my wrists down so that they were at my side. Anethe came into the room. Evan let go of me. She was still in her nightdress, and her hair was braided in a single plait down her back. She was sleepy still, and her eyes were half closed. "Good morning, Maren," she said pleasantly, seemingly oblivious to her husband's posture or the tears on my cheeks, and I thought, not for the first time, that Anethe must be short-sighted, and I then recalled several other times in the past few weeks when I had seen her squinting.

Anethe went to her husband and coiled herself into his embrace so that though she was facing me, his arms were wrapped around her. Evan, unwilling to look at me any longer, bent his head into her hair.

I could not speak, and for a moment, I could not move. I felt raw, as though my flesh had torn, as though a wild dog had taken me in his teeth, sunk his teeth into me, and had pulled and tugged until the flesh and gristle had come away from the bone.

"I must go," Evan said quickly to Anethe, giving her one last quick embrace about the shoulders. "I must collect the nets."

And without a glance in my direction, he took his jacket from the chair and left the room. I knew then that Evan would take great pains never to be left alone in a room again with me.

I turned around and brought my fists close in to my breast. I squeezed my eyes shut and tried to contain the rage and longing within me so that no unwanted sound would slip through my lips. I heard Anethe walk her husband to the door. Evan would take the nets, I knew, to Louis Wagner's room to mend them, even though it was colder in there. When I heard Anethe come back to where I was standing, I made myself relax my eyelids and put my hands on the back of a chair. I was trembling.

"Maren," Anethe said behind me, reaching up to tuck a stray lock of hair into my bun. The touch sent a shiver through my back and down my legs. "I am hopelessly naughty for sleeping so late, but do you think you could forgive me and let me have some of the sausage and cheese from yesterday's dinner for my breakfast?"

I stepped away from her and, with methodical movements, long practiced, long rehearsed, went to the stove, and slowly lifted the kettle up and slowly set it down again upon the fire.

For six weeks during the period that Evan and Anethe lived with John and me, Louis Wagner was with us, and for most of this time he was well and working on the *Clara Bella*. But one day, when the men were still going out, Louis remained behind. He was, he said, experiencing a sudden return of the rheumatism. I know now, of course, that this was a ruse, and I am sorry to have to report here that the inappropriate attraction Louis felt for Anethe had not abated with time, but rather had intensified. And this was due, in part, to the fact that Anethe had taken pity on Louis, fearing for his poverty and loneliness and his inability to get a wife, and had shown him some mild affection in the way of people who are so content with their lot that they have happiness in excess of their needs and thus can share the bounty with others. I believe that Louis, not having had this form of attention, and certainly not from such a lady as Anethe, mistook the young woman's kindness for flirtation and sought to make the most of that advantage. So it happened that on the day that he pretended ill and I had gone to see if he would sit up to take some porridge, he asked me if I would send Anethe forthwith into his chamber in order that she might read to him, and thus divert his attention from his "sore joints." I did see, in Anethe's face, the smallest hesitation when I suggested this, as she had never attended to a man other than her husband in the privacy of his room, and had never nursed the sick, but I imagine that she thought that if I was so willing to be alone with Louis there could be no harm in it. She took a book out of the front door of our kitchen and into the apartment in which Louis was lying.

I do not believe she was in his room for more than ten minutes before I heard a small exclamation, a sound that a woman will make when she is suddenly surprised, and then a muffled but distinctly distressed cry. As there was no noise from Louis, the first thought I had was that the man had fallen out of his bed. I had been on my knees with a dustpan, cleaning the ashes from the stove, and was halfway to my feet when there was a loud thump as though a shoulder had hit the wall that separated Louis's apartment from the kitchen of our own. There was a second bump and then another unintelligible word. I set down the dustpan on the table, wiped my hands on a cloth and called to Anethe through the wall. Before I could wonder at a lack of response, however, I heard the door of Louis's apartment open, and presently Anethe was in our kitchen.

One plait to the side of Anethe's head had pulled loose from its knot and was hanging in a long U at her shoulder. On the bodice of her blouse, a starched, white garment with narrow smocked sleeves, was a dirty smudge, as though a hand had ground itself in. The top button of her collar was missing. She was breathless and held her hand to her waist.

"Louis," she said, and put her other hand to the wall to steady herself.

The color had quite left Anethe's face, and I saw that her beauty was truly in her coloring and animation, for without both she looked gaunt and anemic. I confess I was riveted by the contrast of the dirty smudge on the white breast of her blouse, and I suppose because I am not at all a demonstrative person I found it difficult to speak some comfort to her. It was as though any word I might say to her would sound false and thus be worse than no word at all, and for some reason I cannot now articulate, I was in an odd state of paralysis. And though it shames me deeply, I must confess that I think I might actually have begun to smile in that awful inappropriate way one does when one hears terribly bad news, and the smile just seems automatically, without will, to come to one's lips. I reproach myself greatly for this behavior, of course, and think how easy it might have been to go to my sister-in-law and put my arms around her and console her, or at least help to put behind her the absurd and almost laughable advances of the man next door, but as I say, I was frozen to the spot and able only to utter her name.

"Anethe," I said.

Whereupon the blood left her head altogether, and she fell down in a wondrous sort of collapse that I am sorry to say struck me as somewhat comical in nature, the knees buckling, the arms fluttering out sideways as if she would try to fly, and it was only once she was on the ground that I was able to unlock my limbs and move toward her and raise her head up and in that way help her back to consciousness.

When I had her in her bed, and she had nearly recovered her color, we spoke finally about Louis and about the fearful rage that this incident might provoke in Evan, and it was decided then and there between us that I would not tell my brother, but rather would suggest to my husband that there had been some disappearances of beer and honey and candles in the household for which I could not account, and that without raising a fuss I thought it might be wise to terminate our boarder's lease.

Unfortunately, however, I was not present at Louis Wagner's dismissal and, as a consequence, John did not quite heed or remember my precise advice, and said to Louis that because I had missed certain household items it might be better for Louis to look elsewhere for lodgings. Louis denied these charges vigorously and demanded to see me, but John, of course believing his wife and not his boarder, stood firm and told Louis that he would be leaving the next day. The following morning, as Louis was preparing to board Emil Ingerbretson's schooner for the passage into Portsmouth, I remained in the kitchen, as I did not want an unpleasant confrontation, but just before sailing Louis came up from the cove and sought me out. I heard a noise and turned to see him standing in the open door. He did not speak a word, but merely stared at me with a look so fixed and knowing I grew warm and uncomfortable under his gaze. "Louis," I began, but could not go on, although the expression on his face seemed to dare me to speak. Truthfully, I could think of nothing I could say to him that would not make the situation worse. He smiled slowly at me then and closed the door.

Thus it was that Louis Wagner left Smutty Nose.

I THINK ABOUT THE WEIGHT of water, its scientific properties. A cubic foot of water weighs 62.4 pounds. Seawater is 3.5 percent heavier than freshwater; that is, for every 1,000 pounds of seawater, 35 of those will be salt. The weight of water causes pressure to increase with depth. The pressure one mile down into the ocean is 2,300 pounds per square inch.

What moment was it that I might have altered? What point in time was it that I might have moved one way instead of another, had one thought instead of another? When I think about what happened on the boat, and it was a time that was so brief — how long? four minutes? eight? certainly not even ten — the events unfold with excruciating lethargy. In the beginning, I will need to see the scene repeatedly. I will hunt for details I have missed before, savor tiny nuances. I will want to be left alone in a dark room so that I will not be interrupted. But after a time, I will not be able to stop the loop. And each time the loop plays itself, I will see I have a chance, a choice.

Thomas pulls me by the arms up onto the deck. He

tries to wipe the rain from his eyes with his sleeve. "Where have you been?" he asks.

"Where's Billie?"

"Down below."

"It was my last chance to get any pictures."

"Christ."

"We started back the minute it began to rain." My voice sounds strained and thin, even to myself.

"The wind came up half an hour ago," Thomas says accusingly. "The other boat has already left. I don't know what's going on."

"Billie's all right?"

Thomas combs his hair off his forehead with the fingers of both hands. "I can't get her to put her life jacket on."

"And Adaline?" I ask.

He massages the bridge of his nose. "She's lying down," he says.

Rich hoists himself onto the deck from the dinghy. I notice that Thomas does not extend a hand to his brother. Rich drags the dinghy line to the stern.

"Tom," Rich calls, again using the boyhood nickname. "Take this line."

Thomas makes his way to the stern, and takes the rope from Rich, and it is then that I notice that Thomas is shaking. Rich sees it, too.

"Go inside," Rich says to Thomas quietly. "Put on dry clothes and a sweater. The foul-weather gear is under the bunks in the forward cabin. You, too," he adds, looking at me quickly and then away. He ties the line in his hand to a cleat. "I'll go down and listen to what NOAA has to say. How long ago did the other boat leave?"

"About fifteen minutes," Thomas answers.

"Did she say where she was headed?"

"Little Harbor."

As if in answer to Rich's doubts, the Morgan shudders deep in her hull from the hard bang of a wave. I can feel the stern skid sideways in the water, like a car on ice. The rain is dark, and I can barely make out the shape of the islands around us. The sea is lead colored, dull but boisterous.

I go below to find Billie huddled in her berth. She has her face turned away. I touch her on the shoulder, and she snaps her head around, as though she were raw all over.

I lie down beside her. Gently, I rub her shoulder and her arm. "Daddy was right," I say softly. "You have to put your life jacket on. It's a law, Billie, and there isn't anything we can do about it."

Invoking parental helplessness before a higher authority has usually worked with Billie, as when I tell her that the police will stop me if she doesn't put on her seat belt in a car. The door to the forward cabin is shut. Thomas knocks and enters simultaneously, a gesture that catches my breath. I can see a slim form lying on the left side of the V berth. A head rises. Thomas shuts the door.

My sneakers make squelching sounds on the teak floor grate. I kick them off, and they thwack against a galley cabinet. I strip off my sweatshirt and shorts and underwear and pull from my duffel bag a pair of jeans and a cotton sweater. Billie, hearing the unexpected bumps of the sneakers, rolls over in her berth and looks up at her naked and shivering mother.

"Can't I wear an orange one?" she asks.

"No, those are for adults. Only yours will fit you." I peer down at the life vest, with its Sesame Street motif, on the table.

Thomas opens the door of the forward cabin. I am struggling awkwardly with jeans on wet skin. Rich swings down from the deck. Instinctively, I turn my back.

Thomas drops a muddle of navy and yellow foulweather gear onto the teak table. "There's a small one here," he says and holds it up. "I think it will fit Billie."

"Oh, Daddy, can I have it?" Billie asks, holding out her arms.

I wrestle with my sweater. I bend to Thomas's duffel bag and take out a dry shirt, a sweater, and a pair of khakis. I hold them out to him. I look at Thomas's face, which has gone white and looks old.

At the trial, Mr. Yeaton for the prosecution asked "Mary S. Hontvet" how long she had known Louis Wagner. She answered that he had boarded with her for seven months the previous year, beginning in the spring.

"When did he leave, get through boarding with you?" Mr. Yeaton asked.

"He went into Portsmouth about November," Maren answered.

"What room did he occupy in your house?"

"He had the easterly end of the house, he had a big room there."

"Where did he keep his clothes?"

"He kept his clothes in a little bed-room there hanging up. He had oil skin hanging up in my entry, when he had been out fishing, he took his oil skin off and hung it up in the entry, entry coming into my kitchen."

"Entry in your part?"

"Yes."

Mr. Yeaton then asked what was in Louis Wagner's room.

Maren answered: "He had his bed there, and one big trunk, which belonged to my sister Karen."

"Do you know what was in that trunk?"

"She had clothes, some she wore in the winter time, and she put them in the trunk in the summer, and summer clothes she did not use she put in the trunk, and she had a feather-bed that she had at the time she came over in the steamer."

"Was that in the trunk?"

"Yes, the bed was in the trunk, the big chest."

"While he boarded with you, was Karen a member of the family?"

"She came out visiting me some days."

"Did she sleep there?"

"No, sir."

Mr. Yeaton then asked Maren whether she knew if Karen had a piece of silver money. Maren answered that yes, she had seen the piece of silver money in October or November, and that Karen had said she had gotten the money from boarders at Appledore, and that it was kept in her purse. Mr. Tapley then asked her if she knew if Karen kept anything else in that purse or if Maren had seen Karen on the day of the murders put something in the purse.

"Yes," Maren answered.

"What was it?"

"A button, white button-like."

"Have you any articles of clothing, with similar buttons upon?"

"Yes, have got some."

"Where was the button taken from, if you know?"

"From my sewing basket."

"State what was done with the button, how did it come there."

"She took the sewing basket and looked for a button, and took a button there and handed it to Karen."

"Who took it from the basket?"

"Anethe, and handed it to Karen, and Karen put it in her purse."

"Have you any buttons similar to that?"

"Yes, have them with me."

Maren then produced the buttons.

"Where did you get these buttons?" Mr. Yeaton asked.

"Got them in my sewing basket, found one in the basket and two in my box that I have always kept in my sewing basket. I have a nightdress with similar buttons upon it."

Maren produced the nightdress, and the Court said to Mr. Yeaton that it did not see how the buttons and the nightdress were relevant.

"We will connect them hereafter and offer them again," Yeaton answered.

Rich stands at the chart table, a microphone uncoiled and in his hand. Staticky sounds — a man's even, unemotional voice — drone from the radio over the quarter berth, but I cannot understand what the man is saying. Rich seems to, however, and I watch as he bends closer to the charts, sweeping one away onto the floor altogether and examining another. I am looking for a sweater for Billie.

Rich puts the microphone back into its holder and

makes markings on a chart with a ruler and a pencil. "We've got a front coming in faster than they thought," he says with his back to Thomas and me. "They're reporting gusts of up to fifty miles an hour. Thunderstorms and lightning as well." A wave hits the sailboat side-to and floods the deck. Seawater sprays into the cabin through the open companionway. Rich reaches up with one hand and snaps the hatch shut.

"The wind alone could put us up on the rocks," he says. "I'm going to motor in towards Little Harbor, the same as the other boat, but even if we get caught out in the open, we'll be better off than we'd be here. There's not enough swinging room." He turns and looks from Thomas to me and back to Thomas, and seems to be making lists in his mind. He is still in his wet T-shirt and shorts, though this is a different Rich from the one I saw earlier, organized and in charge. Alarmed, but not panicked.

"Thomas, I need you to put sail ties on the main. Jean, I want you to heat some soup and hot coffee and put it into thermoses, and put dry matches, bread, toilet paper, socks, and so on — you decide — into Ziploc bags. We need to lock down everything in the cabin — drawers, your cameras, the binoculars, anything in the galley that could shift. There are cargo straps in that drawer over there if you need them. Get Adaline to help you. We want all the hatches tightly closed." Rich turns around to the chart table. "And you'll need these."

He opens the slanted desk top and pulls out a vial of pills, which he tosses to Thomas. "Seasickness pills," he says. "Each of you take one — even you, Thomas — and give a half of one to Billie. It could be a little uncomfortable today. And Thomas, there are diving masks under the cushions in the cockpit. Those are sometimes useful in the rain for visibility. Where *is* Adaline?"

Thomas gestures toward the forward cabin.

"She's sick?"

Thomas nods.

I look at my daughter, struggling with the jacket of the foul-weather gear. I open a drawer to retrieve the plastic bags. Beside the drawer, the stove is swinging. I realize that it is not the stove that is swinging, but rather the sloop itself. Seeing this, I feel, for the first time, an almost instantaneous queasiness. Is seasickness in the mind? I wonder. Or have I simply been too busy to notice it before?

Rich goes to the forward cabin and leaves the door open. Adaline is still lying motionless on the berth; she has thrown her arm across her eyes. I watch Rich peel off his wet clothes. How casual we are being with our nakedness, I think.

Rich dresses quickly in jeans and a sweatshirt. I can hear his voice, murmuring to Adaline, but I cannot hear the precise words. I want to know the precise words. He comes out and pulls on a pair of foul-weather pants and a jacket. He slips his feet back into his wet boat shoes. I can see that he is still thinking about the storm, making mental lists, but when he walks past me to go up on deck, he stops at the bottom of the ladder and looks at me.

It is strange enough that just a half hour before I was willing — no, trying — to make love with my brother-in-law. But it seems almost impossibly strange with my daughter in the berth and my husband at the sink. I feel an odd dissonance, a vibration, as though my foot had hit a loose board, set something in motion.

Thomas turns just then from the faucet, where he has been pouring water into a paper cup. In one hand, he holds the cup; in the other, a pill. I believe he is about to say to me, "Drink this," when he sees his brother's face, and then before I can pull away, my own.

Thomas's eyes move briefly from Rich's face to mine. Rich glances away, over toward the radio. I can see images forming in Thomas's mind. He still holds the cup of water with his hand. The other hand with the pill floats in front of me.

"What?" he asks then, almost inaudibly, as if he cannot formulate a whole question. I take the pill and the cup of water. I shake my head quickly, back and forth, small motions.

I hand the cup to Thomas. Rich goes immediately up to the cockpit. Billie calls to me: "Mommy, help me, please. I can't do the snaps."

With the exception of Maren Hontvedt's testimony as an eyewitness to the murders, the prosecution's case was based on circumstantial evidence and a lack of an alibi. It had been a bloody murder, and blood was found on clothing (left in the privy behind his landlady's house) belonging to Louis Wagner. Mrs. Johnson, the landlady in question, identified a shirt as belonging to Wagner by the buttonhole she had once mended. Money had been stolen from the Hontvedt house, and the next morning Wagner had enough money to go to Boston and to buy a suit of clothes. Any man who made the row to Smuttynose and back would have put a lot of wear and tear on a dory; the brand new thole pins in James Burke's dory were worn down. Wagner had talked to John Hontvedt and knew that the women would be alone on Smuttynose. In the weeks prior to the murders, Wagner had said repeatedly that he would have money if he had to murder for it. Wagner could not produce a single witness who had seen him in the city of Portsmouth from seven P.M. on the night of the murders until after seven o'clock the next morning. His landlady testified that Wagner did not sleep in his room that night.

The chief bit of evidence for the prosecution, however, was the white button that was found in Wagner's pocket when he was arrested. The button, the prosecution claimed, had been stolen, along with several coins, from a pocketbook belonging to Karen Christensen the night of the murders. The button matched those of Mary S. Hontvet's nightdress — the one she produced in court.

I slip Maren Hontvedt's document and its translation into a plastic bag and seal it. Into other plastic bags, I put my film and my cameras, my log, Thomas's notebooks, other books, and the provisions Rich has asked for. Rich and Thomas are above; Billie is beside me. I keep her close, throwing my arm in front of her or behind her like a railroad barrier whenever I feel the boat tip or catch a gust of wind. Rich and Thomas have unfastened the boat from the mooring and have turned on the motor. I can hear the cough and kick of the engine, and then a reassuring hum. We leave the Isles of Shoals and head for open water.

"Mommy, is Adaline coming to live with us?"

Billie and I are folding charts and sliding them into Ziploc bags. My daughter likes running her fingers along the seal, the satisfaction of feeling it snap shut.

I crouch down in front of her and sit back on my heels.

"She's not coming to live with us," I say. It is meant to be an answer, but it sounds like a question.

"Oh," Billie says. She looks down at the floor. I notice that water is sloshing over the teak planking.

"Why do you ask?" I put my finger under her chin and lift it just a fraction. There is a note that isn't entirely parental in my voice, and I think she must hear it. She sticks her tongue out the gap made by her two missing front teeth and stares up at the ceiling.

"I forget," she says.

"Billie."

"Um." She stretches her arms high above her head. Her toes are pointed inward. "Well . . . ," she says, drawing out the words. "I think Daddy said."

"Said what?"

She flaps her arms at her sides. "I don't know, do I?"

Shockingly, tears appear at the lower lids of her eyes.

"Billie, what's the matter?" I pull her to me and hold her close. I can feel the oilskin, the damp curl of her hair, the plumpness of her legs.

"Why is the boat moving around like this?" she asks. "It doesn't feel good."

Louis Wagner's defense consisted primarily of attempts to answer prosecution questions in order to convince the jury of a reasonable doubt. Why were his hands blistered and the knuckles bruised the day after the murders? He had helped a man lay crates on a fish cart. Where had he been all night? He had had a glass of ale, then had baited nine hundred hooks for a fisherman whose name he didn't know and who could not be produced at the trial. After that, he had two more mugs of ale and then began to feel poorly. He was sick to his stomach in the street and fell down near a pump. He went back to the Johnsons' at three o'clock to go to sleep, but went in the back door instead of the front, and did not go up to his bed, but slept in the lounge. Later in the morning, he decided to have his beard shaved, then heard the train whistle and thought to go to Boston. There he bought a new suit of clothes and went to stay at his old boardinghouse in North Street, a place he had lived at several times before. How did he happen to have blood on articles of clothing that he had on the night of the murders? It was fish blood, he said, and also he had stabbed himself with a fish-net needle several days earlier. How did he come by the money to go to Boston and to buy a suit of clothes? He had earned twelve dollars earlier in the week baiting trawls for a fisherman, whose name he did not remember, and the night of the murders had earned a further dollar.

Wagner took the stand in his own defense. Mr. Tapley, counsel for the defense, asked Louis Wagner what had happened to him when he was arrested in Boston.

"When I was standing in the door of the boarding master where I boarded five years," Wagner answered, "he came along, shook hands with me and said, halloo, where did you come from. Before I had time to answer him, policeman stepped along to the door. He dropped me by the arm. I ask them what they want. They answered me they want me. I asked him what for. I told him to let me go upstairs and put my boots on. They answered me the slippers are good enough. They then dragged me along the streets and asked me how long I had been in Boston. I was so scared I understand they asked me how long I had been in Boston altogether. I answered him five days, making a mistake to say five years."

"Did you intend to say five years?"

"Yes, sir. Then they asked me if I could read the English newspapers. I told them no. Well, he says, if you could you would have seen what was in it. You would have been in New York at this time."

"Would what?"

"I would have been in New York at this time if I knowed what was in the newspapers. I asked him what was in the newspapers. He asked me if I was not on the Isle of Shoals and killed two women; I answered him that I had not done such a thing. He brought me into station-house, Number One. I found there a man named Johnson, city marshal at Portsmouth."

Mr. Tapley then asked him what happened to him when he was brought to the station house.

Wagner said that City Marshall Johnson had asked him the whereabouts of the tall hat he was supposed to have worn the night before on the Isles of Shoals.

Wagner continued. "I told him I had not been on the Isle of Shoals; had not wore no tall hat in my life. He says the woman on the Isle of Shoals has seen you with a tall hat that night. I asked him what woman. He told me Mrs. Hontvet. He told me that he had the whiskers, that was shaved off my face, in his pocket, that it was shaved off in Portsmouth by such a barber. I told him to show me them whiskers. He told me that he had found the baker where I had been that night and bought bread; that I told the baker that I was going to the Isle of Shoals that night. I asked him to put me before the baker, or put the baker before me that said so. He answered that I soon would see him. When the new clothes was taken from my body I was taken into another room. The city marshal Johnson stripped me bare naked; asked me where I changed them underclothes. I told him that I had them underclothes on my body nearly eight days. He says you changed them this morning when you went to Boston; he says there was no gentleman in the city of Boston could wear underclothes for eight days so clean as them was. I told him I was poor, but I was a gentleman and I could wear clean underclothes just as well as any gentleman in the city of Boston. After my underclothes was overhauled they was put on me and I was brought into the cell; stayed in the cell until the next morning; when I was taken out again from two policemen, and dragged along the street."

"Do you mean from two men?"

"They took me along the street; walked me along the street."

"What do you mean by dragged?"

"They dragged me on my hands; took me into some kind of a house; don't know what it was. I was put on a seat; was kept about ten minutes; all the people had to look at me; was taken then away out of that house where they took my picture; and was brought again to station-house."

"After that, what took place?"

"After that I was closed up again. After a spell I was taken out and brought to the depot. When they took me down to the depot, I asked them where they were going to put me to. They answered me, they were sending me back to Portsmouth, asked me if I did not like to go there. I told them yes."

"Who asked you that?"

"The policeman who took me down there."

"Do you know his name?"

"Yes, one that was here."

"Go on."

"Well, I was brought to Portsmouth. I came to Portsmouth, the street was crowded with peoples, and was hallooing, 'Kill him, kill him.' I was put into station-house. I was closed in about three-quarters of an hour when Mr. Hontvet came there. . . . Mr. Hontvet came to side door and said, Oh! damn you murderer. I said, Johnny, you are mistaken. He says, damn you, you kill my wife's sister and her brother's wife. I told John, I hope you will find the right man who done it. He says, I got him. He says, hanging is too good for you, and hell is too good for you. He says I ought to be cut to pieces and put on to fish-hooks. I told him, that the net that he had spread out for me to drop in he might drop in himself. He says, where is that tall hat that you had on that night when you was on the Shoals. I told him I had no tall hat. He says, what have you been doing with the fish that you bought last night from the schooner, or was going to buy. I told him that I had not bought any fish, and was not out of Portsmouth that night. He told me that the dory was seen that night, between twelve and two o'clock, going on board a vessel that was lying at anchor on Smutty Nose Island."

"What do you mean by dory?"

"Dory pulled on board that schooner and asked that skipper if he had any fish to sell."

"Did he say where the schooner was?"

"Yes, he said that she was lying at anchor on Smutty Nose Island. He said that this dory was seen crossing over to the westward of the island and had hailed another vessel there. I then told him, Johnny, better look after that man that has been pulling that night in the dory. Then he and his brother-in-law answered me, that I was the man. His brother-in-law told Mr. Hontvet to ask me if I could not get the money without killing the vimen."

"Who do you mean by brother-in-law?"

"Evan Christensen. I told him that I never tried to steal money, but if I was a thief I thought I could get money without killing people. He says, you stole thirteen dollars. He says, you took ten-dollar bill out of that pocket-book."

"Who said that?"

"Mr. Hontvet. His brother, Mattheas Hontvet, showed me another pocket-book and said I stole out five dollars out of that. I told him that he was mistaken. They then left me, and some more people was coming to see me."

Blood evidence was introduced into the trial. Horace Chase, a physician who resided at 22 Newbury Street in Boston, testified that he had made a study of the analysis of blood and had examined the blood found on Louis Wagner's clothing. Dr. Chase explained that the red corpuscles of fish blood differ in shape from those of human or mammalian blood. Moreover, he said, it was possible to distinguish human blood from horse blood because of the size of the blood corpuscles. "The average blood corpuscle of man measures 1-3200 of an inch; that is, 3200 laid down in a line would cover one side of a square inch; it would take about 4600 of the corpuscles of a horse; the difference is quite perceptible," he said.

Various articles of clothing had been taken to Dr. Chase in Boston for blood analysis by Mr. Yeaton of the prosecution — overalls, a jacket, and a shirt. Dr. Chase testified that he found human blood on the overalls, human blood on the shirt, and simply mammalian blood on the jacket. During cross-examination, Dr. Chase said that he had not made more than "two or three" blood analysis examinations in criminal cases.

The defense introduced its own blood expert. James F. Babcock, a professor of chemistry at the Massachusetts College of Pharmacy in Boston, testified that it was not possible to distinguish with absolute certainty human blood from other mammalian blood, and that it was not possible to say, after blood had dried on an article of clothing, how old the stain was or whether it had appeared before or after another stain. Nor were there any tests available to determine whether the blood was male or female. Mr. Babcock said that he had examined blood stains in "several" capital cases.

The defense then called Asa Bourne, a fisherman, who testified that he and his sons had been out fishing on the night of the murders, and that the wind was so strong they could not make any headway against it. In his opinion, said Bourne, Wagner could not have rowed to the islands and back.

Dr. John D. Parsons, the physician who had examined the body of Anethe at the undertaker's room at Gerrish & Adams, was recalled to the stand by the defense. He was asked whether or not it was reasonable to suppose that the wounds upon Anethe, from their appearance, were made by a person not very muscular. He replied, "I think the flesh wounds might have been made by a person of not great muscular force."

Finally, the defense made an attempt to dismiss the entire case. In the state of Maine, at that time, a person could not be convicted of murder in the first degree of another person if the victim was not accurately named and that name not accurately spelled in the indictment. When Evan Christensen first testified, he said, "Anethe Christensen was my wife." The indictment, however, reports the victim as Anethe M. Christenson, with the slightly different spelling and the middle initial. Evan was recalled to the stand, whereupon Tapley questioned him.

"What time of day did you say that you went down to that house where your wife was dead?"

No response.

"What time was it?"

No response.

"Do you understand me?"

No response.

"What time of the clock was it, after you heard of your wife's death, that you went to the house the first time, the first morning after the murder?"

No response.

"Did you go inside?"

"Yes, sir."

"Did you go around in the different rooms?"

"I went into other rooms."

"Didn't you find a good deal of blood in those rooms?"

"Yes, sir."

"On the floor?"

"Yes, sir."

"Were you asked, since you were here day before yesterday, what your wife's name was?"

No response.

"Did anybody ask you before you came in this morning what your wife's name was? Didn't somebody ask you?"

No response.

"When did anybody say anything to you about your wife's name since day before yesterday, do you understand?"

No response.

"Are you a Norwegian?"

No response.

"You do not understand, do you?"

"No, sir."

"Did you speak with any one about your wife?"

No response.

"Did you tell anybody your wife's name, before you came here this morning?"

No response.

"What is Karen's full name?"

"Karen Alma Christensen."

"Was your wife's name Matea Annette?"

"Anetha Matea Christensen."

"Was she not sometimes called Matea Annette?"

No response.

"Do you understand my question?"

No response.

"When were you married?"

No response.

"When did you marry your wife?"

No response.

Tapley finally gave up this odd appeal, and the court declared that Anethe M. Christenson, as written, was the victim in the case.

Billie is doubled over at the waist, as if she will be sick. She coughs several times. Her skin has gone a shadowy white, and there is perspiration on her forehead. She cries.

She does not understand what is happening to her. "Mom," she says. "Mom."

The boat catches a gust, and it feels as though we have been hit by a train. We heel over, and I bang my head hard on the chart table. I hear the crash of dishes in the cabinets. A thermos on the counter slides the length of the Formica counter and topples onto its plastic cap. I kneel on the teak planking and hold Billie as best I can. I fight a sense of panic.

"Rich," I call up the ladder. I wait for an answer. I call again. "There's water on the floor," I shout.

It is hard to hear his response. Before the storm, the sounds from the water were soothing. The gentle slap of waves upon the hull. But now there is a kind of churning roar that is not just the engine. It is as though the ocean has become more difficult to slice through, as though the sea were causing resistance. Above this noise, I hear Rich call to Thomas, but I cannot make out the words.

Thomas slides down the ladder. He is soaked despite his slicker. He seems not to have the metal clasps fastened correctly. He sees me with Billie, with Billie bent over and crying. "What's wrong?" he asks.

"I think she's seasick."

He squats down beside us.

"She's frightened," I say. "She doesn't understand."

"Did you give her the half pill?"

"Yes. But it was probably too late."

Thomas reaches for a dishtowel and uses it to wipe Billie's forehead. Then he blots his own face. He is breathing hard, and there is an angry swelling to one side of his cheekbone.

"What happened?" I ask, pointing to the bump.

"It's rough out there," he says. He flips off the hood of the slicker, wipes the top of his head. His hair is mussed in an odd kind of sculpture that would make Billie laugh if she felt better.

He puts his hand down to the teak planking to balance himself. He is still breathing hard. Trying to catch his breath. Our faces aren't a foot apart. I think, looking at him, He's frightened, too.

Thomas yells up the companionway. "There's water over the teak, Rich. I can't tell how much."

We can hear Rich's voice, but again I cannot make out the words. Thomas stands up and leans against the ladder. "OK," he says in answer to something Rich has asked.

I watch Thomas take a tool from a galley drawer and then remove a cushion from the dinette. In the bulkhead is a socket. Thomas puts the metal tool into the socket and begins to ratchet it back and forth. He is awkwardly bent on the bench, and the table is in his way. I have hardly ever seen Thomas perform manual labor before.

"It's the bilge," Thomas says to me. "Rich says the electric is gone."

Thomas works intensely, silently, as if he wishes to exhaust himself.

I hear another sound then, or rather it is the cessation of sound.

"Shit," I hear Rich say loudly.

He comes down the ladder. He lifts a diving mask off his face, and I can see the crazy 8 the rubber has made. The skin around the 8 looks red and raw. "We've lost the engine," he says quickly. He looks at Billie. "What's wrong?" he asks.

"She's seasick," I say.

He sighs heavily and rubs his left eye with his finger. "Can you take the wheel for a minute?" he asks me. "I have to go into the engine compartment."

I look at Billie, who is lost in the isolation of her misery. She has her hands neatly folded at her stomach. "I could put her in with Adaline," I say. I know that Rich would not ask for help unless he really needed it.

"Get her settled," he says, "and come on up, and I'll show you what to do. The sooner the better."

I take Billie to the forward cabin and open the door. The berths make an upside-down V that joins in the middle, so that they form a partial double bed. Below this arrangement, there are large drawers, and to the end of each leg of the V, a hanging locker. Adaline is lying on her side in the berth to my left. She has a hand to her forehead. She glances up as I enter and raises her head an inch.

I hold Billie on my hip. I do not want to give my daughter up. I do not want her to be with Adaline. Billie retches again.

"She hasn't thrown up yet," I say, "but she feels awful. Rich needs me to take the wheel for a minute. Thomas is right here if you need him."

"I'm sorry, Jean," she says.

I turn to Billie. "I have to help Uncle Rich for a minute," I say. "Adaline is going to take care of you. You're going to be all right." Billie has stopped crying, as if she were too sick to expend even the effort to weep.

"Seasickness is awful," I say to Adaline. "Rich and Thomas pride themselves on never getting sick. It's supposed to be in the genes. I guess Billie didn't get them."

"It's one of the first things he told me about himself when I met him," says Adaline.

"Rich," I say, wiping the sweat off Billie's brow.

"No, Thomas."

I feel it then. A billowing in of the available air.

"When did you meet Thomas?" I ask as casually as I can.

There are moments in your life when you know that the sentence that will come next will change your life forever, although you realize, even as you are anticipating this sentence, that your life has already changed. Changed some time ago, and you simply didn't know it.

I can see a momentary confusion in Adaline's face.

"Five months ago?" she says, trying for an offhand manner. "Actually, it was Thomas who introduced me to Rich."

A shout makes its way from the cockpit to the forward cabin.

"Jean!" Rich yells. "I need you!"

"Put Billie down here with me," Adaline says quickly. "She'll be fine."

I think about Thomas's suggestion that we use Rich's boat.

I set Billie beside Adaline, between Adaline and the bulkhead, and as I do, the boat slides again. Billie whacks her head against the wall. "Ow," she says.

I am thinking I just want it to be all over.

I could not have anticipated what it is like above deck, how sheltered we have been below. I did not know that a storm could be so dark, that water could appear to be so black.

There is almost no visibility. Rich takes my arm and turns me around to face the stern and yells into the side of my hood. "This is simple," he shouts. "Keep the seas be-

hind you just like they are now. Whatever you have to do.
I'm running with a piece of sail, but don't bother about
that right now. The main thing is that we don't want the
boat to put its side to the waves. OK?"

"Rich, when did you meet Adaline?"

"What?" He leans closer to me to hear.

"When did you meet Adaline?" I shout.

He shakes his head.

I turn away from him. "How high are those waves?" I
ask, pointing.

"High," he says. "You don't want to know. OK, now,
take the wheel."

I turn and put my hands on wooden spokes at ten and
two o'clock. Immediately the wheel spins out of my control, flapping against the palms of my hands.

"You have to hang on, Jean."

"I can't do this," I say.

"Yes, you can."

I take hold of the wheel again and brace my legs
against the cockpit floor. The rain bites my cheeks and
eyelids.

"Here, put this on," he says.

He bends toward me with a diving mask, and in the
small shelter of our hoods I realize we do not have to
shout. "Rich, where did you meet Adaline?" I ask.

He looks confused. "The Poets and Prose dinner," he
says. "I thought you knew that. Thomas was there. You
couldn't go."

"I couldn't get a babysitter. Why was Adaline there?"

"Bank of Boston was a sponsor. She went as a repre-
sentative."

Rich slips my hood from my hair, and I think it must be

that gesture, the odd tenderness of that gesture, or perhaps it is the fitting of the mask, as you might do for a child, but he bends and kisses my wet mouth. Once, quickly. There is a sudden hard ache inside me.

He lowers the mask onto my face. When I have adjusted it and opened my eyes, he already has his back to me and is headed for the cabin.

I think it will be impossible to do as Rich has asked. I cannot control the wheel without using both hands, so I have to steer with my neck craned to see behind the stern. The boat falls into a trough, and I think the wall of water will spill upon me and swamp the boat. The swell crests at the top, then pushes the boat along with a forward zip. The boat zigzags in my inexpert hands. Several times, I mistake the direction I should turn the wheel, and overcorrect. I do not see how I will be able to keep the waves behind me. My hands become stiff with the wet and cold. The wheel shakes, and I put all my weight into my hands to keep it from spinning away from me. Less than an hour earlier I was on the beach at Smuttynose.

A wave breaks over the railing to my left. The water sloshes into the cockpit, rises to my ankles, and quickly drains away. The water is a shock on the ankles, like ice. The boat, I see, is turning into the swells. I fight the wheel, and then, oddly, there is no resistance at all, just a spinning as if in air. To my right, lightning rises from the water. Then we are lost again in a trough, and I am once more struggling with the steering apparatus. Rich has been gone only a minute, two minutes. There is another lightning skewer, closer this time, and I begin to have a new worry.

The jib snaps hard near the bow. It collapses and snaps

again. I turn the wheel so as to head into the wind. The jib grows taut and steadies.

Adaline emerges from the forward hatch.

I rub the surface of the diving mask with my sleeve. The wheel gives, and I take hold of it again. I am not sure what I am seeing. There is the smoky blur of the Plexiglas hatch rising. I take the diving mask off and feel for my glasses in the pocket of my oilskin. There is a half inch of water in the pocket. I put the glasses on, and it is as though I am looking through a prism. Objects bend and waver.

Adaline sits on the rim of the hatch and lifts her face to the sky, as if she were in a shower. The rain darkens and flattens her hair almost at once. She slips out of the hatch entirely and closes it. She slides off the cabin roof and onto the deck. She holds herself upright with a hand on a metal stay. She comes to the rail and peers out. I yell to her.

She has on a white blouse and a long dark skirt that soaks through immediately. I cannot see her face, but I can see the outline of her breasts and legs. I yell again. She doesn't have a life vest on.

I shout down to Rich, but he doesn't hear me. Even Thomas cannot hear with all the roar.

What is she doing out there? Is she crazy?

I feel then an anger, a sudden and irrational fury, for her carelessness, this drama. I do not want this woman to have entered our lives, to have touched Thomas or Billie, to have drawn them to her, to have distracted them. I do not want this woman to be up on deck. And most of all, I do not want to have to go to her. Instead, I want to shake her for her foolishness, for the theatrical way she carries herself, for her gold cross.

I let the wheel go, bend forward at the waist, and clutch at a stay. The wind flattens the oilskin against my body. I reach for a winch, the handholds in the teak railing. I pull myself forward. She is perhaps fifteen feet from me. My hood snaps off my head.

Adaline leans over the teak rail. Her hair falls in sheets, then blows upward from her head. I see then that she is sick.

I am three, four feet from where she is huddled at the railing. I shout her name.

The boat turns itself into the swells and heels. Adaline straightens and looks at me, an expression of surprise on her face. The jib swings hard, and makes a sharp report, like a shot. She holds out her hand. It seems to float in the air, suspended between the two of us.

I have since thought a great deal about one time when I shut a car door, gave it a push, and in the split second before it closed, I saw that Billie's fingers were in the door, and it seemed to me in the bubble of time that it took for the door to complete its swing that I might have stopped the momentum, and that I had a chance, a choice.

In Alfred, Maine, the jury took less than an hour to reach a verdict of murder in the first degree. Wagner was sentenced to be hanged. He was then taken to the state prison at Thomaston to await execution.

The hanging at Thomaston was a particularly grisly affair and is said to have almost single-handedly brought about the abolition of the death penalty in Maine. An hour before Wagner and another murderer, a man named True

Gordon, who had killed three members of his brother's family with an ax, were to be hanged, Gordon attempted suicide by cutting his femoral artery and then stabbing himself in the chest with a shoemaker's knife. Gordon was bleeding out and unconscious, and the warden of Thomaston was presented with a ghastly decision: Should they hang a man who was going to die anyway before the afternoon was out? The warrant prevailed, and Wagner and Gordon were brought to an abandoned lime quarry, where the gallows had been set up. Gordon had to be held upright for the noose to be put on. Wagner stood on his own and protested his innocence. He proclaimed, "God is good. He cannot let an innocent man suffer."

At noon on June 25, 1873, Louis Wagner and True Gordon were hanged.

Adaline goes over like a young girl who has been surprised from behind by a bullying boy and pushed from the diving board, arms and legs beginning to flail before she hits the water.

The ocean closes neatly over her head. I try to keep my eye fixed on the place where she has gone in, but the surface of the water — its landscape, its geography — twitches and shifts so that what has been there before is not there a moment later.

The sea heaves and spills itself and sends the boat side-to sliding down a trough. Water cascades onto the deck, pinning my legs against the railing. Adaline breaks the surface twenty yards from the place I expected her to be. I shout her name. I can see that she is struggling. Rich comes above to see what has happened to the boat. He takes the wheel immediately.

"Jean!" he shouts. "Get away from the railing. What's going on?"

"Adaline's overboard," I shout back, but the wind is against me, and all he can make out is my lips moving soundlessly.

"What?"

"Adaline!" I yell as loudly as I can and point.

Thomas comes above just then. He has put on a black knit cap, but his oilskins are off. Rich shouts the word *Adaline* to Thomas and gestures toward the life ring. Thomas takes hold of the life ring and pulls himself toward me.

There are thundering voices then, the spooling out of a line, a life ring missed and bobbing in a trough. There is a flash of white, like a handkerchief flung upon the water. There are frantic and sharp commands, and Thomas then goes over. Rich, at the wheel, stands in a semi-crouch, like a wrestler, from the strain of trying to keep the boat upright.

I think then: If I had put out my hand, might Adaline have grabbed it? Did I put out my hand, I wonder, or did a split second of anger, of righteousness, keep my hand at my side?

I also think about this: If I hadn't shouted to Adaline just then, she would not have stood up, and the sail would have passed over her.

When Rich hauls Adaline over the stern, her skirt and underwear are missing. What he brings up doesn't seem like a person we have known, but rather a body we might study. Rich bends over Adaline and hammers at her chest, and then puts his mouth to hers again and again. In the corner of the stern, against the railing, Thomas stands doubled over from the effort to rescue Adaline and to pull himself back into the boat. He wheezes and coughs for breath.

And it isn't me, it isn't even me, it is Rich — angry, frustrated, exhausted, breathless — who lifts his head from Adaline's chest, and calls out: "Where's Billie?"

25 September 1899

I NOW ENCOUNTER MY most difficult task of all, which is that of confronting the events of 5 March 1873, and committing them to paper, to this document, to stand as a true account made by a witness, one who was there, who saw, and who survived to tell the tale. Sometimes I cry to myself, here in the silence of my cottage, with only the candles to light my hand and the ink and the paper, that I cannot write about that day, I cannot. It is not that I do not remember the details of the events, for I do, too vividly, the colors sharp and garish, the sounds heightened and abrasive, as in a dream, a terrible dream that one has over and over again and cannot escape no matter how old one grows or how many years pass.

It was a day of blue sky and bright sun and harsh reflections from the snow and sea and ice crystals on the rocks that hurt the eye whenever one's gaze passed across the window panes or when I went outside to the well or to the hen house. It was a day of dry, unpleasant winds that whipped the hair into the face and made the skin feel like paper. The men had left the house early in the morning to draw their trawls, which they had set the day before, and

John had said to me as he was leaving that they would be back midday to collect Karen and to have a meal before they set out for Portsmouth to sell the catch and purchase bait. I had some errands I wished him to perform, and I spoke to him about these, and it is possible I may have handed him a list on that day, I do not remember. Evan stumbled down the stairs, unshaven, his hair mussed, and grabbed a roll on the table for his breakfast. I urged him to stay a moment and have some coffee, as it would be raw and frigid in the boat, but he waved me off and collected his jacket and his oilskins from the entryway. Matthew was already down at the boat, making it ready, as he did nearly every morning. Indeed, I hardly ever saw Matthew, as he seemed to be on a clock different from the rest of us, rising at least an hour before me, and retiring to his bed as soon as it was dark. Karen, I remember, was in the lounge that morning, and she said to John that she would be dressed and ready to go with him after the dinner meal, and John nodded to her, and I could barely look at her, since she had had all her teeth removed, and her face had a terrible sunken appearance, as one sometimes sees on the dead. Karen, who had been with us since the end of January, had been fired from her job with the Laightons when she had said one day that she would not sweep out or make the beds in a certain room belonging to four male boarders. I suspect that Eliza Laighton had been wanting to let Karen go for some time, since Karen could now speak a rudimentary English and therefore could make her complaints and opinions known, as she had not been able to do when she first arrived. As you may imagine, I was somewhat ambivalent about Karen's presence. Since Evan's arrival, we had not been overly cordial with one another, and, in addition, there were many of us under that roof, under that half-roof I should say, since we all lived in the southwest apartment, so as to be nearer to the heat source during the long winter.

Indeed, I can barely write about that dreadful winter when we were all closed in together for so many weeks in January and February. In the kitchen most hours of the day, there would be myself and John, Evan and Anethe, Matthew of course, and then Karen, and for days on end we would not be able to leave the house or to bathe properly so that there was a constant stale and foul odor in that room, a smell composed of shut-in human beings as well as the stink of fish that was on the oilskins and in the very floorboards themselves, and that no matter how hard I scrubbed with the brush was never able entirely to remove. Even Anethe, I noticed in the last weeks of February, had begun to lose her freshness, and I did observe that her hair, unwashed for so many days, took on a darker and more oily appearance and that her color, too, seemed to have faded in the winter.

It was a severe trial to keep one's temper in that fetid atmosphere. Only Evan seemed to have any enthusiasm for his lot, being content simply to remain in Anethe's presence, though I did notice signs of strain in Anethe herself, and if ever a marriage was put to the test, it was on that island, during those winters, when small tics or habits could become nearly unbearable, and the worst in a person was almost certain to emerge. John used the hours to mend nets and repair trawls, and Matthew was his partner in this work. Matthew would often hum or sing tunes from Norway, and I do remember this as a pleasant diversion. Evan had taken on the building of a wardrobe for

Anethe as a project, so that the room was filled not only with nets and hooks into which one had to be careful not to become entangled, but also with wood shavings and sawdust and nails and various sharp implements with which Evan worked. I took refuge in routine, and I will say here that more than once in my life the repetition of chores has been my salvation. Of the six of us, I was the one who went outdoors the most often, to collect wood or water or eggs from the coop. It was understood that I would keep the house in order, and I have observed that while fishermen do take seasonal rests from their labors, their womenfolk do not, and do not even when the men are too weak from old age to draw a trawl and must retire from their labors. An aging wife can never retire from her work, for if she did, how would the family, or what was left of it, eat?

Karen, during this time, attended to her sewing and her spinning, and I was just as happy not to have her in my way or in constant attendance. In the beginning of Karen's stay, Anethe set out to please this sister of Evan's, rolling the wool that Karen had spun, feigning enthusiasm for the skill of embroidery and offering to braid Karen's hair, but it was not long before I noticed that even Anethe, who previously seemed to have nearly inexhaustible reserves of selflessness, began to tire of Karen's constant querulous whine and started to see as well that pleasing Karen was in itself a futile endeavor. There are some people who simply will not be pleased. After a time, I noticed that Anethe asked me more and more often for chores of her own to perform. I had more than a few to spare, and I took pity upon her, as enforced idleness in such a claustrophobic setting will almost certainly begin to erode joy, if not one's character altogether.

As for me, I had not thought about joy much, and sometimes I felt my character, if not my very soul, to be in jeopardy. I had not prayed since the day that Evan spoke harshly to me in the kitchen, as I no longer had anything compelling to pray for. Not his arrival, not his love, not even his kindness or presence. For though he was in that room all the days, though we were seldom more than a few feet from each other, it was as though we were on separate continents, for he would not acknowledge me or speak to me unless it was absolutely necessary, and even at those times, I wished that he had not had need to speak to me at all, for the indifference of his tone chilled my blood and made me colder than I had been before. It was a tone utterly devoid of warmth or forgiveness, a tone that seeks to keep another being at bay, at a distance. Once, in our bed at night, John asked me why it was that Evan and I seemed not to enjoy each other's company as much as we used to, and I answered him that there was nothing in it, only that Evan was preoccupied and blind to everyone except Anethe.

Since the first day of March, the men had been going out to sea again, and there was something of a sense of relief in this, not only because we had all survived the gruelling weeks of the hard winter, but also because now there would be some breathing room. The men, in particular, were cheered by occupation, and I suppose I was a bit more relaxed not to have so many underfoot. My work did not seem to lighten much, however, since there were the same number of meals to prepare and increased washing now that the men would come back fouled with fish goory in the afternoons.

On the morning of 5 March, I remember that Karen painstakingly dressed in her city clothes, a silver-gray dress with peacock-blue trim, and a bonnet to match, and that once outfitted in this manner, she sat straight-backed in a chair, her hands folded in her lap, and did not move much for hours. I believe she thought that being in city clothes prevented her from taking up a domestic occupation, even one so benign as sewing. It was extremely annoying to me to observe her that day, so stiff and grim, her mouth folded in upon itself, arrested in a state of anticipation, and I know that at least once I was unable to prevent my irritation from slipping out, and that I said to her that it was ludicrous to sit there in my kitchen with her hat on, when the men would not return for hours yet, but she did not respond to me and set her mouth all the tighter. Anethe, by contrast, seemed excessively buoyant that morning, and it was as though the two of us, Anethe and myself, were performing some sort of odd dance around a stationary object. Anethe had a gesture of running the backs of her hands upwards along the sides of her neck and face and gracefully bringing them together at the top of her head and then spreading her arms wide, actually quite a lovely, sensuous movement, and she did this several times that day, and I thought it could not just be that she was glad the men were out of the kitchen, for, in truth, I think she was ambivalent about not being with Evan, and so I asked her, more in jest really, what secret it was that was making her so happy on that day, and she stunned me by replying, "Oh, Maren, I had not thought to tell anyone. I have not even told my husband."

Of course, I knew right away what she meant, and it hit me with so much force that I sat down that instant as though I had been pushed.

Anethe put her hand to her mouth. "Maren, you look shocked. I should not have said —"

I waved my hand. "No, no . . ."

"Oh, Maren, are you not pleased?"

"How can you be sure?" I asked.

"I am late two months. January and February."

"Perhaps it is the cold," I said. It was an absurd thing to say. I could not collect my thoughts and felt dizzy.

"Do you think I should tell him tonight? Oh, Maren, I am amazed at myself that I have kept it from him all this time. Indeed, it is surprising that he himself did not notice, although I think that men —"

"No, do not tell him," I said. "It is too soon. It is bad luck to speak of this so early on. There are so many women who lose their babies before three months. No, no, I am quite sure. We will keep this to ourselves for now." And then I collected myself a bit. "But, my dear, I am happy for you. Our little family will grow bigger now, as it should do."

And then Karen said from the table, "Where will you keep it?" and Anethe, I think somewhat taken aback by the use of the word *it* rather than *the child,* composed herself and looked steadily at her sister-in-law. "I will keep our baby with myself and Evan in our bedroom," she said.

And Karen did not say anything more at that time.

"It is why you have been looking pale," I said, suddenly comprehending the truth of what Anethe was saying. As I looked at her, I had no doubt now that she was pregnant.

"I have felt a bit faint from time to time," she said, "and sometimes there is a bad taste in the back of my mouth, a metallic taste, as if I had sucked on a nail."

"I cannot say," I said, standing up and spreading my hands along my apron skirt. "I have never had the experience."

And Anethe, silenced by the implications of that statement, picked up the broom by the table and began to sweep the floor.

The coroner missed this fact about Anethe in his examination of her body, and I did not like to tell Evan, as I thought it would make his agony all the more unendurable.

About two o'clock of that afternoon, I heard a loud hallooing from the water and looked through the window and saw Emil Ingerbretson waving to me from his schooner just off the cove, and so I ran outside quickly, thinking that perhaps there had been an accident, and I managed to make out, though the wind kept carrying off the words, that John had decided to go straight in to Portsmouth, as he could not beat against the wind. When I had got the message, I waved back to Emil, and he went off in his boat. Once inside, I told the other two women, and Anethe looked immediately disappointed, and I saw that she had meant to tell Evan that day of her news, despite my admonition not to. Karen was quite vexed, and said so, and asked now what would she do all dressed up with her city clothes on, and I replied that I had been asking myself that question all morning. She sighed dramatically, and went to a chair against the wall in the kitchen and lay back upon it.

"They will be back tonight," I said to Anethe. "Let's

have a portion of the stew now, as I am hungry, and you must eat regular meals, and we will save the larger share for the men when they return. I have packed them no food, so unless they feed themselves in Portsmouth, they will be starved when they return."

I asked Karen if she would take some dinner with us, and she then asked me how she would eat a stew with no teeth, and I replied, with some exasperation, as we had had this exchange nearly every day since she had had her teeth removed, that she could sip the broth and gum the bread, and she said in a tired voice that she would eat later and turned her head to the side. I looked up to see that Anethe was gazing at me with a not unkind expression, and I trust that she was nearly as weary of my sister's complaints as I was.

We ate our meal, and I found some rubber boots in the entryway and put them on and went to the well and saw that the water had frozen over and so I went into the hen house to look for the axe, and found it lying by a barrel, and brought it to the well and heaved it up with all my strength and broke the ice with one great crack. I had been used to this chore, since the water often froze over on that island, even when the temperature of the air was not at freezing level, and this was due to the wind. I fetched up three buckets of water and took them one by one into the house and poured them into pans, and when I was done I brought the axe up to the house and laid it by the front door, so that in the morning, I would not have to go to the hen house to get it.

Dusk came early, as it was still not the equinox, and when it was thoroughly dark, and I noticed, as one will notice not the continuous sound of voices in the room but rather the cessation of those voices, that the wind had quieted, I turned to Anethe and said, "So that is that. The men will not be back this night."

She had a puzzled look on her face. "How can you be sure?" she asked.

"The wind has died," I said. "Unless they are right at the entrance to the harbor, their sails will not fill, and if they have not yet left Portsmouth, John will not go out at all."

"But we have never been alone at night before," Anethe said.

"Let us wait another half hour before we are sure," I said.

The moon was in its ascendancy, which had a lovely effect on the harbor and on the snow, outlining in a beautifully stark manner the Haley House and the Mid-Ocean Hotel, both vacant at that time. I went about the lounge lighting candles and the oil lamp. When a half hour had elapsed, I said to Anethe, "What harm can possibly come to us on this island? Who on these neighboring islands would want to hurt us? And anyway, it is not so bad that the men have not come. Without them, our chores will be lighter."

Anethe went to the window to listen for the sound of oars. Karen got up from her chair and walked to the stove and began to spoon broth and soft potatoes into a bowl. I took off my kerchief and stretched my arms.

Anethe wondered aloud where the men would stop to eat. Karen said she thought it likely they would go to a hotel and have a night for themselves. I disagreed and said I thought they would go to Ira Thaxter's on Broad Street, for they would have to beg a meal from a friend, until they sold the catch, the proceeds of which were to have gone for provisions. Karen pointed out to me that Ringe hadn't been fed yet, and I rose from the table and put some stew into his dish. All in all, I was quite amazed that Karen had not muttered something about the men having failed to take her into Portsmouth, but I imagine that even Karen could tire of her own complaints.

While Anethe washed the pots and dishes, nearly scalding her hand from the kettle water, Karen and I struggled with a mattress that we dragged downstairs to lay in the kitchen for her. Anethe asked if she could sleep in my bed to keep from being cold and lonely without Evan that night, and though I was slightly discomfited by the thought of a woman in my bed, and Anethe at that, I did reason that her body would provide some warmth, as John's did, and besides, I did not like to refuse such a personal request. After stoking up the fire for warmth, I believe that the three of us then took off our outer garments and put on our nightdresses, even Karen, who had thought to stay in her city clothes so that she would not have to dress again in the morning, but in the end was persuaded to remove them so as not to muss them unduly. And then, just as I was about to extinguish the lights, Karen took out from the cupboard bread and milk and soft cheese, and said that she was still hungry, and I will not weary the reader with the silly quarrel that ensued, although I had reason to be annoyed with her as we had just cleaned up the kitchen, and finally I said to Karen that if she would eat at this time, she could tidy up after herself and would she please extinguish the light.

Sometimes it is as though I have been transported in my entirety back to that night, for I can feel, as if I were again lying in that bed, the soft forgiveness of the feather mattress and the heavy weight of the many quilts under which Anethe and I lay. It was always startling, as the room grew colder, to experience the contrast in temperatures between one's face, which was exposed to the frigid air, and one's body, which was encased in goose down. We had both been still for some time, and I had seen, through the slit underneath the bedroom door, that the light had been put out, which meant that Karen had finally gone to bed. I was lying flat on my back with my arms at my sides, looking up at the ceiling, which I could make out only dimly in the moonlight. Anethe lay facing me, curled into a comma, holding the covers close up to her chin. I had worn a nightcap, but Anethe had not, and I suppose this was because she had a natural cap in the abundance of her hair. I had thought she was asleep, but I turned my head quickly toward her and back again and saw that she was staring at me, and I felt a sudden stiffening all through me, a response no doubt to the awkwardness of lying in my bed with a woman, and this woman my brother's wife.

"Maren," she whispered, "are you still awake?"

She knew that I was. I whispered, "Yes."

"I feel restless and cannot sleep," she said, "although all day I have felt as though I would sleep on my feet."

"You are not yourself," I said.

"I suppose." She shifted in the bed, bringing her face a little closer to my own.

"Do you think the men are all right? You don't think anything could have happened to them?"

I had thought once or twice, briefly, not liking to linger on the thought, that perhaps John and Evan had met with an accident on the way to Portsmouth, although that seemed unlikely to me, and, in any event, hours had passed since Emil had come with the message, and if some ill had befallen the men, I thought that we would have heard already.

"I believe they are safe in Portsmouth. Perhaps in a tavern even as we speak," I said. "Not minding at all their fate."

"Oh," she said quickly, "I think my Evan would mind. He would not like to sleep without me."

My Evan.

She reached out a hand from the covers and began to stroke my cheek with her fingers. "Oh, Maren," she said, "you are so watchful over us all."

I did not know what she meant by that. My breath was suddenly tight in my chest from the touch of her fingers. I wanted to throw her hand off and turn my back to her, but I was rigid with embarrassment. I was glad that it was dark, for I knew that I must be highly colored in my face. To be truthful, her touch was tender, as a mother might stroke a child, but I could not appreciate this kindness just then. Anethe began to smooth my forehead, to run her fingers through the hair just underneath my cap.

"Anethe," I whispered, meaning to tell her to stop.

She moved her body closer, and wrapped her hands around my arm, laying her forehead on my shoulder.

"Do you and John?" she asked, in a sort of muffled voice. "Is it the same?"

"Is what the same?" I asked.

"Do you not miss him at this moment? All the attentions?"

"The attentions," I repeated.

She looked up at me. "Sometimes it is so hard for me to sit in the kitchen until it is proper to go up to bed. Do you know?" and she moved herself still closer to me so that her length was all against my own. "Oooh," she said. "Your feet are freezing. Here, let me warm them," and she began, with the smooth sole of her foot, to massage the top of my own. "Do you know," she said again, "I have never told anyone this, and I hope you will not be shocked, but Evan and I were lovers before we were married. Do you think that was very wrong? Were you and John?"

I did not know what to say to her or which question to answer first, as I was distracted by the movement of her foot, which had begun to travel up and down the shin of my right leg.

"I no longer know what is right or wrong anymore," I said.

Her body was a great deal warmer than my own, and this warmth was not unpleasant, though I remained stiff with discomfort, as I had never been physically close with anyone except my brother Evan and my husband. I had certainly never been physically close with a female, and the sensation was an odd one. But, as will happen with a child who is in need of comfort and who gradually relaxes his limbs in the continuous embrace of the mother, I began to be calmed by Anethe, and to experience this peace as pleasurable, and, briefly to allow myself to breathe a bit more regularly. I cannot explain this to the reader. It is, I think, a decision the body makes before the heart or the head, the sort of decision I had known with John, when, without any mental participation, my body had seemed to respond in the proper ways to his advances.

In truth, as Anethe laid her head on my chest and began to stroke the skin of my throat, I felt myself wanting to turn ever so slightly toward my brother's wife and to put my arm around her, and perhaps, in this way, return something of the affection and tenderness she was showing to me.

"Do you do it every night?" she asked, and I heard then a kind of schoolgirlish embarrassment in her own voice.

"Yes," I whispered, and I was shocked at my own admission. I wanted to add that it was not my doing, not my doing at all, but she giggled then, now very much like a girl, and said, to my surprise, "Turn over."

I hesitated, but she gently pushed my shoulder, and persisted with this urging, so that finally I did as I was told, putting my back to her, and not understanding what this was for. She lifted herself up onto her elbow and said, close to my ear, "Take up your nightgown."

I could not move.

"I want to rub your back," she explained, "and I cannot do it properly through the cloth." She pushed the covers down and began slightly to tug at the skirt of my nightgown with her hand, and I, though somewhat fearful of the consequences, began to wrestle with the gown and to pull the hem up to my shoulders. I held the bunched cloth to my bosom as I had done once at the doctor's office in Portsmouth when I had had the pleurisy. But shortly I felt the warmth of being attended to, and I surrendered myself to this attention.

Anethe began then to stroke my skin with an exquisite lightness and delicacy, from the top of my spine to my waist, from one side of my back to the other, all around in the most delightful swirls, so that I was immediately, without any reservations, put into a swoon of such all-encompassing proportions that I could not, in those moments, for any reason, have denied myself this touch. It was a sensation I had not experienced in many years. Indeed, I cannot remember, ever in my adult life, being the recipient of such pleasure, so much so that had she stopped before I had had my fill, I would have begged her to continue, would have promised her anything if only she would again touch my skin with her silken fingers. But she did not stop for some time, and I remember having the thought, during that experience, that she must be a very generous lover, and then realizing, when I was nearly in a dream state myself, that her hand had trailed off and that she had fallen asleep, for she began to snore lightly. And hearing her asleep, and not wishing to wake her, and also not wanting the trance I had fallen into to be broken, I did not move or cover myself, but drifted into a deep sleep while the moon set, for I remember being confused and struggling for sense when I heard my dog, Ringe, barking through the wall.

What a swimming up is there from the bath of a sensuous dream to the conscious world, from a dream one struggles desperately not to abandon to the frigid shock of a startled voice in the darkness. Ringe barked with loud, sudden yips. I raised my arms up from the bed before I was even fully awake. I thought that Karen was stumbling about in an attempt to go to the privy, and that she had woken Ringe, who normally slept with me. I was about to call out to her with some irritation to be quiet and go back to bed and to send my dog into the bedroom, when I heard her say, in the clearest possible voice, "My God, what have you done?"

It was all so much simpler, so much simpler, than I said.

I sat up in my bed and saw that my sister was standing at the open door of the bedroom and that to my great embarrassment, the bedclothes were still at the foot of the bed, and that most of my naked body was exposed. I hastily pulled the cloth of my nightdress down to my feet.

I can remember the awful surprise in Karen's face, and, even now, the horror of her mouth folded in upon itself, sputtering words to me in a voice that had become more metallic, more grating with the years, and the way the words issued from that black hole of a mouth.

"First our Evan and now Anethe!" she shouted. "How can you have done this? How can you have done this to such a sweet and innocent woman?"

"No, Karen . . . ," I said.

But my sister, in an instant, had progressed from shock to moral righteousness. "You are shameless and have always been so," she went on in that terrible voice, "and I shall tell our Evan and John also when they return, and you will be banished from this household as I should have done to you many years ago, when I knew from the very beginning you were an unnatural creature."

"Karen, stop," I said. "You don't know what you say."

"Oh, but I do know what I say! You have borne an unnatural love for our brother since your childhood, and he has fought to be free of you, and now that he is married, you have thought to have him by having his wife, and I have caught you out in the most heinous of sins, Maren, the most heinous of sins."

Beside me, Anethe struggled to waken. She lifted herself up upon one elbow and looked from me to Karen. "What is it?" she asked groggily.

Karen shook her head furiously back and forth, back and forth. "I have never loved you, Maren, I have never loved you. I have not even liked you, and that is the truth. And I think it is true also that our Evan has found you selfish and self-dramatic, and that he grew so tired of you he was glad when you went away. And now you are grown old, Maren, old and fat, and I see that your own husband does not really love, nor does he trust you, for you would do anything to get what you want, and now, rebuffed, you have committed the worst possible of sins, a sin of corruption, and have chosen to steal your brother's wife, and seduce her in the most shameful manner."

No one can say with any certainty, unless he has lived through such an experience, how he will react when rage overtakes the body and the mind. The anger is so swift and so piercing, an attack of all the senses, like a sudden bite on the hand, that I am not surprised that grown men may commit acts they forever regret. I sat, in a stiffened posture on the bed, seconds passing before I could move, listening to the outrageous litany against me which I knew that Anethe was being forced to hear as well, and the beating of my heart against my breastbone became so insistent and so loud that I knew I must silence Karen or surely I would die.

I pushed myself from my bed, and Karen, observing me, and coward that she was and always had been, backed away from me and into the kitchen. At first she put her hand to her mouth, as if she might actually be frightened, but then she took her hand away and began to sneer at me most scornfully.

"Look at you in your silly nightdress," she said, "grown fat and ugly in your middle age. Do you imagine you can scare me?" She turned her back to me, perhaps to further show her scorn by dismissing me. She bent over her trunk and opened it, and took up a great armful of linens. Or perhaps she was looking for something. I have never known.

I put my hands on the back of a chair and gripped that chairback so hard my knuckles whitened.

Karen staggered two or three steps under the blows from the chair and, twisting around, turned towards me, held out her arms and dropped the linens on the floor. I am not sure if she did this in entreaty or if she meant only to protect herself. A small exclamation escaped me, as I stood there with the chair in my hands.

Karen stumbled into my bedroom and fell upon the floor, weakly scrabbling against the painted wood like a strange and grotesque insect. I think that Anethe may have gotten out of the bed and taken a step backwards toward the wall. If she spoke, I do not remember what she said. The weight of the wood caused the chair to swing from my arms so that it fell upon the bed. I took hold of Karen's feet and began to pull her back into the kitchen, as I did not want this sordid quarrel to sully Anethe. The skirt of Karen's nightgown raised itself up to her waist, and I remember being quite appalled at the white of her scrawny legs.

I write now of a moment in time that cannot be retrieved, that took me to a place from which there was never any hope of return. It all seemed at the time to happen very quickly, somewhere within a white rage in my head. To retell these events is exceedingly painful for me now, and I will doubtless horrify the reader, but because my desire is to unburden myself and to seek forgiveness before I pass on, I must, I fear, ask the reader's patience just a moment longer.

When Karen was across the threshold, I moved to the door, shut it and put a slat through the latch so that there would be only myself and my sister in the kitchen. I think that Karen may have struggled to stand upright, and then fallen or been thrown against the door, for there was a small shudder against the wood, and it must have been then that Anethe, on the other side of the door, pushed our bed against it. I heard Karen cry out my name.

I would not have harmed Anethe. I would not. But I heard, through the wall, the sound of the window being opened. Anethe would have run to the beach. Anethe would have called for help, alerted someone on Apple-dore or Star, and that person would have rowed across the harbor and come up to the house and found myself and Karen. And then what would I have done? And where could I go? For Karen, possibly, was dying already.

In truth, the axe was for Karen.

But when I picked up the axe on the front stoop, I found I was growing increasingly concerned about Anethe. Therefore I did not return just then to the kitchen, but stepped into the entryway and put on the rubber boots, and went outside again and kept moving, around to the side of the house, where the window was. I remember that Ringe was barking loudly at my feet, and I think that Karen was crying. I don't believe that Anethe ever said a word.

She was standing just outside the window, her feet in the snow up to the hem of her nightgown. I was thinking that her feet must be frozen. Her mouth was open, and she was looking at me, and as I say, no sound emerged from her. She held a hand out to me, one hand, as though reaching across a wide divide, as though asking for me, so that I, too, might lay my hand over that great expanse and help her to safety. And as I stood there, gazing upon her fingers, looking at the fearful expression in my brother's wife's face, I remembered the tenderness of her touch of just hours ago, and so I did extend my hand, but I did not reach her. She did not move, and neither then could I.

It is a vision I have long tried to erase, the axe in the air. Also as well the sight of blood soaking the nightgown and the snow.

On more than one occasion, I have waited for the sunrise. The sky lightens just a shade, promising an easy dawn, but then one waits interminably for the first real shadows, the first real light.

I had to leave the boots back at the house, in keeping with the first and hasty suggestions of a story, and as a consequence, I had cut my feet on the ice. I could no longer feel them, however, as they had gone numb during the night. I held my dog, Ringe, for warmth, and I think that if I had not done so, I would have frozen entirely.

During those awful hours in the sea cave, I wept and cried out and battered my head back against the rock until it bled. I bit my hand and my arm. I huddled in my hiding place and wished that the rising tide might come in to my cave and wash me out to sea. I relived every moment of the horrors that had occurred that night, including the worst moments of all, which were those of cold, calculated thought and of arranging facts to suit the story I must invent. I could not bear the sight of Karen's body, and so I dragged her into the northeast apartment and left her in the bedroom. And also, just before I fled the house, I found I did not like to think of Anethe in the snow, and so I hauled her inside the cottage.

I have discovered in my life that it is not always for us to know the nature of God, or why He may bring, in one night, pleasure and death and rage and tenderness, all intermingled, so that one can barely distinguish one from the other, and it is all that one can do to hang onto sanity. I believe that in the darkest hour, God may restore faith and offer salvation. Toward dawn, in that cave, I began to pray for the first time since Evan had spoken harshly to me. These were prayers that sprang from tears shed in the blackest moment of my wretchedness. I prayed for the souls of Karen and Anethe, and for Evan, who would walk up the path to the cottage in a few hours, wondering why his bride did not greet him at the cove, and again for Evan, who would be bewildered by the cluster of men who stood about the doorstep, and once more for Evan, who would stagger away from that cottage and that island and never return again.

And also I prayed for myself, who had already lost Evan to his fathomless grief. For myself, who would be inexplicably alive when John saw the bodies of Karen and Anethe. For myself, who did not understand the visions God had given me.

When the sun rose, I crawled from the rock cave, so stiff I could barely move. The carpenters on Star Island, working on the hotel, dismissed me as I waved my skirt. Around the shore I limped on frozen feet until I saw the Ingerbretson children playing on Malaga. The children heard my cries and went to fetch their father. In a moment, Emil ran to his dory and paddled over to where I was standing on the shore of Smutty Nose. My eyes were swollen, my feet bloody, my nightgown and hair dishevelled, and, in this manner, I fell into Emil's arms and wept.

At the Ingerbretsons', I was laid upon a bed. A story came out, in bits and pieces, the pieces not necessarily in their correct order, the tale as broken as my spirit. And it was not until later that day, when I heard the story told to another in that room, that I understood for the first time all that I had said, and from that moment on, this was the precise story I held to.

I kept to my lurid story that day and the next, and throughout the trial, but there was a moment, that first morning, as I lay on a bed in the Ingerbretson house, and was speaking to John and was in the midst of my story, that my husband, who had been holding his head in his hands in a state of awful anguish, looked up at me and took his hands away from his face, and I knew he had then the first of his doubts.

And what shall I say of my meeting with Evan, who, shortly after John left, stumbled into the room, having been blasted by the scene at Smutty Nose, and who looked once at me, not even seeing me, not even knowing I was there in that room with him, and who turned and flung his arm hard against the wall, so hard he broke his bones, and who howled the most piteous wail I have ever heard from any human being?

The white button that was found in Louis Wagner's pocket was an ordinary button, quite common, and only I knew, apart from Louis, although how could he admit to the manner in which he had come by it without showing that he was capable of an attack on a woman and thus aiding in his own conviction, that the button had come loose from Anethe's blouse on the day that he had feigned illness and had made advances to her in his bedroom. Following the discovery of the button, which was widely reported, I removed the buttons from the blouse, which I subsequently destroyed, and put them on my nightgown.

I often think of the uncommon love I bore my brother and of how my life was shaped by this devotion, and also of John's patience and of his withdrawal from me, and of the beauty and the tenderness of my brother's wife. And I think also of the gathering net Evan threw into the water, and how he let it sink, and how he drew it up again, and how it showed to us the iridescent and the dark, the lustrous and the grotesque.

Last night, lying awake with the pain, I could take no nourishment except water, and I understand that this is a sign of the end, and to be truthful, I cannot mind, as the pain is greater than the ability of the girl who attends to me to mollify it with the medicine. It is in my womb, as I always knew it would be, knew it from the time I lay ill with the paralysis and my womanhood began. Or perhaps I knew it from the night my mother died, knew that I, too, would one day perish from something that would be delivered from the womb, knew that one day my blood, too, would soak the sheets, as it did that night, so long ago, that night of my mother's death, when Evan and I lay together in the bed, and occasionally I am addled and confused and think myself a young woman again and that my monthly time has come, and then I remember, each time with a shock that leaves me breathless, that I am not young but am old, and that I am dying.

In a few weeks, we will have a new century, but I will not be here to see it.

I am glad that I have finished with my story, for my hand is weak and unsteady, and the events I have had to write about are grim and hideous and without any redemption, and I ask the Lord now, as I have for so many years, Why was the punishment so stern and unyielding? Why was the suffering so great?

The girl comes early in the morning and opens the curtains for me, and once again, as I did each day as a child, I look out onto Laurvig Bay, the bay constantly changing, each morning different from the one before or indeed any morning that has ever come before that. When the girl arrives, I am always in need of the medicine, and after she has given it to me, I watch from the chair as she changes the filthy sheets, and goes about the cottage, tidying up, making the thin soup that until recently I was able to drink, speaking to me occasionally, not happy with her lot, but not selfish either. And in this way, she very much reminds me of myself when I was at the Johannsen farm, though in this case, she will have to watch me die, will have to sit beside me in this room and watch the life leave me, unless she is fortunate enough to have me go in the night, and I hope, for her sake, that it will be an easy passage, without drama and without agony.

26 September 1899, Maren Christensen Hontvedt.

I SIT IN THE SMALL BOAT in the harbor and watch the light begin to fade on Smuttynose. I hold in my hand papers from the cardboard carton.

Not long ago, I had lunch with Adaline in a restaurant in Boston. I hadn't been in a restaurant since the previous summer, and I was at first disoriented by the space — the tall ceilings, the intricately carved moldings, the mauve banquettes. On each table was a marble vase filled with peonies. Adaline was waiting for me, a glass of wine by her right hand. She had cut her hair and wore it in a sleek flip. I could see more clearly now how it might be that she was an officer with Bank of Boston. She was wearing a black suit with a gray silk shell, but she still had on the cross.

Our conversation was difficult and strained. She asked me how I was, and I had trouble finding suitable words to answer her. She spoke briefly about her job. She told me she was getting married. I asked to whom, and she said it was to someone at the bank. I wished her well.

"Have you seen Thomas?" I asked her.

"Yes. I go down there . . . well, less now."

She meant Hull, Thomas's family home, where he lived with Rich, who looked after him.

"He's writing?"

"No, not that any of us can see. Rich is gone a lot. But he says that Thomas just sits at the desk, or walks along the beach."

I was privately amazed that Thomas could bear to look at water.

"He blames himself," said Adaline.

"I blame myself."

"It was an accident."

"No, it wasn't."

"He's drinking."

"I imagine."

"You haven't seen him since . . . ?"

She was unable to say the words. To define the event.

"Since the accident," I said for her. "We were together afterwards. It was excruciating. I suppose I will eventually go down to see him. In time."

"Sometimes a couple, after a tragedy, they find comfort in each other."

"I don't think that would be the case with me and Thomas," I said carefully.

During the hours following the discovery that Billie was missing, Thomas and I had said words to each other that could never be taken back, could never be forgotten. In the space of time it takes for a wave to wash over a boat deck, a once tightly knotted fisherman's net had frayed and come unraveled. I could not now imagine taking on the burden of Thomas's anguish as well as my own. I simply didn't have the strength.

"You're all right, then?" she asked. "In your place?"

"The apartment? Yes. As fine as can be."

"You're working?"

"Some."

"You know," she said, "I've always been concerned . . ." She fingered the gold cross. "Well, it doesn't seem very important now. But I've always been concerned you thought Thomas and I . . ."

"Were having an affair. No, I know you weren't. Thomas told me."

"He held me once in the cockpit when I was telling him about my daughter."

"I know. He told me that, too." I picked up a heavy silver spoon and set it down. All around me were animated women and men in suits.

"And there's another thing," she said. "Thomas indicated that you thought . . . well, Billie must have misheard a casual invitation from Thomas to me. Billie somehow thought I might be coming to live with you."

I nodded. "You were lucky," I said. "Not having a life vest."

She looked away.

"Why did you leave her?" I asked suddenly, and perhaps there was an edge of anger in my voice.

I hadn't planned to ask this of Adaline. I had promised myself I wouldn't.

Her eyes filled. "Oh, Jean, I've gone over and over this, a thousand times. I didn't want to be sick in front of Billie. I wanted fresh air. I'd been looking through the hatch all morning. I didn't think. I just opened it. I just assumed she wouldn't be able to reach it."

"I don't think she went out the hatch," I said.

Adaline blew her nose. I ordered a glass of wine. But

already I knew that I would not be there long enough to drink it.

"She was a wonderful girl," I said to Adaline.

I think often of the weight of water, of the carelessness of adults.

Billie's body has never been found. Her life jacket, with its Sesame Street motif, washed up at Cape Neddick in Maine. It is my theory that Billie had the life jacket on, but not securely. That would have been like Billie, unclipping the jacket to readjust it, to wear it slightly differently, backwards possibly, so that she could satisfy herself that some part of her independence had not been lost. It is my theory that Billie came up the companionway looking for me or for Adaline to help her refasten the waist buckle. I tell myself that my daughter was surprised by the wave. That it took her fast, before thoughts or fear could form. I have convinced myself of this. But then I wonder: Might she have called out *Mom,* and then *Mom?* The wind was against her, and I wouldn't have heard her cry.

I did not return Maren Hontvedt's document or its translation to the Athenaeum. I did not send in the pictures from the photo shoot, and my editor never asked for them.

This is what I have read about John Hontvedt and Evan Christensen. John Hontvedt moved to a house on Sagamore Street in Portsmouth. He remarried and had a daughter named Honora. In 1877, Evan Christensen married Valborg Moss at St. John, New Brunswick, where he had gone from Portsmouth, and where he worked as a carpenter and cabinetmaker. After his marriage, the couple moved to Boston. They had five children, two of whom died in infancy.

I think about the accommodations Evan Christensen would have had to make to marry another woman. What did he do with his memories?

Anethe and Karen Christensen are buried side by side in Portsmouth.

I sometimes think about Maren Hontvedt and why she wrote her document. It was expiative, surely, but I don't believe she was seeking absolution. I think it was the weight of her story that compelled her — a weight she could no longer bear.

I slide the handful of papers into the water. I watch them bob and float upon the water's twitching surface, and I think they look like sodden trash tossed overboard by an inconsiderate sailor. Before morning, before they are found, the papers will have disintegrated, and the water will have blurred the ink.

I think about the hurt that stories cannot ease, not with a thousand tellings.

Acknowledgments

I could not have written this book without the aid of the various guidebooks to the Isles of Shoals as well as the several published accounts of the Smuttynose murders, in particular *Murder at Smuttynose and Other Murders* by Edmund Pearson (1938), *Moonlight Murder at Smuttynose* by Lyman Rutledge (1958), *The Isles of Shoals: A Visual History* by John Bardwell (1989), *The Isles of Shoals in Lore and Legend* by Lyman Rutledge (1976), "A Memorable Murder" by Celia Thaxter (1875), *A Stern and Lovely Scene: A Visual History of the Isles of Shoals* by the Art Galleries at the University of New Hampshire (1978), *Sprays of Salt* by John Downs (1944), and, of course, my much thumbed copy of *Ten Miles Out: Guide Book to the Isles of Shoals* by the Isles of Shoals Unitarian Association (1972). To these authors and to others who have written about this wonderful and mysterious archipelago, I am indebted.

I am also extremely grateful to my editor, Michael Pietsch, and my agent, Ginger Barber, for their incisive comments and advice.

Finally, I am most grateful to John Osborn for his tireless research and emotional intelligence.

ABOUT THE AUTHOR

Anita Shreve received the PEN / L. L. Winship Award
and the New England Book Award for fiction in 1998.
Her bestselling novels include *Fortune's Rocks,*
The Pilot's Wife, Resistance, Where or When,
Strange Fits of Passion, and *Eden Close*

. . . AND HER MOST RECENT NOVEL

In April 2001 Little, Brown and Company will publish
The Last Time They Met.
Following is a preview.

S HE HAD COME from the plane and was even now
forgetting the ride from the airport. This was in a
northern city in the month of April, spring not even
tantalizingly near in such a climate. The rain darkened her
stocking as she stepped from the pearl-colored car, the
driver unknown to her and mercifully silent for the now-
forgotten trip to the hotel. She strained to emerge with
some dignity to an audience of a doorman in a uniform
and another man in a dark coat moving through a revolv-
ing door, but the gravity of inanimate objects made her
graceless. As she stood, a rain-stung gust of wind lifted
her hair from the back of her neck and blew it upwards
from the nape, and had she worn a hat, she would have
lost it. The man in the dark coat hesitated, taking a moment to open an umbrella that immediately, in one fluid
motion, blew itself inside out. And he, looking abashed,
and then purposefully amused — for now she was his audience — tossed the useless appendage into a bin and
moved on.

She did not need the doorman and wished he would not

take her suitcase, and might have, but for the ornate gold leaf of the canopy and the perfectly polished brass of the entryway, told him it wasn't necessary. She had not expected the tall columns that rose to a ceiling she could not see clearly without squinting, or the rose carpet through those columns that was long enough for a coronation. The doorman wordlessly gave the suitcase, inadequate in this grandeur, to a bellman, as if handing off a secret. She moved past empty groupings of determinedly costly furniture to a desk marked Reception.

Linda, who had once struggled constantly to overcome the commonness of her name, gave her credit card when asked, wrote her signature on a piece of paper and accepted a pair of keys, one plastic, the other reassuringly real. She followed directions to a bank of elevators, noting on a mahogany table a bouquet of hydrangeas and day lilies as tall as a ten-year-old boy. Despite the elegance of the hotel, the music in the elevator was cloying and banal, and she wondered how it was this detail had been overlooked. She followed signs and arrows along a wide, hushed corridor built during an era when space was not a luxury.

The white paneled door of her room was heavy and opened with a soft click. There was a mirrored entryway that seemed to double as a bar, a sitting room with heavily-draped windows, and French doors veiled with sheers that opened to a bedroom larger than her living room at home. The weight of unwanted obligation was, for the moment, replaced with wary acceptance of being pampered. But then she looked at the ivory linen pillows on the massive bed and thought of the waste when it was only herself who would sleep there, she who might have been satisfied with a narrow bed in a narrow room, she who no longer thought of beds as places where love or sex was offered or received.

She sat for a moment in her wet raincoat, waiting for the bellman to bring her suitcase to her. She closed her eyes and tried to relax, a skill for which she had no talent, she who had never been to a yoga class, never meditated, unable to escape the notion that such strategies constituted a surrender, an admission that she could no longer bear to touch the skin of reality, her old lover; as if she would turn her back against a baffled husband, she who had once been so greedy.

She answered the door to a young bellman, overtipping the man to compensate for the size of her suitcase. She was aware of scrutiny on his part, impartial scrutiny simply because she was a woman and not entirely old. Abandoning the suitcase in the doorway, she crossed to the windows and drew back the drapes, and even the dim light of a rainy day was a shock to the gloom of the room. There were blurred buildings, the gleam of wet streets, glimpses of gray lake between skyscrapers. Three nights in one hotel room. Perhaps by Sunday morning she would know the number, would not have to ask at the front desk, as she so often had to do, her confusion, she was convinced, as the desk clerks clearly were not, a product simply of physics: She had too much to think about and too little time in which to do it. She had long ago accepted the need for excessive amounts of time to think (more, she had observed, than others seemed to need or want), and for years she had let herself believe that this was a product of her profession, her art, when of course it was much the other way around: The spirit sought and found the work, and discontent began when it could not.

And, of course, it was a con, this art. Which was why she could not help but approach a podium, any podium, with a mantle of slight chagrin that she could never quite manage to hide, her shoulders hunched inside her jacket or her blouse, her eyes not meeting those in the audience, as if the men and women in front of her might challenge her, accuse her of fraud. Which, in the end, only she appeared to understand she was guilty of. There was nothing easier nor more agonizing than writing the long, narrative verses that her publisher put in print — easy in that they were simply daydreams written in ink; agonizing the moment she returned to consciousness (the telephone rang; the heat kicked on in the basement), and she looked at the words on the blue-lined page and saw, for the first time, the dishonest images, the manipulation, the conniving couplets and wily quatrains, all of which, when it had been a good day, worked well for her. She wrote poetry, she had been told, that was *accessible,* a fabulous and slippery word that could be used in the service of both scathing criticism and excessive praise, neither of which she thought she deserved. Her greatest wish was to write anonymously, though she no longer mentioned this to her publishers, for they seemed slightly wounded at these mentions, at the apparent ingratitude for the long — and tedious? — investment they had made in her that was finally, after all these years, beginning to pay off. Some of her collections were selling now (and one of them was selling very well indeed) for reasons no one had predicted and no one seemed to understand, the unexpected sales attributable to that vague and unsettling phenomenon called "word of mouth."

She covered the chintz bedspread with her belongings: the olive suitcase (slim and soft for the new stingy over-heads); the detachable computer briefcase (the detaching a necessity for the security checks); and her microfiber purse with its eight compartments for her cell phone, notebook, pen, driver's license, credit cards, hand cream, lipstick and sunglasses. She used the bathroom with her coat still on and then searched for her contact lens case so that she could remove the miraculous plastic irritants from her eyes, the lenses soiled with airplane air and smoke from an airport bar, a four-hour layover in Dallas ending in capitulation to a plate of nachos and a Diet Coke. And seeping around the edges, she began to feel the relief that hotel rooms always provided: a place where no one could get to her.

She sat again on the enormous bed, two pillows propped behind her. Across from her was a gilded mirror that took in the entire bed, and she could not look into such a mirror without thinking of various speakable and unspeakable acts that had almost certainly been per-formed in front of that mirror (she thought of men as being particularly susceptible to mirrors in hotel rooms), a speculation that led inevitably to consideration of cer-tain substances that had spilled or fallen onto that very bedspread (how many times? thousands of times?), and the room was immediately filled with stories: A married man who loved his wife but could make love to her but once a month because he was addicted to fantasizing about her in front of hotel mirrors on his frequent busi-ness trips, her body the sole object of his sexual imaginings; a man cajoling his business partner into performing one of the speakable acts upon him, enjoying the image of her subservient and bobbing head in the mirror over the dresser and then, when he had collapsed into a sitting position, confessing, in a moment that would ultimately cost him his job, that he had Herpes (why were her thoughts about men today so hostile?); a woman who was not beautiful, but was dancing naked in front of the mirror, as she would never do at home, might never do again (there, that was better). She took her glasses off so that she could not see across the room. She leaned against the headboard and closed her eyes.

She had nothing to say. She had said it all. She had written all the poems she would ever write. Though something large and subterranean had fueled her images, she was a minor poet only. She was, possibly, an overachiever. She would coast tonight, segue early into the Q&A, let the audience dictate the tenor of the event. Mercifully, it would be short. She appreciated literary festivals for precisely that reason: She would be but one of many novelists and poets (more novelists than poets), most of whom were better known than she. She knew she ought to examine the program before she went to the cocktail party on the theory that it sometimes helped to find an acquaintance early on so that one was not left stranded, looking both unpopular and easy prey; but if she glanced at the program, it would pull her too early into the evening, and she resisted this invasion. How protective she had recently grown of herself, as if there were something of value to protect.

From the street, twelve floors below, there was a clanging of a large machine. In the corridor there were voices, those of a man and a woman, clearly disturbed.

It was pure self-indulgence, the writing. She could still remember (an antidote to the chagrin?) the exquisite pleasure, the texture, so early on, of her first pencilled letters on their stout lines, the practiced slant of the blue-inked cursive on her first copy book (the lavish F of Frugality, the elegant E of Envy). She collected them now, old copy books, small repositories of beautiful handwriting. It was art, found art, of that she was convinced. She had framed some of the individual pages, had lined the walls of her study at home with the prints. She supposed the copy-books (mere schoolwork of anonymous women, long dead) were virtually worthless — she had hardly ever paid more than five or ten dollars for one in a second-hand book store — but they pleased her nevertheless because she was convinced that for her the writing was all about the act of writing itself, even though her own penmanship had deteriorated to an appalling level, nearly that of code.

She stood up from the bed and put her glasses on. She peered into the mirror. Tonight she would wear long earrings of pink Lucite. She would put her lenses back in and use a lipstick that didn't swear with the Lucite, and that would be that. Seen from a certain angle, she might simply disappear.

Why did she continue to present herself to the world?

The party was in a room reserved for such occasions. Presumably, the view outside attracted, though the city now was gray and darkening yet. Lights twinkled at random, and it was impossible not to think: In this room or that, women will be undressing and men, with ties undone, will be pouring drinks. Though one did not know, and there were other, more grotesque scenarios, to contemplate.

The window shuddered with a gust similar to the one that had taken her hair. For a moment, the lights dimmed, causing a stoppage in the conversation of equal duration, a pause in which one could not help but think of panic in a blackened hotel, of hands groping. Some dreadful music, cousin to the malevolently bland tunes in the hotel elevator, seeped between the talk. She saw no recognizable face, which was disconcerting. There were, perhaps, twenty-five people in the suite when she arrived, most already drinking, and most, it would appear, already bonded into clusters. Along one wall, a table had been laid with hors d'oeuvres of a conventional sort. She set her purse under a chair by the door and walked to the bar. She asked for a glass of wine, guessing that the chardonnay would not live up to the rose coronation carpet and the bouquets as big as boys, and in this she was not wrong.

A woman said her name, and Linda turned to an outstretched hand belonging to a slight woman in a woolen suit, its cloth the color of irises. It was pleasant to see a woman not dressed in black, as she herself was, but then this might be taken as insult for being provincial. Linda shook the proferred hand, her own wet and cold from her wine glass.

"I'm Susan Sefton, one of the organizers of the Festival. I am such a fan. I wanted to thank you for coming."

"Oh. Thank you," Linda said. "I'm looking forward to it," she lied.

The woman had feral teeth but lovely green eyes. Did she do this for a living?

"In about half an hour, we'll all be heading down to the front of the hotel, where we'll be taken by bus to a restaurant called Le Matin. It's a bistro. Do you like French?"

The answer couldn't matter, though Linda nodded yes. The idea of being carted out to dinner put her in mind of senior citizens, an image not dispelled in the next instant when she was informed that dinner would be early because of the various reading schedules.

"And then each author will be taken to his or her event. There are four separate venues." A vinyl binder with colored tabs was consulted. "You are in Red Wing Hall. You're reading at 9:30."

Which would insure a smallish crowd, Linda thought but didn't say. Most people with tickets to a festival — authors included — would be ready to go home by 9:30.

"Do you know Robert Seizek?"

The name was vaguely familiar, though Linda could not then have named a title or even a genre. She made a motion with her head that might be construed as a nod.

"You and he will be sharing a stage," the organizer said, and Linda heard the demotion implicit in the fraction, a sense of being only half an entertainment. "It was in the program," the woman said defensively, perhaps in response to a look of disappointment. "Didn't you get your packet?"

Linda had, but could hardly admit now to ownership, it being deliberately rude not even to have glanced at it.

"I'll see you get one," said the organizer. The feral teeth were gone now, the smile having faded. Linda would be but one of many wayward writers Susan Sefton was in charge of, most too disorganized or self-absorbed to do what was expected. She looked pointedly at Linda's breast.

"You have to wear a badge to all events. It's in the packet," she said. A rule against which writers surely would rebel, Linda thought, looking around at a room filled with white badges encased in plastic and pinned onto lapels and bodices. "Have you met Robert yet? Let me introduce you," Susan Sefton nodded, not waiting for an answer to her question.

The woman in the iris-colored suit interrupted a conversation amongst three men, none of whom seemed to need or want interruption. The talk was of computers (Linda might have guessed this) and tech stocks one might have bought if only one had known. Seizek had a large head — leonine one would have to say — and an even larger body that spoke of appetites, one of which was much in evidence in his nearly lethal breath and in the way in which he swayed slightly, as if attached to a different gyroscope than the rest of them. Perhaps she would be solo on the stage after all. One of the two remaining authors had an Australian accent that was pleasant to listen to, and Linda deduced (as if tuning into a radio broadcast that had already begun) that he was a novelist about whom it had been said just the Sunday previous in a prominent book review that his prose was "luminous and engaging," his insights "brilliant and incisive." (A novel about an Australian scientist? She tried to remember. No, an engineer.) And it was impossible, despite the overused and thus devalued words of praise, not to regard the man with more interest than she had just seconds earlier, a fact she despised about herself. One bowed to power conferred. And she saw, as she had not before, that the other two men were turned slightly in the direction of the newly annointed, as though their bodies had been drawn just slightly off course by a powerful magnet.

"And you, Ms. Fallon," Seizek said thickly, suggesting that she might at any minute be sprayed with sibilants, "would you say that your understanding of love came more from love itself or from reading about love?"

Another conversation she had only bits of. The third writer looked at her not at all, as if she were invisible. It would not be fair to say that he was gay. How odd, she thought, that men would talk of love, had been talking of love before she had even joined them, a topic it was supposed was of interest only to women.

"Experience," she said without hesitation. "No one has ever accurately described a marriage."

"A novel can't, can it?" the Australian, in broad antipodean accent, asked. "A marriage doesn't lend itself to art. Certainly not to satisfying structure or to dialogue worth reading."

"You write of love," the man who could not be called gay said to Linda, rendering her suddenly visible; and she could not help but be pleased that someone knew her work.

"I do," she said, not embarrassed to state her claim in this arena. "I believe it to be the central drama of our lives." Immediately, she qualified her bold pronouncement. "For most of us, that is."

"Not death?" asked Seizek, a drunk looking for debate.

"I count it as part of the entire story," she said. "All love is doomed, seen in the light of death."

"I take it you don't believe that love survives the grave," the Australian offered.

And she did not, though she had tried to. After Vincent.

"Why central?" asked the third man, who had a name after all: William Wingate.

"It contains all theatrical possibilities," she said. "Passion, jealousy, betrayal, risk. And is nearly universal. It is something extraordinary that happens to ordinary people."

"Not fashionable to write about love, though, is it?" Seizek said dismissively.

"No," she said, agreeing. "But in my experience, fashion doesn't have a great deal to do with validity."

"No, of course not," he said quickly, not wanting to be thought invalid.

Linda drifted to the edges of the talk, assaulted by a sudden hunger. She hadn't had a proper meal (if one didn't count the small, inedible paper carton of nachos) since breakfast in her hotel room in a city seven hundred miles away. She asked the men if they wanted anything from the buffet table, she was just going to get a cracker, she was starved, she hadn't eaten since breakfast. No, no, the men did not want, but of course she must get it herself. The salsa was decent, they said, and they wouldn't be eating for another hour anyway. And, by the way, did anyone know the restaurant? And she reflected, as she turned away from them, that just a year ago, or maybe two, one of the men would have followed her to the buffet table, would have viewed the occasion as opportunity. Such were the ironies of age, she thought. When the attention had been ubiquitous, she had minded.

Small colored bowls of food left the guest to guess at their identity: the green might be guacamole, the red was doubtless the decent salsa, and the pink possibly a shrimp or crab dip. But she was stumped as to the grayish-beige, not a good color for food under the best of circumstances. She reached for a small paper plate — the management had not provided for large appetites — and heard the hush before she understood it, a mild hush as if someone had lowered the volume a notch or two. From the corner, she heard a whispered name. It couldn't be, she thought, even as she understood it could. She turned to see the source of the reverential quiet.

He stood in the doorway, as if momentarily blinded by the unfamiliar. As if having been injured, he was having to re-learn certain obvious cues to reality: pods of men and women with drinks in hand, a room attempting to be something it was not, faces that might or might not be familiar. His hair was silver now, the shock of that, badly cut, atrociously cut really, too long at the sides and at the back. How he would be hating this, she thought, already taking his side. His face was ravaged in the folds, but you could not say he was unhandsome. The navy eyes were soft and blinking, as if he had come out of a darkened room. A scar, the old scar that seemed as much a part of him as his mouth, ran the length of his left cheek. He was greeted as a man might who had long been in a coma; as a king who had for years been in exile.

She turned around, unwilling to be the first person he saw in the room.

There were other greetings now, a balloon of quiet but intense attention. Could this be his first public appearance since the accident, since he had taken himself into seclusion, retired from the world? It could, it could. She stood immobile, plate in hand, breathing in a tight, controlled manner. She raised a hand slowly to her hair, tucked a stray strand behind her ear. She rubbed her temple softly with her finger. She picked up a cracker and tried to butter it with a crumbly cheese, but the cracker broke, disintegrating between her fingers. She examined a fruit bowl of strawberries and grapes, the latter having gone brown at the edges.

Someone said, too unctuously, "Let me get you a drink." Another crowed, "I am so pleased." Still others murmured: "You cannot know," and "I am such."

It was nothing, she told herself as she reached for a glass of water. Years had passed, and all of life was different now.

She could feel him moving toward her. How awful that after all this time, she and he would have to greet in front of strangers.

He said her name, her very common name.

"Hello, Thomas," she said, turning, his name as common as her own, but his having the weight of history.

He had on an ivory shirt and a navy blazer, the cut long out of style. He had grown thicker through the middle, as might have been anticipated, but still, one thought, looking at him: A tall man, a lanky man. His hair fell forward onto his forehead, and he brushed it away in a gesture that swam up through the years.

He moved across the space between them and kissed her face beside her mouth. Too late, she reached to touch his arm, but he had retreated, leaving her hand to dangle in the air.

Age had diminished him. She watched him take her in, she who would be seen to have been diminished by age as well. Would he be thinking: *Her hair gone dry, her face not old?*

"This is very strange," he said.

"They are wondering about us already."

"It is comforting to think we might provide a story." His hands did not seem part of him; they were pale, soft, writer's hands, hints of ink forever in the creases of the middle finger of the right hand. "I've followed your career."

"What there's been of it."

"You've done well," he said.

"Only recently."

The others moved away from them like boosters falling from a rocket. There was conferred status in his knowing her, not unlike the Australian writer with the good review. A drink appeared for Thomas, who took it and said thank-you, disappointing the bearer, who hoped for conversation.

"I haven't done this sort of thing in years," he began and stopped.

"When are you reading?" she asked.

"Tonight," he answered.

"And me as well."

"Are we in competition?"

"I certainly hope not," she said.

It was rumored that after many barren years, Thomas was writing again and that the work was extraordinarily good. He had in the past, inexplicably, been passed over for the prizes, though it was understood, by common agreement, that he was, at his best, the best of them.

"You got here today?" she asked.

"Just."

"You've come from . . . ?"

"Hull."

She nodded.

"And you?" he asked, each question seemingly written in a code she could not quite decipher.

"I'm finishing a tour."

He tilted his head and half-smiled, as if to say, *Condolences.*

A man hovered near Thomas's elbow, waiting for admission. "Tell me something," Thomas said, ignoring the man beside him and leaning forward so that only she could hear, "did you become a poet because of me?"

She remembered that Thomas's questions were often startling and insulting, though one forgave him always. "It's how we met," she said, reminding him.

He took a longish sip of his drink.

"It was out of character for me," she said, "that class."

"In character, I should think. The rest was fraud."

"The rest?"

"The pretending to be fast."

Fast. She hadn't heard the word used that way in decades.

"You're more in character now," he said.

"How could you possibly know?" she asked, challenging him.

He heard the bite in her voice. "Your body and your gestures give you the appearance of having grown into your character, what I perceive to be your character."

"It's only middle-age," she said, at once devaluing both of them.

"Lovely on you," he said.

She turned away from the compliment. The man beside Thomas would not go away. Behind him there were others who wanted introductions to the reclusive poet. She excused herself and moved through all the admirers and the sycophants, who were, of course, not interested in her. *This was nothing,* she told herself again as she reached the door. *Years had passed, and all of life was different now.*

Look for these other novels by Anita Shreve

FORTUNE'S ROCKS

"Fortune's Rocks kept me reading long into the night. . . . Shreve renders an adolescent girl's plunge into disastrous passion with excruciating precision and acuteness."
—*Boston Globe*

"A beautifully written narrative, rich in detail and in a style that has the perfection of a snowflake and all the passion and intensity of first love."
—*Seattle Times*

THE PILOT'S WIFE

"Gripping. . . . You don't want to stop turning the pages once Kathryn has opened her door."
—*Washington Post Book World*

"Highly readable. . . . Shreve is extremely skillful at showing the stages by which someone learns to live with the unthinkable."
—*San Francisco Chronicle*

Available in paperback wherever books are sold

Also by Anita Shreve

RESISTANCE

❧

"Anita Shreve's perceptive novel relates a simple story set in terrible times in a clear, dispassionate voice. . . . I reached the last chapter with hungry eyes, wanting more."
—*Los Angeles Times Book Review*

"From the first sentence, Anita Shreve draws in the reader with the quiet poetry of her narrative voice. . . . *Resistance* is a turn-off-the-phone, put-the-kids-in-bed-early, stay-up-till-two-in-the-morning-on-a-work-night reading experience."
—*Detroit Free Press*

Available in paperback wherever books are sold